Richard Doddridge Blackmore

Cradock Nowell - A Tale of the New Forest

Vol. I

Richard Doddridge Blackmore

Cradock Nowell - A Tale of the New Forest
Vol. I

ISBN/EAN: 9783337024437

Printed in Europe, USA, Canada, Australia, Japan

Cover: Foto ©Andreas Hilbeck / pixelio.de

More available books at **www.hansebooks.com**

CRADOCK NOWELL

A Tale of the New Forest.

BY

RICHARD DODDRIDGE BLACKMORE,

AUTHOR OF " CLARA VAUGHAN."

" You have said : whether wisely or no, let the forest judge."
As You Like It, Act III. Sc. 2.

IN THREE VOLUMES.

VOL. I.

LONDON :

CHAPMAN AND HALL, 193, PICCADILLY.

1866.

[The right of Translation is reserved.]

To the Memory

OF

MY DEAR FRIEND

THOMAS JAMES SCALÉ,

THIS WORK

(IN WHICH, FROM MONTH TO MONTH, HE TOOK THE KINDEST
INTEREST)

IS

IN GRATITUDE, AFFECTION, AND AFFLICTION,

DEDICATED.

R. D. B.

CRADOCK NOWELL.

CHAPTER I.

WITHIN the New Forest, and not far from its western boundary, as defined by the second perambulation of the good King Edward the First, stands the old mansion of the Nowells, the Hall of Nowelhurst. Not content with mere exemption from all feudal service, their estate claims privileges, both by grant and custom. The benefit of Morefall trees in six walks of the forest, the right of digging marl, and turbary illimitable, common of pannage, and license of drawing akermast, pastime even of hawking over some parts of the Crown land,—all these will be catalogued as claims quite indefeasible, if the old estates come to the hammer, through the events that form my story. With many of these privileges the Royal Commissioners will deal in a spirit of scant courtesy, when the Nowell influence is lost in the neighbouring boroughs; but as yet these claims have not been treated like those of some poor commoners.

"Pooh, pooh, my man, don't be preposterous: you know, as well as I do, these gipsy freedoms were only allowed to balance the harm the deer did."

And if the rights of that ancient family are ever called in question, some there are which will require a special Act to abolish them. For Charles the Second, of merry memory (saddened somewhat of late years), espied among the maids of honour an uncommonly pretty girl, whose name was Frances Nowell. He suddenly remembered, what had hitherto quite escaped him, how old Sir Cradock Nowell—beautiful Fanny's father—had saved him from a pike-thrust during Cromwell's "crowning mercy." In gratitude, of course, for this, he began to pay most warm attentions to the Hampshire maiden. He propitiated that ancient knight with the only boon he craved—craved hitherto all in vain—a plenary grant of easements in the neighbourhood of his home. Soon as the charter had received the royal seal and signature, the old gentleman briskly thrust it away in the folds of his velvet mantle. Then taking the same view of gratitude which his liege and master took, home he went without delay to secure his privileges. When the king heard of his departure, without any kissing of hands, he was in no wise disconcerted; it was the very thing he had intended. But when he heard that lovely Fanny was gone in the same old rickety coach, even ere he began to whisper, and with no leave of the queen, His Majesty swore his utmost for nearly half an hour. Then having spent his fury, he laughed at the " sell," as he would have called it if the slang had been invented, and turned his royal attention to another of his wife's young maidens.

Nowelhurst Hall looks too respectable for any loose doings of any sort. It stands well away from the weeping of trees, like virtue shy of sentiment, and therefore has all the wealth of foliage shed, just where it pleases, around it. From a rising ground the house has sweet view of all the forest changes, and has seen three hundred springs wake in glory, and three hundred autumns waning. Spreading away from it wider, wider, slopes " the Chase," as they call it, with great trees stretching paternal arms in the vain attempt to hold it. For two months of the twelve, when the heather is in blossom, all that chase is a glowing reach of amaranth and purple. Then it fades away to pale orange, dim olive, and a rusty brown when Christmas shudders over it ; and so throughout young green and russet, till the July tint comes back again. Oftentimes in the fresh spring morning the blackcocks—" heathpoults" as they call them—lift their necks in the livening heather, swell their ruffing breasts, and crow for their rivals to come and spar with them. Below the chase the whiskers of the curling wood converge into a giant beard, tufted here and there with hues of a varying richness ; but for the main of it, swelling and waving, crisping, fronding, feathering, coying, and darkening here and there, until it reach the silver mirror. of the spreading sea. And the seaman, looking upwards from the war-ship bound for India, looking back at his native land, for the last of all times it may be, over brushwood waves, and billows of trees, and the long heave of the gorse-land: "Now, that's the sort of place," he says, as the distant gables glisten; "the right sort of berth for our jolly old admiral, and me for his butler, please God, when we've licked them Crappos as ought to be."

South-west of the house, half a mile away, and scattered along the warren, the simple village of Nowelhurst digests its own ideas. In and out the houses stand, endwise, crossways, skewified, any-how except upside down, and some even tending that way. It looks like a game of dominoes, when the leaves of the table have opened and gape betwixt the players. Nevertheless, it is all good English; for none are bitterly poor there; in any case of illness, they have the great house to help them, not proudly, but with feeling; and, more than this, they have a parson who leads instead of driving them. There are two little shops exceed-ingly anxious to under-sell each other, and one mild alehouse conducted strictly upon philosophic principles. Philosophy under pressure, a caviller would call it, for the publican knows, and so do his customers, that if poachers were encouraged there, or any. uproarious doings permitted (except in the week of the old and new year), down would come his license-board, like a flag hauled in at sunset.

Pleasant folk, who there do dwell, calling their existence "life," and on the whole enjoying it more than many of us do; forasmuch as they know their neighbours far better than themselves, and perceive each cousin's need of trial, and console him when he gets it. Not but what we ourselves partake the first and second advantages, only we miss the fruition of them, by turning our backs on the sufferer.

Nowelhurst village is not on the main road, but keeps a straggling companionship with a quiet parish highway which requires much encouragement. This little highway does its best to blink the many difficulties, or, if that may not be, to compromise them, and establish a pleasant footing upon its devious wandering course from the Lymington road to Ringwood. Here it goes zig to escape the frown of a heavy-browed crest of furzery, and then it comes zag when no soul expects it, because a little stream has babbled at it. It even seems to bob and dip, or jump, as the case may be, for fear of prying into an old oak's storey or dusting a piece of grass land. The hard-hearted traveller who lives express, and is bound for the train at Ringwood, curses, too often, up hill and down dale, the quiet lane's inconsistency. What right has any road to do anything but go straight on end to its purpose? What decent road stops for a gossip with flowers—flowers overhanging the steep ascent, or eavesdropping on the rabbit-holes? And as for the beauty of ferns—confound them, they shelter the horse-fly—that horrible forest-fly, whose tickling no civilized horse can endure. Even locusts he has heard of as abounding in the New Forest; and if a swarm of them comes this very hot weather, good-bye to him, horse and trap, newest patterns, sweet plaid, and chaste things.

And good-bye to thee, thou bustling "traveller" —whether technically so called or otherwise,—a very good fellow in thy way, but not of nature's pattern. So counter-sunk, so turned in a lathe, so pressed and rolled by steam-power, and then condensed hydraulically, that the extract of flowers upon thy shirt is but as the oil of machinery. But we who carry no chronometer, neither puff locomotively—now he is round the corner—let us saunter down this lane beyond the mark-oak and the blacksmith's, even to the sandy rise whence the Hall is seen. The rabbits are peeping forth again, for the dew is spreading quietude : the sun has just finished a good day's work and is off for the western waters. Over the rounded heads and bosses, and then the darker dimples of the many-coloured foliage—many-coloured even now with summer's glory fusing it—over heads and shoulders, and breasts of heaving green, floods the lucid amber, trembling at its own beauty—the first acknowledged leniency of the July sun. Now every moment has its difference. Having once

acknowledged that he may have been too downright in his ride of triumph, the sun, like every
generous nature, scatters broadcast his amends.
Over holt, and knoll, and lea, and narrow dingle,
scooped with shadow where the brook is wimpling,
and through the breaks of grass and gravel, where
the heather purples, scarcely yet in prime flush,
and down the tall wood overhanging, mossed and
lichened, green and grey, as the grove of Druids—
over, through, and under all flows pervading sunset. Then the birds begin discoursing of the
thoughts within them—thoughts that are all
happiness, and thrill and swell in utterance.
Through the voice of the thicket-birds—the mavis,
the whinchats, and the warblers—comes the tap
of the yaffingale, the sharp, short cry of the
honey-buzzard above the squirrel's cage, and the
plaining of the turtle-dove.

But from birds and flowers, winding roads and
woods, and waters where the trout are leaping,
come we back to the only thing that interests a
man much—the life, the doings, and the death of
his fellow-men. From this piece of yellow road,
where the tree-roots twist and wrestle, we can see
the great old house; winking out of countless
windows, deep with sloping shadows, mantling
back from the clasp of the forest, in a stately,
sad reserve. It looks like a house that can endure
and not talk about affliction, that could disclose
some tales of passion were it not undignified, that
remembers many a generation, and is mildly sorry

for them. Oh! house of the Nowells, grey with
shadow, wrapped in lonely grandeur, cold with the
dews of evening and the tone of sylvan nightfall,
never through twenty generations hast thou known
a darker fortune than is gathering now around
thee, growing through the summer months, deep-
ening ere the leaves drop! All men, we know,
are born for trial, to work, to bear, to purify; but
some there are whom God has marked for sorrow
from their cradle. And strange as it appears to
us, whose image is inverted, almost always these
are they who *seem* to lack no probation. The
gentle and the large of heart, the meek and unpretending, yet gifted with a rank of mind that
needs no self-assertion, trebly vexed in this way-
faring, we doubt not they are blest tenfold in the
everlasting equipoise.

Perhaps it was the July evening that made me
dream and moralise; but now let us gaze from that
hill again, under the fringe of autumn's gold, in the
ripeness of October. The rabbits are gone to bed
much earlier—comparatively, I mean, with the
sun's retirement—because the dew is getting cold,
and so has lost its flavour; and a nest of young
weasels is coming abroad, "and really makes it
unsafe, my dear," says Mrs. Bunny to her third
family, "to keep our long-standing engagements."
"Send cards instead," says the timid Miss Cony;
"I can write them, mamma, on a polypod."

Now though the rabbits shirk their duty, we can
see the congregation returning down the village
from the church, which is over the bridge, towards

Lymington, and seems set aside to meditate. In straggling groups, as gossip lumps them, or the afternoon sermon disposes, home they straggle, wondering whether the girl has kept the fire up. Kept the fire "blissy" is the bodily form of the housethought. But all the experienced matrons of the village have got together; and two, who have served as monthly nurses, are ready to pull sidehair out. There is nothing like science for setting people hard by the ears and the throat-strings. But we who are up in the forest here can catch no buzz of voices, nor even gather the point of dispute, while they hurry on to recount their arguments, and triumph over the virile mind, which, of course, knows nothing about it.

The question is, when Lady Nowell will give an heir to the name, the house, the village, the estates, worth fifty thousand a year—an heir long time expected, hoped for in vain through six long years, now reasonably looked for. All the matrons have settled that it must be on a Sunday; everybody knows that Sunday is the day for all grand ceremonies. Even Nanny Gammon's pigs —— But why pursue their arguments—the taste of the present age is so wonderfully nice and delicate. I can only say that the Gammers, who snubbed the Gaffers upon the subject, miscarried by a fortnight, though right enough hebdomadally. They all fixed it for that day fortnight, but it was done while they were predicting. And not even the monthly nurses anticipated, no one ever guessed at the contingency of—twins.

CHAPTER II.

"WHISHTREW, whishtrew, every bit of me!
Whativer will I do, God knows.   The blue ribbon
there forenint me, and the blessed infants one to
aich side!"

The good nurse fell against a chest of drawers,
as she uttered this loud lament; the colour ebbed
from her cherry cheeks, and her sturdy form shook
with terror.   She had scarcely turned her back,
she could swear, upon her precious charges; and
now only look at the murder of it!   Two little
cots stood side by side, not more than four feet
asunder; and on each cot fast asleep lay a fine
baby, some three or four days old.   Upon the floor
between them was a small rosette of blue ribbon.
The infants were slumbering happily; and breathing as calmly as could be.   Each queer little dump
of a face was nestled into its pillow; and a small
red podge, which was meant for an arm, lay cross-
wise upon the flannel.   Nothing could look more
delicious to the eyes of a fine young woman.

Nevertheless, that fine young woman, Mrs. Biddy O'Gaghan, stood gazing from one cot to the other, in hopeless and helpless dismay. Her comely round face was drawn out with horror, her mouth wide open, and large tears stealing into her broad blue Irish eyes.

"And the illigant spots upon them, as like as two Blemishing spannels; nor the blissed saints in heaven, if so be they was tuk to glory, afore they do be made hairyticks, cudn't know one from the ither, no more nor the winds from the brazes. And there go the doctor's bell again! Oh whurra-strew, whurra, whurra!"

Now Biddy O'Gaghan would scarcely have been head-nurse at Nowelhurst Hall, before she was thirty years old, but for her quick self-reliance. She was not the woman therefore to wring her hands long, and look foolish. Her Irish wit soon suggested so many modes of solution, all so easy, and all so delightfully free from reason, that the only question was how to listen to all at once. First she went and bolted carefully both the doors of the nursery. Then, with a look of triumph, she rushed to her yellow workbox, snatched up a roll of narrow tape, some pins, and a pair of scissors, and knelt upon the floor very gingerly, where the blue ribbon lay. Then, having pinned one end of the tape to the centre of the rosette, and the rosette itself to the carpet, she let the roll run with one hand, and drew the tape tight with the other, until it arrived at the nose of the babe

ensconced in the right-hand cot. There she cut it
off sharply, with a snip that awoke the child, who
looked at her contemplatively from a pair of large
grey eyes. Leaving him to his meditations, she
turned the tape on the pin, and drew it towards the
nasal apology of the other infant. The measure
would not reach; it was short by an inch and a
half. What clearer proof could be given of the
title to knot and pendency?

But alas for Biddy's triumph! The infant last
geometrised awoke at that very moment, and lifting
his soft fat legs, in order to cry with more comfort,
disclosed the awkward fact that his left knee was
nearer by three inches to the all-important rosette,
than was any part of his brother. Biddy shook
anew, as she drew the tape to the dimples. What
is the legal centre of a human being? Upon my
word, I think I should have measured from the
ὀμφαλός.

Ere further measurement could be essayed, all
the premises were gone utterly; for the baby upon
the right contrived to turn in the flannels, as an
unsettled silkworm pupa rolls in his cocoon. And
he managed to revolve in the wrong direction; it
was his fate through life. Instead of coming towards the rosette, as a selfish baby would have done,
away he went, with his grey eyes blinking at the
handle of the door. Then he put up his lips, like
the ring of a limpet, and poked both his little fists
into his mouth.

"Well, I never," cried Bridget; "that settles it

altogether. Plase the saints an' he were a rogue,
it's this way he'd ha' come over on his blessed little
empty belly. My darlin' dumplin' dillikins, it's
you as it belongs to, and a fool I must be to doubt
of it. Don't I know the bend o' your nose, and the
way your purty lips dribbles, then? And to think
I was near a robbing you! What with the sitting
up o' nights, and the worry of that carroty spal-
peen, and the way as they sends my meals up,
Paddy O'Gaghan, as is in glory, wud take me for
another man's wife."

With great relief and strong conviction, Mrs.
O'Gaghan began to stitch the truant rosette upon
the cap of the last-mentioned baby, whence (or
from that of the other) it had dropped through
her own loose carelessness, before they were
cuddled away. And with that ribbon she stitched
upon him the heritage of the old family, the name
of "Cradock Nowell," borne by the eight last
baronets, and the largest estates and foremost rank
in all the fair county of Hants.

"Sure an' it won't come off again," said Biddy
to the baby, as she laid down her needle, for, like
all genuine Irishwomen, she despised a thimble;
"and it's meself as is to blame, for not taking a
nick on your ear, dear. A big fool I must be only
to plait it in afore, and only for thinkin' as it wud
come cross-ways, when you wint to your blissed
mammy, dear. And little more you be likely to
get there, I'm afeared, me darlin'. An' skeared
anybody would be to hoort so much as a hair o'

your skull, until such time as you has any, you little jule of jewels, and I kisses every bit on you, and knows what you be thinking on in the dead hoor of the night. Bless your ticksy-wicksies, and the ground as you shall step on, and the childer as you shall have."

Unprepared as yet to contemplate the pleasures of paternity, Master Cradock Nowell elect opened great eyes and great mouth, in the untutored wrath of hunger; while from the other cot arose a lusty yell, as of one already visited by the injustice of the world. This bitter cry awoke the softness and the faint misgivings of the Irishwoman's heart.

"And the pity of the world it is ye can't both be the eldest. And bedad you should, if Biddy O'Gaghan had the making of the laws. There shan't be any one iver can say as ye haven't had justice, me honey."

Leaving both the unconscious claimants snugly wrapped and smiling, she called to her assistants, now calmly at tea in an inner room. "Miss Penny, run down now just, without thinking, and give my compliments, Mrs. O'Gaghan's kind compliments to the housekeeper's room, and would Mrs. Toaster oblige me with her big square scales? No weights you needn't bring, you know. Only the scales, and be quick with them."

"And please, ma'am, what shall I say as you wants them for?"

"Never you mind, Jane Penny. Wait you till your betters asks of you. And mayn't I weigh my

grandfather's silver, without ask you, Jane Penny?
And likely you'd rather not, and good reason for
that same, I dessay, after the way as I leaves it
open."

Overlooking this innuendo, as well as the slight
difficulty of weighing, without weights, imaginary
bullion, Miss Penny hurried away; for the wrath
of the nurse was rising, and it was not a thing to
be tampered with. When Jane returned with the
beam of justice, and lingered fondly in the doorway to watch its application, the head-nurse sidled
her grandly into the little room, and turned the
key upon her.

"Go and finish your tea, Miss Penny. No
draughts in this room, if you please, miss. Save
their little sowls, and divil a hair upon them.
Now come here, my two chickabiddies."

Adjusting the scales on the bed, where at night
she lay with the infants warm upon her, she took
the two red lumps of innocence in her well-rounded
arms, and laid one in either scale. As she did so,
they both looked up and smiled: it reminded them,
I suppose, of being laid in their cradles. Blessing
them both, and without any nervousness—for to
her it could make no difference—she raised by the
handle the balance. It was a very nice question—
which baby rose first from the counterpane. So
very slight was the difference, that the rosette itself
might almost have turned the scale. But there
was a perceptible difference, of perhaps about half
an ounce, and that in favour of the sweet-tempered

babe who now possessed the ribbon; and who, as the other rose slowly before him, drew up his own little toes, and tried prematurely to crow at him. Prematurely, my boy, in many ways.

No further mistrust was left in the mind of Mrs. O'Gaghan. Henceforth that rosetted infant is like to outweigh and outmeasure his brother, a hundred-fold, a thousandfold, in every balance, by every standard, save those of self, and of true love, and perhaps of the kingdom of Heaven.

CHAPTER III.

THE reason why Mrs. O'Gaghan, generally so prompt and careful, though never very lucid, had neglected better precautions in a matter so important, was simply and solely this—Lady Nowell, the delicate mother, was dying. It had been known, ever since the birth, that she had scarcely any chance of recovery. And Biddy loved her with all her warm heart, and so did every one in the house who owned a heart that could love. In the great anxiety,. all things were upside down. None of the servants knew where to go for orders, and few could act without them; the housekeeper was all abroad; house-steward there was none; head-butler Hogstaff cried in his pantry, and wiped his eyes with the leathers; and, as for the master of them all, Sir Cradock Nowell himself, he rarely left the darkened room, and when he did he could not see well.

A sweet frail creature the young mother was,
wedded too early, as happens here more often than
we are aware of. Then disappointed, and grieving
still more at her husband's disappointment, she had
set her whole heart so long and so vainly upon
prospective happiness, that now it was come she had
not the strength to do anything more than smile at
it. And smile she did, very sweetly, all the time
she knew she was dying; she felt so proud of those
two fine boys, and could not think how she had
them. Ever so many times Sir Cradock, hanging
fondly over her wan, sweet face, ordered the little
wretches away, who would keep on coming to
trouble her. But every time she looked up at him
with such a feeble glory, and such a dash of
humour,—"You've got them at last, and now you
don't care a bit about them; but oh! please do for
my sake;" every time her fading eyes followed them
to the door, so that the loving husband, cold with
the shadow of the coming void, had to whisper,
"Bring them back, put them here between us."

Although he knew that she was dying, he could
not feel it yet; the mind admitted that fearful
truth, but the heart repulsed it. Further as she
sunk, and further yet, from his pleading gaze, the
closer to her side he crept, the more he clasped her
shadowy hands, and raised her drooping neck; the
fonder grew the entreating words, the whispers of
the love-time, faint smiles that hoped to win her
smile, although they moved in tears. And smile
she did once more on earth, through the ashy hue

—the shadow of the soul's wings fluttering—when two fresh lives, bought by her death, were shown for the farewell to her.

"And if it's wrong, then, she'll make it right," thought the conscientious Biddy. "I can take my oath on't she knowed the differ from the very first, though nobody else couldn't see it, barring the caps they was 'put in. Now, if only that gossoon will consent to her see them once more, and it can't hurt the poor darlin'—and the blessing as comes from the death's gaze——"

Mrs. O'Gaghan's doubts were ended by the entrance of the doctor, a spare, short man, with a fiery face, red hair, and quick little eyes. He was not more than thirty years old, but knew his duties thoroughly; nevertheless, he would not have been there but for the sudden emergency. He was now come to fetch the nurse, having observed that the poor mother's eyes were gleaming feebly, once and again, towards the door that led to the nursery; and at last she had tried to raise her hand, and point in that direction. So in came Biddy, sobbing hard, with a babe on either arm; 'and she curtseyed cleverly to Sir Cradock without disturbing the equipoise. But the mother's glance was not judicial, as poor Biddy had expected—her heart and soul were far beyond rosettes, and even titles. In one long, yearning look, she lingered on her new-born babes, then turned those hazy eyes in fondness to her kneeling husband's, then tried to pray or bless the three, and shivered twice, and died.

For days and weeks Sir Cradock Nowell bore
his life, but did not live. All his clear intellect and
strong will, noble plans, and useful labours, all his
sense of truth and greatness, lay benumbed and
frozen in the cold track of death. He could not
bear to see his children, he would not even hear of
them; "they had robbed him of his loved one,
and what good were they? Little red things;
perhaps he would love them when they grew like
their mother." Those were not his expressions, for
he was proud and shy; but that was the form his
thoughts would take, if they could take any. No
wonder that he, for a time, was lost beyond the
verge of reason; because that blow, which most of
all stuns and defeats the upright man, had descended
on him—the blow to the sense of justice. This a
man of large mind feels often from his fellow-men,
never from his Maker. But Sir Cradock was a man
of intellect, rather than of mind. To me a large
mind seems to be strong intellect quickened with
warm heart. Sir Cradock Nowell had plenty of intellect, and plenty of heart as well, but he kept the
two asunder. So much the better for getting on in
the world; so much the worse for dealing with
God. A man so constituted rarely wins, till over-
borne by trouble, that only knowledge which falls
(like genius) where our Father listeth. So the
bereaved man measured justice by the ells and
inches of this world.

And it did seem very hard, that he who had
lived for twenty years, from light youth up to the
balance age of forty, not only without harming any

fellow-mortal, but, upon fair average, to do good in the world—it seemed, I say—it was, thought he —most unjust that such a man could not set his serious heart upon one little treasure without losing it the moment he had learned its value. Now, with pride to spur sad memory—bronze spurs to a marble horse — he remembered how his lovely Violet chose him from all others. Gallant suitors crowded round her, for she was rich as well as beautiful; but she quietly came from out them all for him, a man of twice her age. And he who had cared for none till then, and had begun to look on woman as a stubby-bearded man looks back at the romance of his first lather, he first admired her grace and beauty, then her warmth of heart and wit, then, scorning all analysis, her own sweet self; and loved her.

A few days after the funeral he was walking sadly up and down in his lonely library, caring no whit for his once-loved books, for the news of the day, or his business, and listless to look at anything, even the autumn sunset; when the door was opened quietly, and shyly through the shadows stole his schoolfellow of yore, his truest friend, John Rosedew. With this gentleman I take a very serious liberty; but he never yet was known to resent a liberty taken honestly. That, however, does not justify me. "John Rosedew" I intend to call him, because he likes it best; and so he would though ten times a Bachelor of Divinity, a late Vice-Principal of his college, and the present Rector of Nowelhurst. Formerly I did my best, loving well the character, to describe that simple-minded, tender-hearted yeoman, John Huxtable, of Tossil's Barton, in the county of Devon. Like his, as like any two of Nature's ever-varied works, were the native grain and staple of the Rev. John Rosedew. Beside those little inborn and indying variations which Nature still insists on, that she may know her sons apart, those two genial Britons differed both in mental and bodily endowments, and through education. In spite of that, they were, and are, as like to one another as any two men can be who have no smallness in them. Small men run pretty much of a muchness; as the calibre increases, so the divergence multiplies.

Farmer Huxtable was no fool; but having once learned to sign his name, he had attained his maximum of literary development; John Rosedew, on the other hand, although a strong and well-built man, who had pulled a good oar in his day, was not, in bulk and stature, a match for Hercules or Milo. Unpretending, gentle, a lover of the truth, easily content with others, but never with himself, even now, at the age of forty, he had not overcome the bashfulness and diffidence of a fine and sensitive nature. And, first-rate scholar as he was, he would have lost his class at Oxford solely through that shyness, unless a kind examiner, who saw his blushing agony, had turned from some common-place of Sophocles to a glorious passage of Pindar. Then, carried away by the noble poet, John Rose-dew forgot the schools, the audience, even the row of examiners, and gave grand thoughts their grand expression, breathing free as the winds of heaven. Nor till his voice began to falter from the high emotion, and his heart beat fast, though not from shame, and the tears of genius touched by genius were difficult to check, not till then knew he, or guessed, that every eye was fixed upon him, that every heart was thrilling, that even the stiff exa- miners bent forward like eager children, and the young men in the gallery could scarcely keep from cheering. Then suddenly, in the full sweep of magnificence, he stopped, like an eagle shot.

Now the parson, ruddy cheeked, with a lock of light brown hair astray upon his forehead, and his pale, blue eyes looking much as if he had just awoke and rubbed them, came shyly and with deep embarrassment into the darkening room. For days and days he had thought and thought, but could not at all determine whether, and when, and how, he ought to visit his ancient friend. His own heart first suggested that he ought to go at once, if only to show the bereaved one that still there were some to love him. To this right impulse—and the im- pulse of a heart like this could seldom be a wrong one—rose counter-checks of worldly knowledge, such little as he had. And it seemed to many people strange and unaccountable, that if Mr. Rosedew piqued himself upon anything whatever, it was not on his learning, his purity, or benevo- lence, it was not on his gentle bearing, or the chivalry of his soul, but on a fine acquirement,

whereof in all opinions (except, indeed, his own)
he possessed no jot or tittle—a strictly-disciplined
and astute experience of the world. Now this
supposed experience told him that it might seem
coarse and forward to offer the hard grasp of
friendship ere the soft clasp of love was cold;
that he, as the clergyman of the parish, would
appear to presume upon his office ; that no proud
man could ever bear to have his anguish pryed
into. These, and many other misgivings and ob-
jections, met his eager longings to help his dear old
friend.

Suddenly and to his great relief—for he knew
not how to begin, though he felt how and mis-
trusted it—the old friend turned upon him from
his lonely pacing, and held out both his hands.
Not a word was said by either ; what they meant
required no telling, or was told by silence. Long
time they sat in the western window, John Rosedew keeping his eyes from sunset, which did not
suit them then. At last he said, in a low voice,
which it cost him much to find—

"What name, dear Cradock, for the younger
babe ? Your own, of course, for the elder."

"No name, John, but his sweet mother's; unless
you like to add his uncle's."

John Rosedew was puzzled lamentably. He
could not bear to worry his friend any more upon
the subject; and !yet it seemed to him sad, false
concord, to christen a boy as "Violet." But he
argued that, in botanical fact, a violet is male as

well as female, and at such a time he could not think of thwarting a widower's yearnings. In spite of all his worldly knowledge, it never occurred to his simple mind that poor Sir Cradock meant the lady's maiden surname, which I believe was "Incledon." And yet he had suggestive precedent brought even then before him, for Sir Cradock Nowell's brother bore the name of "Clayton;" which name John Rosedew added now, and found relief in doing so.

Thus it came to pass, that the babe without rosette was baptized as "Violet Clayton," while the owner of the bauble received the name of "Cradock"—Cradock Nowell, now the ninth in lineal succession. The father was still too broken down to care about being present; godfathers and godmothers made all their vows by proxy. Mrs. O'Gaghan held the infants, and one of them cried, and the other laughed. The rosette was there in all its glory, and received a tidy sprinkle; and the wearer of it was, as usual, the one who took things easily. As the common children said, who came to see the great ones "loustering," the whole affair was rather like a white burying than a baptism. Nevertheless, the tenants and labourers moistened their semi-regenerate clay with many a fontful of good ale, to ensure the success of the ceremony.

CHAPTER IV.

It is not pleasant to recur, to have a relapse of
chronology, neither does it show good management
on the part of a writer. Nevertheless, being free
of time among these forest by-ways, I mean to let
the pig now by the ear unfold his tail, or curl it
up, as the weather suits him. And now he runs
back for a month or two, trailing the rope from his
left hind-leg.

Poor Lady Nowell had become a mother, as indeed we learned from the village gossip, nearly a
fortnight before the expected time. Dr. Jellicorse
Buller, a very skilful man, in whom the Hall had
long confided, was suddenly called to London, the
day before that on which we last climbed the hill
towards Ringwood. With Sir Cradock's full consent, he obeyed the tempting summons. So in the
hurry and flutter of that October Sunday, it seemed
a most lucky thing to obtain, in a thinly-peopled
district, the prompt attendance of any medical
man. And but that a gallant regiment then hap-

pened to be on the march from Dorchester to
Southampton, there to embark for India, no masculine aid would have been forthcoming till after the
event. But the regimental surgeon, whose name
was Rufus Hutton, did all that human skill could
do, and saved the lives of both the infants, but
could not save the young mother. Having earned
Sir Cradock's lasting gratitude, and Biddy O'Gaghan's strong execrations, he was compelled to
rejoin his regiment, then actually embarking.

The twins grew fast, and throve amain, under
Mrs. O'Gaghan's motherly care, and shook the
deep-rooted country faith, that children brought
up by hand are sure to be puny weaklings. Nor
was it long till nature reasserted her authority,
and claimed her rights of compensation. The
father began to think more and more, first of
his duty towards the dead mother, and then of
his duty towards ·his children; and ere long
affection set to work, and drove duty away till
called for, which happened as we shall see presently. By the time those two pretty babies were
"busy about their teeth," Cradock Nowell the
elder was so deep in odontology, that Biddy herself could not answer him, and was afraid to ask
any questions. He watched each little white
cropper, as a girl peers day by day into a starting
hyacinth. Then, when they could walk, they followed daddy everywhere, and he never was happy
without them. It was a pretty thing to see them
toddling down the long passages, stopping by the

walls to prattle, crawling at the slippery parts,
where the newly-invented tiles shone. And the
father would dance away backwards from them,
forgetting all about the grand servants, clapping
his hands to encourage them, and holding an
orange as prize for a crawling-race—then whisk
away round a corner, and lay his cheek flat to the
wainscot, to peep at his sons, and learn which of
them was the braver. And in those days, I think,
he was proud to find that Cradock Nowell, the
heir of the house, was by far the more gallant baby.
Which of the two was the prettier, not even sharp
Biddy could say; so strongly alike they were, that
the palm of beauty belonged to the one who had
taken least medicine lately.

Then, as they turned two years and a half, and
could jump with both feet at once, without the
spectator growing sad on the subject of biped defi-
ciencies, their father would lie down on the carpet,
and make them roll and jump over him. He
would watch their little spotted legs with intense
appreciation; and if he got an oral sprinkle from
childhood's wild sense of humour, instead of de-
pressing him, I declare it quite set him up for the
day, sir. And he never bothered himself or them
by attempts to forecast their destinies. There
they were enjoying themselves, uproariously happy,
as proud as Punch of their exploits, and the father
a great deal prouder. All three as blest for the
moment, as full of life and rapture, as God meant
His creatures to be, so often as they are wise

enough; and, in the name of God, let them be so!

But then there came a time of spoiling, a time of doing just what they liked, even after their eyes were opening to the light and shadow of right and wrong. If they smiled, or pouted, or even cried—though in that they were very moderate—in a fashion which descended to them from their darling mother, thereupon great right and law, and even toughest prejudice, fell flat as rolled dough before them. So they toddled about most gloriously, with a strong sense of owning the universe.

Next ensued a time of mighty retribution. Astræa, with her feelings hurt, came down for a slashing moment. Fond as he was, and far more weak than he ever had been before, Sir Cradock Nowell was not a fool. He saw it was time to check the license, ere mischief grew irretrievable. Something flagrant occurred one day; both the children were in for it; they knew as well as possible that they were jolly rogues together, and together in their childish counsel they resolved to stand it out. The rumour was that they had stolen into Mrs. Toaster's choicest cupboard, and hardly left enough to smell at in a two-pound pot of greengage jam. Anyhow, there they stood, scarlet in face and bright of eye, back to back, with their broad white shoulders, their sturdy legs set wide apart, and their little heels stamping defiantly. Mrs. Toaster had not the heart to do anything but

kiss them, with a number of "O fies!" and they
accepted her kisses indignantly, and wiped their
lips with their pinafores. They knew that they
were in the wrong, but they had not tried to conceal it, and they meant to brazen it out. They
looked such a fine pair of lords of the earth, and
vindicated their felony with so grand an air, such
high contempt of all justice, that Cookey and
Hogstaff, empannelled as jury, said, "Drat the
little darlings, let 'em have the other pot, mem!"
But as their good star would have it, Mrs. O'Gaghan came after them. Upsetting the mere *nisi
prius* verdict, she marched them off, one in either
hand, to the great judge sitting *in banco*, Sir Cradock himself, in the library. With the sense of
heavy wrong upon them, the little hearts began to
fail, as they climbed with tugs instead of jumps,
and no arithmetic of the steps, the narrow flight of
stone stairs that led from regions culinary. But
they would not shed a tear, not they, nor even say
they were sorry, otherwise Biddy (who herself was
crying) would have let them go with the tap of a
battledore.

Poor little souls, they got their deserts with very
scanty ceremony. When Biddy began to relate
their crime, one glance at their father's face was
enough; they hung behind, and dropped their
eyes, and flushed all under their curling hair. Yet
little did they guess the indignity impending. Hogstaff had followed all the way, and so had Mrs.
Toaster, to plead for them. Sir Cradock sent them

both away, and told Biddy to wait outside. Then he led his children to an inner room, and calmly explained his intentions. These were of such a nature that the young offenders gazed at each other in dumb amazement and horror, which very soon grew eloquent as the sentence was being executed. But the brave little fellows cried more, even then, at the indignity than the pain of it.

Then the stern father ordered them out of his sight for the day, and forbade every one to speak to them until the following morning; and away the twins went, hand in hand, down the cold cruel passage, their long flaxen hair all flowing together, and shaking to the sound of their contrite sobs and heart-pangs. At the corner, by the steward's room, they turned with one accord, and looked back wistfully at their father. Sir Cradock had been saying to himself, as he rubbed his hands after the exercise—"A capital day's work: what a deal of good it will do them; the self-willed little rascals!" but the look cast back upon him was so like their mother's when he had done anything to vex her, that away he rushed to his bedroom, and had to wash his face afterwards.

But, of course, he held to his stern resolve to see them no more that evening, otherwise the lesson would be utterly thrown away. Holding to it as he did, the effect surpassed all calculation. It was the turning-point in their lives.

"My boy, you know it hurts me a great deal more than you," says the hypocritical usher, who

rather enjoys the cane-swing. The boy knows it
is hypocrisy, and is morally hurt more than phy-
sically. But wholly different is the result when
the patient knows and feels the deep love of the
agent, and cannot help believing that justice has
flogged the judge. And hitherto their flesh had
been intemerate and inviolable; the strictest orders
had been issued that none should dare to slap
them, and all were only too prone to coax and pet
the beautiful angels. Little angels: treated so,
they would soon have been little devils. As for
the warning given last week, they thought it a bit
of facetiousness: so now was the time, of all times,
to strike temperately, but heavily.

That night they went to bed before dark, without having cared for tea or toast, and Biddy's soft
heart ached by the pillow, as they lay in each
other's arms, hugged one another, having now
none else in the world to love, and sobbed their
little troubles off into moaning slumber.

On the following morning, without any concert
or debate, and scarcely asking why, the little
things went hand in hand, united more than ever
by the recent visitation, as far as the door of their
father's bedroom. There they slank behind a
curtain; and when he came out, the rings above
fluttered with fear and love and hope. Much as
the father's heart was craving, he made believe to
walk onward, till Craddy ran out, neck or nothing,
and sprang into his arms.

After this great event, their lives flowed on very

happily into boyhood, youth, and manhood. They heartily loved and respected their father; they could never be enough with John Rosedew; and although they quarrelled and fought sometimes, they languished and drooped immediately when parted from one another. As for Biddy O'Gaghan, now a high woman in the household, her only difficulty was that she never could tell of her two boys which to quote as the more astounding.

"If you plase, ma'am," she always concluded, "there'll not be so much as the lean of a priest for anybody iver to choose atwane the bootiful two on them. No more than there was on the day when my blissed self—murder now!—any more, I manes, nor the differ a peg can find 'twane a murphy and a purratie. And a Murphy I must be, to tark, so free as I does, of the things as is above me. Says Patrick O'Geoghegan to meself one day—glory be to his sowl, and a gintleman every bit of him, lave out where he had the small-pux—'Biddy,' he says, 'hould your pratie-trap, or I'll shove these here bellises down it.' And for my good it would have been, as I am thankful to acknowledge that same, though I didn't see it that day, thank the Lord. Ah musha, musha, a true gintleman he were, and lave me out his fellow, ma'am, if iver you comes acrass him."

But, in spite of Biddy's assertion, there were many points of difference, outward and inward too, between Cradock and Clayton Nowell. By this time the "Violet" was obsolete, except with Sir

Cradock, who rather liked it, and with young Crad,
who had corrupted it into the endearing "Viley."
John Rosedew had done his utmost to extinguish
the misnomer, being sensitive on the subject, from
his horror of false concord, as attributed to himself.   Although the twins were so much alike in
stature, form, and feature that it required care to
discern them after the sun was down, no clear-
sighted person would miscall them when they both
were present, and the light was good.   Clayton
Nowell's eyes were brown, Cradock's a dark grey;
Cradock's hair was one shade darker, and grew
more away from his forehead, and the expression
of his gaze came from a longer distance.   Clayton
always seemed up for bantering ; Cradock anxious
to inquire, and to joke about it afterwards, if occasion offered.   Then Cradock's head inclined, as he
walked, a little towards the left shoulder ; Clayton's
hung, almost imperceptibly, somewhat to the right ;
and Cradock's hands were hard and dry, Clayton's
soft as good French kid.

And, as regards the inward man, they differed
far more widely.   Every year their modes of
thought, fancies, tastes, and habits, were diverging
more decidedly.   Clayton sought command and
power, and to be admired ; Cradock's chief ambi-
tion was to be loved by every one.   And so with
intellectual matters ; Clayton showed more dash
and brilliance, Cradock more true sympathy, and
thence more grasp and insight.   Clayton loved the
thoughts which strike us, Cradock those which

move us subtly. But, as they lived not long together, it is waste of time to *finesse* between them.
Whatever they were, they loved one another, and
could not bear to be parted.

Meanwhile, their " Uncle John" as they always
called Mr. Rosedew—their uncle only in the spirit
—was nursing and making much of a little
daughter of his own. Long before Lady Nowell's
death, indeed for ten long years before he obtained
the living of Nowelhurst, with the little adjunct
of Rushford, he had been engaged to a lady-love
much younger than himself, whose name was Amy
Venn. Not positively engaged, I mean, for he
was too shy to pop the question to any one but
himself, for more than seven years of the ten.
But all that time Amy Venn was loving him, and
he was loving her, and each would have felt it a
grievous blow, if the other had started sideways.
Miss Venn was poor, and had none except her
widowed mother to look to, and hence the parson
was trebly shy of pressing a poor man's suit. He,
a very truthful mortal, had pure faith in his Amy,
and she had the like in him. So for several years
he shunned the common-room, and laid by all he
could from his fellowship, college-appointments,
and professorship. But when his old friend Sir
Cradock Nowell presented him to the benefice—
not a very gorgeous one, but enough for a quiet
parson's family—he took a clean white tie at once,
vainly strove to knot it grandly, actually got his
scout to brush him, and after three glasses of

D 2

common-room port, strode away to his Amy at Kidlington.   There he found her training the apricot
on the south wall of her mother's cottage, one of
the three great apricot-trees that paid the rent so
nicely.   What a pity they were not peaches; they
would have yielded so fit a simile.   But peach-
bloom will not thrive at Kidlington, except upon
ladies' faces.

Three months afterwards, just when all was
arranged, and Mrs. Venn was at last persuaded
that Hampshire is not all pigs and rheumatism,
forests, and swamps, and charcoal, when John,
with his voice rather shaky, and a patch of red
where his whiskers should have been, had proclaimed his own banns three times—for he was a
very odd fellow in some things, and scorned the
" royal road" to wedlock—just at that time, I say,
poor Lady Nowell's confinement upset all calculation, and her melancholy death flung a pall on
wedding-favours.   Not only through respect, but
from real sympathy with the faithful friend, John
Rosedew and Amy held counsel together, and de-
ferred the long-pending bridal.   " Ὅσῳ μακρότερον,
τόσῳ μακάρτερον," said John, who always thought in
Greek, except when Latin hindered him; but few
young ladies will admit — and now-a-days they
all understand it—that the apophthegm is applied
well.

. However, it did come off at last ; John Rosedew,
when his banns had been rolling in his mind, in

the form of Greek senarii, for six months after the
first time of out-asking, set to and read them all
over again in public; to revive their efficacy, and
to surrebut all let and hindrance. He was accustomed now to so many stops, that he felt surprised
when nobody rose to interpellate. And so the
banns of John Rosedew, bachelor, and Amy Venn,
spinster, &c., were read six times in Nowelhurst
Church, and six times from the desk at Kidlington. And, sooth to say, it was not without
significance.

> "Tantæ molis erat to produce our beautiful Amy."

On the nuptial morning, Sir Cradock, whom
they scarcely expected, gathered up his broken
courage, sank his own hap in another's, and was
present and tried to enjoy himself. How shy
John Rosedew was, how sly to conceal his blushes,
how spry when the bride glanced towards him,
and nobody else looked that way—all this very
few could help observing; but they liked him too
well to talk of it. Enough that the friend of his
youth, thoroughly understanding John, was blessed
with so keen a perception of those simple little
devices, that at last he did enjoy himself, which he
deserved to do for trying.

When the twins were nearly three years old,
Mrs. Rosedew presented John with the very thing
he wished for most, an elegant little girl. And
here the word "elegant" is used with forethought,

and by prolepsis; though Mrs. O'Gaghan, lent for
a time to the Rectory, employed that epithet at the
first glance, even while announcing the gender.

"Muckstraw, then, and she's illigant intirely;
an' it's hopin' I be as there'll only be two on her,
one for each of me darlin' boys. And now cudn't
you manage it, doctor dear?"

But alas! the supply was limited, and no dupli-
cate ever issued. Lucina saw John Rosedew's
pride, and was afraid of changing his character.
To all his Oxford friends he announced the fact
of his paternity in letters commencing—"Now
what do you think, my dear fellow, what do you
think of this—the most astounding thing has happened," &c. &c. He thought of it himself so
much, that his intellect grew dreamy, and he forgot all about next Sunday's sermon, until he was
in the pulpit. And four weeks after that he made
another great mistake, which horrified him desperately, though it gratified the parish.

It had been arranged between his Amy and
himself, that if she felt quite strong enough, she
should appear in church on the Sunday afternoon,
to offer the due thanksgiving. In the grey old
church at Nowelhurst, a certain pew had been set
apart, by custom immemorial, for the use of good-
wives who felt grateful for their safe deliverance.
Here Mrs. Rosedew was to present herself at the
proper period, with the aid of Biddy's vigorous
arm down the hill from the Rectory. As yet she
was too delicate to bear the entire service. The

August afternoon was sultry, and the church doors stood wide open, while the bees among the church-yard thyme drowsed a sleepy sermon. As luck would have it, a recruiting sergeant, toling for the sons of Ytene, finding the road so dusty, and the alehouse barred against him, came sauntering into the church during the second lesson, for a little mild change of air. Espying around him some likely rustics, he stationed himself in the vacant " churching pew," because the door was open, and the position prominent. " All right," thought the rector, who was very short-sighted, " how good of my darling Amy to come! But I wonder she wears her scarlet cloak to come to church with, and in such weather! But perhaps Dr. Buller ordered it, for fear of her catching cold." So at the proper moment he drew his surplice round him, looked full at the sergeant standing there by the pillar, and commenced majestically, though with a trembling voice—

" Forasmuch as it hath pleased Almighty God of His goodness to give you safe deliverance, and hath preserved you in the great danger of child-birth, you shall therefore give hearty thanks unto God and say——"

The sergeant looked on very primly, with his padded arms tightly folded, and his head thrown back, calling war and victory into his gaze, for the credit of the British army. Then he wondered angrily what the —— those chawbacons could see in him to be grinning at.

"I am well pleased," &c., continued John Rosedew, sonorously ; for he had a magnificent voice,
and still regarding the sergeant with a look of
tender interest. Even Sir Cradock Nowell could
scarcely keep his countenance; but the parson went
through the whole of it handsomely and to the
purpose, thinking only, throughout it, of God's
great mercies to him. So beloved he was already,
and so much respected, that none of the congregation had the heart to tell him of his mistake, as he
talked with them in the churchyard; though he
thought even then that he must have his bands, as
he often had, at the back of his neck.

But on his way home he overtook an old hobbler,
who enjoyed a joke more than a scruple.

"How are you, Simon Tapscott? How do you
do to-day? Glad to see you at church, Simon,"
said the parson, holding his hand out, as he always
did to his parishioners, unless they had disgraced
themselves.

"Purty vair, measter ; purty vair I be, vor a
woald galley baggar as ave bin in the Low Coun-
tries, and dwoant know sin from righteousness."
This last was a gross perversion of a passage in the
sermon which had ruffled ancient Simon. "Can't
goo much, howiver, by rason of the rhymatics.
Now cud 'e do it to I, measter? cud 'e do it to I,
and I'll thraw down bath my critches? Good vor
one sojer, good vor anoother."

"Do what for you, Simon? Fill your old

canteen, or send you a pound of baccy?" asked
the parson, mildly chaffing.

"Noo, noo; none o' that.   There baint noo
innard parts grace of the Lord in that.   Choorch
I handsomely, zame as 'e dwoed that strapping
soger now jist."

"What, Simon!   Why, Simon, do you know
what you are saying——"   But I cannot bear to
tell of John Rosedew humiliated; he was humble
enough by nature.   So fearful was the parson of
renewing that recollection within the sacred walls,
that no thanks were offered there for the birth of
sweet Amy Rosedew, save by, or on behalf of, that
recruiting sergeant.

CHAPTER V.

WHEN Cradock and Clayton were ten years old,
they witnessed a scene which puzzled them, and
dwelt long in their boyish memories. Job Hogstaff was going to Ringwood, and they followed
him down the passage towards the entrance-hall,
emphatically repeating the commissions with which
they had charged him. Old Job loved them as if
they were his grandsons, and would do his utmost
to please them, but they could not trust his
memory, or even his capacity.

"Now, Job," cried little Cradock, pulling at his
coat-lappet, "it's no good pretending that you
know all, when you won't even stop to listen. I'm
sure you'll go and make some great mistake, as
you did last Tuesday. Mind you tell Mr. Stride
it's for Master Cradock Nowell, and they must be
sure to give you a good one, or I shall send it back.
Now just tell me what I have told you. I ought
to have written it down, but I wasn't sure how to
spell 'groove.'"

"Why, Master Crad, I'm to say a long spill, very sharp at the end."

"Sharp at the *point*, Job, not blunt at the end like a new black-lead pencil."

"And whatever you do, Job, don't forget the catgut for my cross-bow, one size larger than last time."

"Hold your jaw, Viley, till I've quite finished; or he'll ask for a top made of catgut."

Both the boys laughed at this; you could hear them all down the long passage. Any small folly makes a boy laugh.

"Well, Master Crad, you *must* think me a 'muff,' as you call it. And the groove is to go quite up to the spill; there must be two rings below the crown of it."

"Below the crown, indeed! On the fat part, I said three times. Now, Viley, you know you heard me."

"Well, well," cried Job in despair, "two rings on the fat part, and no knot at all in the wood, and at least six inches round, and, and, well—I think that's all of it, thank the Lord."

"All of it, indeed! Well, you *are* a nice fellow! Didn't I tell you so, Viley? Why, you've left out altogether the most important point of all, Job. The wood must be a clear bright yellow, or else a very rich gold colour, and I'm to pay for it next Tuesday, because I spent my week's money yesterday, as soon as ever I got it, and—oh, Viley! can't you lend a fellow sixpence?"

44   CRADOCK NOWELL :

"No, not to save my life, sir. Why, Craddy, you know I wouldn't let you go tick if I could."

The boys rushed at one another, half in fun and half in affection, and, seizing each other by the belt of the light-plaid tunic, away they went dancing down the hall, while Hogstaff whistled a polka gently, with his old eyes glistening after them. A prettier pair, or better matched, never set young locks afloating. Each put his healthy, clear, bright face on the shoulder of the other, each flung out his short-socked legs, and pointed his dainty feet. You could see their shapely calves jerked up as they went with double action, and the hollow of the back curved in, as they threw asunder recklessly, then clasped one another again, and you thought they must both reel over. Sir Cradock Nowell hated trousers, and would not have their hair cropped, because it was like their mother's; otherwise they would not have looked one quarter so picturesque.

Before the match was fairly finished—for they were used to this sort of thing, and the object always was to see which would give in first—it was cut short most unexpectedly. While they were taking a sharp pirouette down at the end of the hall—and as they whirled round I defy their father to have known the one from the other—the door of the steward's room opened suddenly, and a tall dark woman came out. The twins in full merriment dashed up against her, and must have fallen if she had not collared them with strong and bony arms. Like little gentlemen, as they were, every atom of them, they turned in a moment to apologise, and their cheeks were burning red. They saw a gaunt old woman, wide-shouldered, stern, and forcible.

"Oo, ah! a bonnie pair ye've gat, as I see in all my life lang. But ye'll get no luck o' them. Tak' the word o' threescore year, ye'll never get no luck o' them, you that calls yoursel' Craydock Nowell."

She was speaking to Sir Cradock, who had followed her from the steward's room, and who seemed as much put out as a proud man of fifty ever cares to show himself. He made no answer, and the two poor children fell back against a side-bench.

"I'll no talk o' matters noo. You've a gi'en me my refoosal, and I tak' it once for all. But ye'll be sorry for the day ye did it, Craydock Nowell."

To the great amazement of Hogstaff, who was more taken aback than any one else, Sir Cradock Nowell, without a word, walked to the wide front door with ceremony, as if he were leading a peeress out. He did not offer his arm to the woman, but neither did he shrink from her; she gathered her dark face up again from its softening glance at the children, and without another word or look, but sweeping her skirt around her, away she walked down the broad front road, as stiff and as stern as the oak-trees.

CHAPTER VI.

THE lapse of years made little difference with
the Reverend John Rosedew, except to mellow
and enfranchise the heart so free and rich by
nature, and to pile fresh stores of knowledge in the
mind so stored already. Of course the parson had
his faults. In many a little matter his friends
could come down upon him sharply, if minded so
to do. But any one so minded would not have
been fit to be called John Rosedew's friend.

His greatest fault was one which sprang from
his own high chivalry. If once he detected a
person, whether taught or untaught, in the attempt
to deceive or truckle, that person was to him
thenceforth a thing to be pitied and prayed for.
Large and liberal as his heart was, charitable and
even lenient to all other frailties, the presence of a
lie in the air was to it as ozone to a test-paper.
And then he was always sorry afterwards when he
had shown his high disdain. For who could dis-

prove that John Rosedew himself might have been
a thorough liar, if trained and taught to consider
truth a policeman with his staff drawn?

Another fault John Rosedew had—and I do not
tell his foibles (as our friends do) to enjoy them—
he gave to his books and their bygone ages much
of the time which he ought to have spent abroad
in his own little parish. But this could not be
attributed to any form of self-indulgence. Much
as he liked his books, he liked his flock still better,
but never could overcome the idea that they would
rather not be bothered. If any one were ailing,
if any one were needy, he would throw aside his
Theophrastus, and be where he was wanted, with a
mild sweet voice and gentle eyes that crannied
not, like a crane's bill, into the family crocks and
dustbin. It was a part, and no unpleasant one,
of his natural diffidence, that he required a poor
man's invitation quite as much as a rich one's, ere
ever he crossed the threshold; unless trouble over-
flowed the impluvium. In all the parish of Nowelhurst there was scarcely a man or a woman who
did not rejoice to see the rector pacing his leisurely rounds, carrying his elbows a little out, as
men with large deltoid muscles do, wearing his old
hat far back on his head, so that it seemed to
slope away from him, and smiling quietly to himself at the children who tugged his coat-tails for
an orange or a halfpenny. He never could come
out but what the urchins of the village were down
upon him as promptly as if he were apple-pie;

and many of them had the impudence to call him
"Uncle John" before his hair was grey.

Instead of going to school, the boys were ap-
prenticed to him in the classics; and still more
pleasantly he taught them to swim, and fish, and
row. Of riding he knew but little, except from
the treatise of Xenophon, and a paper on the Pele-
thronian Lapiths; so they learned it as all other
boys do, by dint of crown and hard bumpage.
Moreover, Mark Stote, head gamekeeper, took them
in hand very early as his pupils in woodcraft and
gunnery. To tell the truth, Uncle John objected
to this accomplishment; he thought that the
wholesome excitement and exercise of shooting
afforded scarcely a valid reason for the destruction
of innocent life. However, he recollected that he
had not always thought so—his conversion having
been wrought by the shrieks of a wounded hare—
neither did he expect to bind all the world with
his own girdle. Sir Cradock insisted that the
young idea should be taught to shoot, and both the
young ideas took to it very kindly.

Perhaps on the whole they were none the worse
for the want of public-school training. What
they lost thereby in quickness, suspicion, and
effrontery, was more than balanced by the gain in
purity, simplicity, love of home, and kindliness.
For nature had not gifted them with that vulgar
arrogance, for which the best prescription is " cal-
citration nine times a day, and clean the boots for
kicking you." Every year their father took them

for a month or two to London, to garnish with
some courtly frilling the knuckles of his Hampshire hams. But they only hated it; thorough
agricoles they were, and well knew their own
blessings : and sweet and gladsome was the morning after each return, though it might be blowing
a gale of wind, or drizzling through the ash-leaves.
And then the headlong rush to see beloved Uncle
John. Nature they loved in any form, sylvan, agra-
rian, human, when that human form was such as they
could climb and nestle in. And there was not in
the parish, nor in all the forest, any child so rough
and dirty, so shock-headed, and such a scamp, that
it could not climb into the arms of John Rosedew's fellow-feeling.

But I must not dwell on these pleasant days, the
father's glory, the hopes of the sons, the love of all
who came near them, and the blessings of Mrs.
O'Gaghan.

They were now to go to Oxford, and astonish
the natives there, by showing that a little *hic, hæc,
hoc*, may come even out of Galilee ; that a youth
never drawn through the wire-gauge of Eton,
Harrow, or Rugby, may carry still the electric
spark, and be taper and well-rounded. Half their
learning accrued *sub dio*, in the manner of the
ancients. Uncle John would lead them between
the trees and down to some forest dingle, the boy
on his right hand construing aloud or parsing
very slowly, the little spark at his left all glowing
to explode at the first mistake. Δεξιόσειρος made

the running, until he tripped and fell mentally,
and even then he was set on his legs, unless the
other was down upon him ; but in the latter case
the yoke-mate leaped into the harness. The
stroke-oar on the river that evening was awarded
to the one who paced the greatest number of stades
in the active voice of expounding. The accuracy,
the caution, born of this warm rivalry, became at
last so vigilant, that the boy who won the toss for
the right-hand place at starting, was almost sure
of the stroke-oar.

So they passed the matriculation test with con-
summate ease, and delighted the college tutor
by their clear bold writing. They had not read
so much as some men have before entering the
University, but all their knowledge was close
and firm, and staunch enough for a spring-board.
And they wrote most excellent Latin prose, and
Greek verse easily flowing. However, Sir Cradock
was very nervous on the eve of their departure for
the first term of Oxford residence, and led John
Rosedew, in whose classical powers he placed the
highest confidence, into his private room, and
there begged him, as a real friend, tested now for
forty years, to tell him bluntly whether the boys
were likely to do him credit.

"Don't spare me, John, and don't spare them :
only let us have no disappointment about it."

"My dear fellow, my dear fellow !" cried John,
tugging at his collar, as he always did when non-
plussed, for fear of losing himself; "how on earth

can I tell? Most likely the men know a great deal more in the University now than they did when I had lectures. Haven't I begged you fifty times to have down a young first-classman?"

"Yes, I know you have, John. But I am not quite such a fool, nor so shamelessly ungrateful. To upset the pile of your ten years' labour, and rebuild it upon its apex! And talk to me of young first-classmen! Why, you know as well as I do, John, that there is not one of them, however brilliant, with a tenth part of your knowledge. It could never be, any more than a young tree can carry the fruit of an old one. Why, when you took your own first-class, they could only find one man to put with you, and you have never ceased to read, read, read, ever since you left old Oriel, and chiefly in taste and philology. And such a memory as you have! John, I am ashamed of you. You want to impose upon me."

And Sir Cradock fixed the parson's eyes with that keen and point-blank gaze, which was especially odious to the shy John Rosedew.

"I am sure I don't. You cannot mean that," he replied, rather warmly, for, like all imaginative men, when of a diffident cast, he was desperately matter-of-fact the moment his honour was played with. His friend began to smile at him, drawing up his grey moustache, and saying, "Yes, John, you are a donkey."

"I know that I am," said John Rosedew, shutting his eyes, as he loved to do when he got on a favour-

E 2

ite topic; "by the side of those mighty critics of the sixteenth and seventeenth centuries—the Scaligers, the Casaubons, the Vossii, the Stephani,— what am I but a starving donkey, without a thistle left for him? But as regards our English critics —at least too many of them—I submit that we have been misled by the superiority of their Latin, and their more slashing style. I doubt whether any of them had a tenth part of the learning, or the sequacity of genius——"

"Come, John, I can't stand this, you know; and the boys will be down here directly, they are so fond of brown sherry."

"Well, to return to the subject—I own that I was surprised and hurt when a former Professor of Greek actually confounded the Æolic form of the *plusquam perfectum* of so common a verb as——"

"Yes, John, I know all about that, and how it spoiled your breakfast. But about the boys, the boys, John?"

"And again, as to the delicate sub-significance, not the well-known tortuousness of παρά in composition, but——"

"Confound it, John. They've got all their things packed. They'll be here in a moment, pretending to rollick for our sakes; and you won't tell me what you think of them."

"Well, I think there never were two finer fellows to jump a gate since the days of Castor and Pollux. '*Hunc equis, illum superare pugnis.*' You remember how you took me down for construing '*pugnis*' wrongly, when we were at Sherborne?"

"Yes, and how proud I was, John! You had been at the head of the form for three months, and none of us could stir you; but you came back again next day in the fifth Æneid. But here come the villains—now it's all over."

And so the boys went away, and their father could not for his life ascertain what opinion his ancient friend had formed as to the chances of their doing something good at Oxford. Simple and straightforward as Mr. Rosedew was, no man ever lived from whom it was harder to force an opinion. He saw matters from so many aspects, everything took so many facets, shifting lights, and playing colours, from the versatility of his mind, that whoso could fix him at such times, and extort his real sentiments, might spin a diamond ring, and shave by it. He had golden hopes about his "nephews," as he often called them, but he would not pronounce those hopes at present, lest the father should be disappointed. And so the boys went up to Oxford, half a moon before the woodcocks came.

CHAPTER VII.

. I DO not mean to write at large upon University
life, because the theme has been out-thesed by men
of higher powers. It is a brief Olympic, a Derby
premature, wherein to lose or win depends—training, health, ability,. and industry being granted—
upon the early stoning or late kernelling of the
brain. Without laying claim to much experience,
any one may protest that our brains are worked a
deal too hard at the time of adolescence. We lose
thereby their vivific powers and their originality.
The peach throws off at the critical period all the
fruit it cannot ripen ; the vine has no such abjective
prudence, and cripples itself by enthusiasm.

The twins were entered at Merton, and had the
luck to obtain adjoining garrets. Sir Cradock had
begun to show a decided preference for Clayton, as
he grew year by year more and more like his
mother. But this was not the only reason why he
would not listen to some fool's suggestion, that

Cradock, the heir to the property, should be ranked as a "gentleman-commoner." That stupid distinction he left for men who require self-assertion, admiring as he did the sense and spirit of that Master, well known in his day, who, to some golden cad insisting that his son should be entered in that college as a gentleman-commoner, angrily replied, "Sir, *all* my commoners are gentlemen."

But the brothers were very soon parted. Clayton got sleeved in a scholar's gown, while Cradock still fluttered the leading-strings. "*Et tunicæ manicas*—you effeminate Viley!" said Cradock, admiring hugely, when his twin ran up to show himself off, after winning a Corpus scholarship; "and the governor won't allow me a chance of a parasol for my elbows." Sir Cradock, a most determined man, and a very odd one to deal with, had forbidden his elder son to stand for any scholarship, except those few which are of the University corporate. "A youth of your expectations," he exclaimed, with a certain bitterness, for he often repined in secret that Clayton was not the heir, "a boy placed as you are, must not compete for a poor young lad's *viaticum*. You may go in for a University scholarship, though of course you will never get one; an examination does good, I have heard, to the unsuccessful candidates. But don't let me hear about it, not even if, by some accident, you should be the lucky one." Craddy was deeply hurt; he had long perceived his father's partiality for the son more dashing, yet more effeminate, more pretentious, and less persistent. So Cradock set his heart upon winning Craven, Hertford, or Ireland, and never even alluding to it in the presence of his father. Hence it will be evident that the youth was proud and sensitive.

"Amy *amata, peramata a me*," cried the parson to his daughter, now a lovely girl of sixteen, straight, slender, and well-poised; "how glad and proud we ought to be of Clayton's great success!"

"Pa, dear, he would never have got it, I am quite certain of that, if Cradock had been allowed to go in; and I think it is most unfair, shamefully unjust, that because he is the eldest son he is never to have any honour." And Amy coloured brilliantly at the warmth of her own championship; but her father could not see it.

"So I am inclined to think"—John Rosedew was never positive, except upon great occasions—"perhaps I should say perpend, if I were fond of hybrid English. I don't mean about the unfairness, Amy; for I think I should do the same if I were in Sir Cradock's place. I mean that our Crad would have got it, instead of Clayton, with health and fortune favouring. But it stands upon a razor's edge, ἐπὶ ξυροῦς ἵσταται ἀκμῆς. You can construe that, Amy?"

"Yes, pa, when you tell me the English. How the green is coming out on the fir-trees! So faint and yet so bright. Oh, papa, what Greek subsignificance, as you sometimes call it, is equal to that composition?"

"Well, my poppet, I am so short-sighted, I would much rather have a triply composite verb——"

"Than three good kisses from me, daddy?" Well, there they are, at any rate, because I know you are disappointed." And the child, herself more bitterly disappointed, as becomes a hot partisan, ran away to sit under a sprawling larch, just getting new nails on its fingers, for the spring was awaking early.

It was not more than a week after this, and not very far from All-Fools'-day, when Clayton, directly after chapel, rushed into Cradock's garret, hot, breathless, and unphilosophical. Cradock, calm and thoughtful, as he usually was, poked his head through the open slide of the dusthole called a scout's room, and brought out three willow-pattern plates, a little too retentive of the human impress, and an extra knife and fork, dark-browed at the tip of the handle. Then he turned up a corner of tablecloth, where it cherished sombre memories of a tearful teapot, and set the mustard-pot to control it. Nor long before he doubled the coffee in the strainer of the biggin, and shouted "Corker!" thrice, far as human voice would gravitate, down the well of the staircase. Meanwhile Master Clayton stood fidgeting, and doffed not his scholarly toga. Corker, the scout, a short fat man, came up the stairs with dignity and indignation contending. He was amazed that any freshman "should have the cheek to holler so." Mr.

Nowell was such a quiet young man, that the scout
looked for some apology. "Corker, a commons of
bread and butter, and a cold fowl and some tongue.
Be quick now, before the buttery closes. And, as
I see I am putting you out in your morning work,
get a quart of ale at your dinner-time." "Yes, sir,
to be sure, sir; I wish all the gentlemen was as
thoughtful."

"No, Craddy, never mind that," cried his brother, reddening richly, for Clayton was fair as a
lady, "I only want to speak to you about—well,
perhaps, you know what it is I have come for. Is
that fellow gone from the door?"

"I am sure I don't know. Go and look yourself. But, dear Viley, what is the matter?"

"Oh, Cradock, you can so oblige me, and it
can't matter much to you. But to me, with nothing to look to, it does make such a difference."

Cradock never could bear to hear this—that his
own twin-brother should talk, as he often did, so
much in the pauper strain. And all the while
Clayton was sure of 50,000*l.* under their mother's
settlement. But Crad was full of wild generosity,
and had made up his mind to share Nowelhurst, if
he could do so, with his brother. He began to
pull Clayton's gown off; he would have blacked
his shoes if requested. He always thought himself
Viley's prime minister.

"Whatever it is, my boy, Viley, you know I
will do it for you, if it is only fair and honourable."

" Oh, it is no great thing. I was sure you would do it for me. To do just a little bit under your best in this hot scrimmage for the Ireland. I am not much afraid of any man, Crad, except you, and Brown, of Balliol."

" Viley, I am very sorry that you have asked me such a thing. Even if it were in other ways straightforward, I could not do it, for the sake of the father, and Uncle John, and little Amy."

" Don't you know that the governor doesn't want *you* to get it? You are talking nonsense, Cradock, downright nonsense, to cover your own selfishness. And that frizzle-headed Amy, indeed!"

" I would rather talk nonsense than fraud, Clayton. And I can't help telling you that what you say about my father may be true, but is not brotherly; and your proposal does you very little honour; and I never could have thought it of you; and I will do my very utmost. And as for Amy, indeed, she is too good for you to speak of—and—and——" He was highly wroth at the sneer about Amy's hair, which he admired beyond all reason, as indeed he did every bit of her, but without letting any one know it. He leaned upon the table, with his thumb well into the mustard-pot. This was the first real quarrel with the brother he loved so much; and it felt like a skewer poked into his heart.

" Well, elder brother by about two seconds," cried Clayton, twitching his plaits up well upon his coat-collar, "I'll do all I can to beat you. And I hope Brown will have it, not you. There's the cash for my commons. I know you can't afford it, until you get a scholarship."

Clayton flung half-a-crown upon the table, and went down the stairs with a heavy tramp, knocking over a dish with the college arms on, wherein Corker was bringing the fowl and the tongue. Corker got all the benefit of the hospitable doings, and made a tidy dinner out of it, for Cradock could eat no breakfast. It was the first time bitter words had passed between the brothers since the little ferments of childhood, which are nothing more than sweetwort the moment they settle down. And he doubted himself; he doubted whether he had not been selfish about it.

It was the third day of the examination, and when he appeared at ten o'clock among the forty competitors, he was vexed anew to see that Clayton had removed to a table at the other end of the room, so as not to be even near him. The piece of Greek prose which he wrote that morning dissatisfied him entirely; and then again he rejoiced at the thought that Viley need not be afraid of him. He had never believed in his chance of success, and went in for the scholarship to please others and learn the nature of the examination. Next year he might have a fairer prospect; this year—as all the University knew—Brown, of Balliol, was sure of it.

Nevertheless, by the afternoon he was in good

spirits again, and found a mixed paper which suited him as if Uncle John had set it. One of the examiners had been, some twenty years ago, a pupil of John Rosedew, and this, of course, was a great advantage to any successor alumnus; though neither of them knew the other. It is pleasant to see how the old ideas germinate and assimilate, as the olive and the baobab do, after the fires of many summers.

Clayton, a placable youth (even when he was quite in the wrong, as in the present instance), came to Craddy's rooms that evening, begged him not to apologise for his expressions of the morning, and compared notes with him upon the doings of the day.

"Bless you, Crad," he cried, after a glass of first-rate brown sherry—not the vile molassied stuff, thick as the sack of Falstaff, but the genuine thing, with the light and shade of brown olives in the sunset, and not to be procured, of course, from any Oxonian wine-dealer;—"oh, Crad, if we could only wallop that Brown, of Balliol, between us, I should not care much which it was. He has booked it for such a certainty, and does look so cocky about it. Did you see the style he walked off, before hall, arm in arm with a Master of Arts, and spouting his own iambics?"

"First-rate ones, I dare say, Viley. Have a pipe, old fellow. After all, it doesn't matter much. Folk who have never been in them think a deal the most of these things. The wine-merchant laughs at beeswing; and so, I suppose, it is with all trades." Cradock was not by any means prone to the discourse sententious; and the present lapse was due, no doubt, to the reaction ensuing upon his later scene with Viley, wherein each had promised heartily to hold fast by the brotherhood.

On the following Saturday morning, John Rosedew's face flushed puce-colour as he opened his letters at breakfast-time. "Hurrah! Amy, darling; hurrah, my child! *Terque quaterque, et novies evoe!* Eat all the breakfast, melimel; I won't tell you till I come back."

"Oh, won't you, indeed?" cried Amy, with her back against the door and her arms in mock grimness folded. "I rather think you will, papa; unless you have made up your mind to choke me. And you are half way towards it already."

John saw that peculiar swell of her throat which had frightened him so often—her dear mother had died of bronchitis, and he knew nothing of medical subjects—and so he allayed her excitement at once, gave her over to Miss Eudoxia, who was late in her bedroom as usual, and then set off at his utmost speed to tell his old friend, Sir Cradock. And a fine turn of speed he still could show, though the whiskers under his college-cap (stuck on anyhow in the hurry) were as white as the breast of a martin quivering under the eaves. Since he lost his wife he had never cared to walk fast, subsiding into three miles an hour, as thoughtful and placid men will do, when they begin to thumb their waistcoats. But now through the waking life of "the Chase," where the brown fern-stalks bent over the Ammon horn of the lifting frond, and the fescue grass was beading rough with dew already, here and among the rabbit-holes, nimbly dodging the undermine, ran as hard as a boy of twelve, the man of threescore, John Rosedew. Without stopping to knock as usual, he burst in upon Sir Cradock, now sitting all alone at his simple, old-fashioned breakfast. Classical and theological training are not locomotive, as we all know to our cost; and the rector stood gasping ever so long, with both hands pressed to his side.

"Why, John; quick, quick! You frighten me. Is your house on fire?"

"Old fellow—old fellow; such news! Shake hands—ever since the *charta forestæ*; shake hands again. Oh, I feel rather sick; pray excuse me; ἄνω κάτω στρέφεται."

"What is it, John? Do be quick. I must send for Mrs. O'Gaghan and the stomach-pump." Biddy was now the licensed doctoress of the household, and did little harm with her simples, if she failed of doing good.

"*Times* there? Open it; look, University news! Crad and Clayton."

Wondering, smiling, placidly anxious, Sir Cradock tore open the paper, and found, after turning a great many corners, the University news. Then he read out with a trembling voice, after glancing over it silently:

"The Ireland scholarship has been awarded to
Cradock Nowell, of Merton College. Proxime
accessit Clayton Nowell, scholar of Corpus Christi.
Unless we are misinformed, these gentlemen are
twin-brothers."

> " Grintie, grintie, grunt,
> Oos be arl tew blunt;
> Naw oose Hampshire hogs,
> But to zhow the way in bogs."

So John Rosedew quoted in the fulness of his
glory from an old New Forest rhyme. John's
delight transcended everything, because he had
never expected it. He had taken his own degree
ere ever the Ireland was heard of; but three pupils
of his had won it while he was still in residence.
Of that he had not thought much. But now to
win it by proxy in his extreme old age, as he began
to consider it, and from all the crack public school-
men, and with his own pet alumni, whom no one
else had taught anything—such an Ossa upon Pe-
lion, such an Olympus on Ossa—no wonder that the
snow of his whiskers shook and the dew trembled
under his eyelids.

Sir Cradock, on the other hand, had never a
word to say, but turned his head like one who waits
for a storm of dust to go by.

"Why, Cradock, old friend, what on earth is
the matter? You don't seem at all delighted."

"Yes, I am, of course, John; as delighted as I
ought to be. But I wish it had been Viley; he
wants it so much more, and he is so like his
mother."

"So is Crad; every bit as much; an enlarged and grander portrait. Can't you see the difference between a large heart and a mere good one? Will no one ever appreciate my noble and simple Craddy?"

John Rosedew spoke warmly, and was sorry before the breath from his lips was cold. Not that he had no right to say it, but because he felt that he had done far more harm than good.

CHAPTER VIII.

HONOURS flash in the summer sun, as green
corn does in the morning; then they gleam mature
and mellow at the time of reaping; they are
bagged, perhaps by a woman's arm, with a cut
"below the knees;" set on their butt for a man to
sit under while eating his bread and cheese; then
they wither, and are tossed into chaff by a contu-
melious steam-engine with a leathern strap in-
flexible.

Cradock's "Ireland" has gone by, and another
has succeeded it, and this has fallen, as most things
fall, to the sap of perseverance, steel-tipped with
hard self-confidence—this Ireland has fallen to the
lot of Brown Balliolensis. Clayton would not go
in for it; his pride, or rather vanity, would not
allow him to do so. Was he going to take Cradock's leavings, and be a year behind him, when
he was only two minutes younger? However,
he went in for the Hertford, and, what was a great

deal more, he got it ; for Cradock would not stand ;
and, even if he had, perhaps the result would
have been the same. Viley had made up his mind
to win it, and worked very hard indeed ; and so
won it very easily. Cradock could usually beat
him in Greek, but not so often in Latin. And
Clayton wrote the prettiest, most tripping, co-
quettish, neat-ankled hendecasyllables that ever
whisked roguishly round a corner, wondering
where Catullus was.

Ah ! light-hearted poet, sensitively sensuous,
yet withal deep-hearted, with a vein of golden philosophy, and a pensive tenderness, now-a-days we
overlook thee. Horace is more fashionable, more
suited to a flippant age, because he has no passion.

Early on a sunripe evening in the month of
June, " when the sun was shifting the shadows of
the hills, and doffed the jaded oxen's yoke, distri-
buting the lovetime from his waning chariot," a
forest dell, soft, clear, and calm, was listening to
its thrushes. And more than at the throstle's flute,
or flageolet of the blackbird, oaks and chestnuts
pricked their ears at the voice of a gliding maiden.
Where the young fern was pluming itself, arching,
lifting, ruffling in filigree, light perspective, and
depth of Gothic tracery, freaked by the nip of
fairy fingers, tremulous as a coral grove in a crystal
under-current, the shyer fronds still nestling home,
uncertain of the world as yet, and coiled like
catherine-wheels of green; where the cranesbill
pushed like Zedekiah, and the succory reared its

sky-blue windmill (open for business till 8 P.M.);
where the violet now was rolled up in the seed-pod,
like a stylite millipede, and the great bindweed, in
its crenate horn, piped and fluted spirally, had forgotten the noonday flaunt: here, and over the
nibbled sward, where the crisp dew was not risen
yet, here came wandering the lightest foot that
ever passed, but shook not, the moss-bed of the
glow-worm. Under the rigorous oaks (so corded,
seamed, and wenned with humps of grey), the
stately, sleek, mouse-coloured beech, the dappled,
moss-beridden ash, and the birch-tree peeling sil-
verly, beneath the murmuring congress of the sun-
proof leaves; and again in the open breaks and
alleys, where light and shade went see-saw; by and
through and under all, feeling for and with every
one, glanced, and gleamed, and glistened, and listened the loveliest being where all was love, the
pet in the nest of nature.

Of all the beauty in that sweet dell, where the
foot of man came scarcely once in a year; of all
the largesse of earth and heaven; of all the grace
which is Nature's gratitude to her heavenly Father:
there was not one, from the lily-bell to the wild rose
and the heather-sprig, fit for a man to put in his
bosom, and look at Amy Rosedew.

It is told of a certain good man's child, whose
lineage still is cherished, that when she was asked
by her father (half-bantering, half in earnest) to
tell him the reason why everybody loved her so, she
cast down her eyes with a puzzled air, then opened

them wide, as a child does to the sunrise of some great truth—" Father, perhaps it is because I love everybody so." Lucan has it in a neater form: " amorem quæris amando." And that was Amy Rosedew's secret, by herself undreamed of—lovely, because she could not help loving all our God has made. And of all the fair things He has made, and pronounced to be very good, since sunshine first began to gleam, to glow, and to fade away, what home has beauty found so bright, so rich in varied elegance, so playfully receptive of the light shed through creation—the light of the Maker's smile—as a young maiden, pure of heart, natural, true, and trusting?

She came to the brink of a forest pool, and looked at herself in the water. Not that she thought more than she could help of the outward thing called " Amy," but that she wondered how her old favourites, Cradock and Clayton Nowell, would esteem her face and style of dress now she was turned seventeen. Most likely they had seen ever so many girls, both at Oxford and in London, compared with whom poor Amy was but a rustic Phidyle, just fit to pick sticks in the New Forest.

The crystal mirror gave her back even the shade on her own sweet face, which fell from the cloud of that simple thought; for she stood where the westering sunshine failed to touch the water, but flushed with rich relief of gold the purity of her figure. Every sapling, dappled hazel, sloughing birch, or glabrous maple, glistened with the

plumes of light, and every leaf was twinkling.
The columns of the larger trees stood like metal
cylinders, whereon the level gleam rules a streak,
and glints away round the rounding. Elbows,
arms, and old embracings, backed with a body-
ground of green, laced with sunset's golden bodkin,
ever shifting every eyelet,—branch, and bough,
and trunk, and leaves, ruffling and twisting, or
staunch and grand, they seemed but a colonnade
and arch, for the sun to peep through at the
maiden, and tell of her on the calm waters.

Floating, fleeting, shimmering there, in a frame
of stately summer flags, vivid upon the crystal
shade, and twinkling every now and then to the
plash of a distant moorhen, or the dip of a swal-
low's wing, lay her graceful image, wondering in
soft reply to her play of wonder. She took off
her light chip hat, and laughed; lo! the courteous
picture did the same. She offered, with a mincing
air, her little frail of wood-strawberries; and the
shadowy Amy put them back with the prettiest
grace ever dreamed of. Then she cast the spark-
ling night of her tresses down the white shoulders
and over her breast; and the other Amy was
looking at her through a ripple of cloudiness, with
the lissom waist retiring. She smoothed her hair
like a scarf around her, withdrew her chin on the
curving neck, and bowed the shapely forehead,
well pleased to see thus the foreshortening undone,
and the pure, bright oval shown as in a glass.

Then, frightened almost at the lustrous depth of her large grey eyes, deep-fringed with black, she thought of things all beyond herself, and woke, from Nature's innocent joy in her own brief luck of beauty, to the bashful consciousness, the down of a maiden's dreamings. Bridling next at her mirrored face, with a sudden sense of humour, all the time she watched the red lips, and the glimmer of pearls between them, "Amy," she cried, "now, after this, don't come to me for a character, unless you want one, you pretty dear, for conceit and self-admiration."

So saying, she tossed her light head at herself, and looked round through her flickering cloudlets. What did she see? What made the dark water flame upon the instant with a richer glow than sunset? The delicate cheeks, the fair forehead and neck, even the pearly slope of the shoulders, were flooded with deepest carmine. Her pride fell flat, as the cistus stamen at a touch droops away on the petal. Then she shrank back into a flowering broom, and cowered among the spikelets, and dared not move to wipe away the tears she was so mad with. Oh! the wretched abasement earned by a sweet little bit of vanity!

How she hated herself, and the light, and the water, her senseless habit of thinking aloud, above all, her despicable fancy that she was growing— what nonsense!—such a pretty girl! Thenceforth and for ever, she felt quite sure, she never could

look in a glass again, unless it were just for a
moment, to put her hair to rights, when she got
home.

"To think of my hair all down my neck, and
the way I had turned in the gathers!"—the poor
little thing had been making experiments how she
would look in a low-necked dress—"Oh! that was
the worst thing of all. I might have laughed at
it but for that. And now I am sure I can never
even peep at his face again. Whatever will he
think of me, and what would my papa say?"

After crying until she began to laugh, she resolved to go straight home, and confess all her
crime to Aunt Eudoxia, John Rosedew's maiden
sister, who had come to live with him when he lost
his wife, three dreary years agone. So Amy
rolled up her long hair anyhow, without a bit of
pride in it, shrank away and examined herself, to
be sure that all was right, and, after one peep,
came bravely forth, trying to look as much as
possible like her good Aunt Doxy; then she walked
at her stateliest, with the basket of strawberries,
picked for papa, in one hand, and the other tightly
clasped upon the bounding of her heart. But her
eyes were glancing right or left, like a fawn's
when a lion has roared; and even the youngest
trees saw quite well that, however rigid with Miss
Eudoxia the gliding form might be, it was poised
for a dart and a hide behind them at every crossing
shadow.

But fortune favours the brave. She won her

own little sallyport without the rustle of a black-
berry-leaf, and thereupon rushed to a hasty and
ostrich-like conclusion. She felt quite sure that,
after all, none but the waters and winds could tell
the tale of her little coquetry. Beyond all doubt,
Cradock Nowell was deep in the richest mental
metallurgy, tracing the vein of Greek iambics, as
he did before his beard grew; and she never, never
would call them " stupid iambics" again.

Cradock, who had seen her, but turned away
immediately (as became a gentleman), did not, for
the moment, know his little Amy Rosedew. A
year and a half had changed her from a stripling,
jumping girl to a shy and graceful maiden, dreadfully afraid of sweethearts. She had not been
away from Nowelhurst throughout that year and
a half, for her father could not get on without her
for more than a month at a time, and all that
month he fretted. But the twins had spent the
last summer in Germany, with a merry reading
(or talking) party; and their Christmas and Easter
vacations were dragged away in London, through
a strange whim of Sir Cradock Nowell; at least,
they thought it strange, but there was some reason
for it.

Young Cradock Nowell was not such a muff as
to be lost in Greek senarii; no trimeter acata-
lectics of truest balance and purest fall could
be half so fair to scan; not "Harmony of
the golden hair," and her nine Pierid daughters
round the crystal spring, were worth a glance of

the mental eye, when fortune granted bodily vision of our unconscious Amy. But he did not stand there watching mutely, as some youths would have done; for a moment, indeed, he forgot himself in the flush of admiration. The next moment he remembered that he was a gentleman; and he did what a gentleman must have done—whether marquis or labourer: he slipped away through the bushes, feeling as if he had done some injury. Then the maiden, glancing round, caught one startled glimpse, as Nyssia did of the stealthy Gyges, or Diana of Actæon. From that one glimpse she knew him, though he was so like his brother; but he had failed to recognise the Amy of his boyhood.

CHAPTER IX.

Miss Eudoxia was now the queen of the little household, and the sceptre she bore was an iron one to all except her niece. John—that easy, good-natured parson, who, coming in from the garden or parish, any summer forenoon, would halt in the long low kitchen, if a nice crabbed question presented itself, take his seat outright upon the corner of the ancient dresser, and then and there discuss some moot point in the classics, or tie and untie over again some fluffy knot historical (which after all is but a pucker in the tatters of a scarecrow); and all the while he would appeal to the fat cook or the other maid—for the house only kept two servants; and all the while Miss Amy, διαφυλάττουσα θέσιν, would poke in little pikepoints of impudence and ignorance—John, I must confess at last, was threatened so with dishclouts, pepper, and even rolling-pins, that the cook began to forget the name of Plato (which had struck her), and the housemaid could not justly tell what Tibullus says of Pales.

"John, you are so lamentably deficient in moral dignity! And the mutton not put down yet, and the kidney-beans getting ropy! If you must sit there, you might as well begin to slice the cucumber. I dare say you'd do that even."

"To be sure, Doxy; so I will. I sharpened my knife this morning."

"Doxy, indeed! And before the servants! I am sure Johanna must have heard you, though she makes such a rattle in there with the rolling-pin, like a doctor's pestle and mortar. She always does when I come out, to pretend she is so busy; and most likely she has been listening for half an hour, and laughing at your flummery. What do I care about Acharnius?—now don't tell me any jokes, if you please, brother John; with butter on both your legs, too! Oh, if I could only put you in a passion! I might have some hopes of you then. But I should like to see the woman that could; you have so little self-respect."

"Eudoxia, that is the very converse of Seneca's proposition."

"Then Seneca didn't know how to converse, and I won't be flouted with him. Seneca to me, indeed, or any other heathen! Let me tell you one thing, John Rosedew"—Miss Eudoxia now was wrathful, not nettlesome only, but spinous; perhaps it would be rude to hint that in this latter word may lurk the true etymon of "spinster"—"let

me tell you one thing, and perhaps you'll try to remember it; for, with all your wonderful memory,
you never can tell to-morrow what I said to-day.

"Surely not, dear Doxy, because you talk so
much. It is related of that same Seneca that he
could repeat——"

"Fiddlesticks. Now you want to turn off the
home-truth you feel to be coming. But you shall
have it, John Rosedew, and briefly, it is this:
Although you do sit on the dresser, your taste is
too eclectic. You are a very learned man, but
your learning gilds foul idols. You spend all your
time in pagans' company, while the epistles and
gospels have too little style for *you*."

"Oh, Aunt Eudoxia, how dare you talk to my
papa like that, my own daddy, and me to hear you?
And just now you flew into a pet because you
fancied Johanna heard him call you 'Doxy.' I
am astonished at it, Aunt Doxy; and it is not true,
not a word of it. Come with me, father, dearest,
and we won't say a word to her all the afternoon."

Even young Amy saw that her father was hit
very hard. There was so much truth in the accusation, so much spiteful truth—among thy beauties,
nuda veritas, a smooth skin is not one—that poor
John felt as if Aristophanes were sewn up henceforth in a pig-sack. He slunk away quietly to his
room, and tried to suck some roots Hebraic, whence
he got no satisfaction. He never could have become
a great theological scholar. After all, a man must
do what God has shaped his mind for. So in a

week John Rosedew got back to his native element; but sister Doxy's rough thrust made the
dresser for many a month like the bottom of a pin-
cushion, when the pins are long, and the bran has
leaked out at the corner.

Now Miss Eudoxia Rosedew was always very
sorry when she had indulged too much in the pleasure of hurting others. It was not in her nature
to harm any living creature; but she could not
understand that hurt is the feminine of harm—the
feminine frequentative, if I may suggest that ano-
maly. She had a warm, impulsive heart, and sided
almost always with the weaker party. Convinced
profoundly, as she was, of her brother's great
ability, she believed, whenever a question arose,
that the strength was all·on his side, and so she
went "dead against him." One thing, and the
most material one, she entirely overlooked, as a
sister is apt to do: to wit, the breadth and modesty
of her brother's nature. One thing, I say, for the
two are one, so closely are they united.

It is a goodly sight to see John Rosedew and his
sister upon their way to church. She supporting
the family dignity, with a maid behind her to carry
the books—that it may please thee to defend us
with a real footman!—just touching John's arm
with the tips of her glove, because he rolls so
shockingly, and even his Sunday coat may be
greasy; then, if a little girl comes by, "Lady
Eudoxia"—as the village, half in joke, and half in
earnest, has already dubbed her—Lady Eudoxia
never looks at her (they are so self-important now,

even those brats of children!), but she knows by instinct whether that little girl has curtseyed. If she has, it is nicely acknowledged; but if she has not, what a chill runs down the lady's rigid spine!

"John, did you see that?"

"See what, Doxy?—Three sugar-plums, my little dear, and a few of our cough-lozenges. I heard you cough last Sunday; and you may suck them in the sermon time, because they don't smell of peppermint, and they are quite as nice as liquorice. How is your mammy, my darling?"

"Well, John — well, Mr. Rosedew! — If you have no more sense of propriety—and so near the house of God——"

And Miss Eudoxia walks on in front, while the girl who failed to curtsey has thrust one brown hand long ago into the parson's ample palm, and with the other is stoking that voracious engine whose vernacular name is "mouth." Amy, of course, is at the school, where this little girl ought by rights to have been, only for her cough, which would come on so dreadfully when the words were hard to spell; and, when they meet Amy by the gate (the double gate of the churchyard—both sides only opened for funerals), how smooth, and rich, and calm she looks—calm, yet with a heart of triumph, as her own class clusters round her, and won't even glimpse at the boys—not even the very smallest boy—one of whom has the cheek to whistle, and pretends that he meant the "Old Hundredth."

But, in spite of all this Eudoxian grandeur, there

was not a poor man in Nowelhurst—no, nor even a
woman—who did not feel, in earnest heart, faith
and good-will towards her. For the worldly nonsense was cast aside when she stood in the presence
of trouble, and her native kindness and vigour
shone forth, till the face of grief was brightened.
Then she forgot her titled grandmother—so often
quoted and such a bore, the Countess of Driddledrum and Dromore—and glowed and melted, as all
must do who are made of good carbon and water.
So let her walk into the village church with the
pride which she is proud of, her tall and comely
figure shown through the scarf of lavender crape,
her dark silk dress on the burial flags, wiping dust
from the memory of John Stiles and his dear wife
Susan. And oh, Johanna, thou goodly fat cook-
maid, dishing up prayer-books, and Guides to the
Altar, and thy gloves on the top ostentatiously—
gloves whose fingers are to thine as vermicelli to
sausages : Johanna, spoil not our procession by
loitering under the hollow oak to wink at thy sweetheart, Jem Pottles. Neither do thou, oh hollow
oak, look down upon us, and tell of the tree only
one generation before thee. Under thy branches,
the Arab himself had better not talk of lineage.
Some acorn spat forth, half-crunched and be-
dribbled, by the deer or the swine of the forest,
and in danger perhaps of being chewed afterwards
by the ancestors of royalty—our family-trees are
young fungus to thee, and our roots of nobility
pignuts.

CHAPTER X.

THE scenery of the New Forest is of infinite variety; but the wooded parts may be ranged, perhaps, in a free, loose-branching order (as befits the subject), into some three divisions, which cross and interlace each other, as the trees themselves do.

First, and most lovely, the glades and reaches of gentle park and meadow, where the beech-tree invades not seriously, or, at any rate, not with discipline, but straggles about like a tall centurion amused by ancient Britons. Here are the openings winged with fern, and ruffling to the west wind; and the crimped oval leaves of the alder rustle over the backs of the bathing cows. In and out we glance, or gaze, through the groined arcade of trees, where the sun goes wandering softly, as if with his hand before his eyes. Of such kind is the Queen's Bower Wood, beside the Boldre Water.

Of the second type, most grand and solemn, is

VOL. I.   G

the tall beech-forest, darkening the brow of some
lonely hill, and draping the bosomed valleys.   Such
is Mark Ash Wood, four miles to the west of
Lyndhurst.   Overhead, is the vast cool canopy;
underfoot, the soft brown carpet, woven by a
thousand autumns.   No puny underwood foils the
gaze, no coppice-whispers circulate; on high there
moves one long, unbroken, and mysterious murmur,
and all below grey twilight broods in a lake of
silent shadow.   Through this the ancient columns
rising, smooth, dove-coloured, or glimpsed with
moss, others fluted, crannied, bulging, hulked at
the reevings of some great limb; others twisted
spirally and tortuously rooting; a thousand giants
receding, clustering, opening lattice-peeps between
them, standing forth to stop the view, or glancing
some busy slant of light—in the massive depth of
gloom they seem almost to glide.

The third and most rudely sylvan form is that
of the enclosures, where the intolerant beech is
absent, and the oak, the spruce, and the Spanish
chestnut protect the hazel, the fern and bramble,
the dog-rose and the honeysuckle.

In a bowering, gleaming, twinkling valley, such
as I have first described, we saw Miss Amy Rosedew admiring her own perfections; and now, some
three months afterwards, a certain young lady, not
wholly unlike her, is roaming in a deep enclosure,
thick with oaks and underwood.   It lies about a
furlong from the western lodge of Nowelhurst, and
stretches away towards the sunset, far from the eye

of house or hut. Even the lonely peatman, who camps (or camped, while so allowed) beneath the open sky, wherever the waste yields labour freely, and no prescription bars him—even he finds nothing here to draw his sauntering footstep. The gorse prefers more open places, the nuts are few and hard to reach, the fuel-turf is not worth cutting, and the fuel-wood he dare not hew. In short, there is nothing there to tempt him. As for shade, and solitude, and the crystal rill, he gets a deal too much of that sort of thing already.

By the side of that crystal rill, and where the trees hung thickest, in the grey gloom of that Michaelmas evening, walked the aforesaid maiden, and (what we had not bargained for) a gentle youth beside her. The light between the lapping boughs and leaves—whose summer whisper grew hoarse in autumn's rustle—the clouded light fell charily, but showed the figures comely, as either could wish of the other.

The maiden's face was turned away, but one hand lay in her lover's; with the other she was drawing close the loose folds of her mantle—her flushing cheek was glad of shade, and the grass thought her feet were trembling.

His eager, glistening, wavering eyes told of hope with fear behind it; and all his life was waiting for a word or look. But for the moment neither came. She trembled more and more before him, and withdrew a little, as the silver-weed at her feet withdrew from the runnel's passion. She thought he would yet say more—she longed for him to say more; oh that her heart would be quiet!

But never another word he said, till she turned to him, sadly and proudly, with her soft eyes full of tears.

"Mr. Nowell, you are very eloquent; but you do not know what love is."

She lifted her left hand towards her heart, but was too proud to put it there, and dropped it, hiding the movement.

"I not know what love is! And I have been saying things I should have laughed at any fellow for saying, though I am fit to cry while I say them. Oh, how cold-blooded you are; for I cannot make you feel them!"

He looked at her so ardently, that her sweet gaze fell like a violet in the May sun.

"No, Mr. Clayton Nowell, I am not cold-blooded; but, at least, my blood is pure, though not in the eyes of the world so high and refined as your own."

"What has that got to do with it? My own—own—own——" He was in a great hurry to embrace her, because she looked at him tenderly, to palliate the toss of her head.

"Wait, if you please. Throughout all your rhapsody" (here she smiled so that none could be angry) "you have not said a single word to show whether—that is—I mean to say whether——"

She burst into tears, turned from him, and clung to the dead arm of the old oak.

"Whether what?" asked Clayton, sharply, in spite of her deep distress; for he began to doubt if he truly were loved, and to tire of the high-strung suspense. "Whether I have got money enough to support us both *respectably?* Isn't that the proper word for it? And because I am the younger son?"

He frowned very hard at the bark of the oak, and crushed the grey touchwood under his foot, though his hand was still seeking for hers. Then she turned full upon him suddenly, too proud to dissemble her tears.

"Oh, Clayton, Clayton Nowell, can you think me so mean as that? Though my father would cast me off, perhaps, in his gratitude to Sir Cradock, do you think I would care for all the world, so long as I only had you? What I meant was only that you never said if you meant me to be— to be—your wife." Her long lashes fell on her glistening cheeks, like the willow-leaves over the Avon.

"Why, what—well, that beats cockfighting!— why, what else did you suppose I meant, you darling of all born darlings?"

"I am sure I don't know, Clayton. Only I beg your pardon."

He gave her no time to beg it twice, with those wistful eyes upon him, but made her earn it thoroughly, with her round arms on his neck, and other proceedings wherewithal we have no right to meddle.

"Yes, you may call me now your own"—ever so many interruptions—"your own; yours only, for ever."

"And you would rather have me than my elder brother?"

"Sooner than a thousand elder brothers, all as grave as Methusalem."

Clayton was so delighted hereat, that he really longed to squeeze her, although it is a thing which young ladies now-a-days never think of allowing. Let them hope that he did not do it. The probabilities are in their favour.

"Oh, Clayton, how can I be such a simpleton? What *would* my father say to me?"

"What do I care, my gem, my jewel, my warm delicious pearl? For three long months I have been dying to kiss you; and now I won't be cheated so. Surely you are not afraid of me, my beautiful wild rose?"

Her gardening hat had fallen off, her eyes were bright with tears, and the glow upon her cheeks had faded to a pellucid gleam. So have I seen the rich red Aurora weep itself, in a pulse-throb, to a pearly and waxen pink.

"No, Clayton, I am not afraid of you. I know that you are a gentleman."

"Well," thought Clayton, "she must be a witch, or the cleverest girl in the universe, as well as the most beautiful. She knows the way to manage me, as if we had been married fifty years."

He looked so disconcerted at the implied rebuke, that she could have found it in her sweet heart to give him fifty kisses; but, with all her warmth of passion, she was a pure and sensitive maiden, full of self-respect. Though abashed for the moment, and bowing her head to the sunrise of young affection, she possessed a fine and very sensible will and way of her own. She was just the wife for Clayton Nowell—a hot, impulsive, wayward youth; proud to be praised by every one, more than proud of deserving it. With such a wife, he would ripen and stiffen into a fine, full character; with a weak and volatile spouse, he would swing to and fro to his ruin. His goodness as yet was in the material; only a soft, firm hand could fashion it.

So she kept him at his distance; except every now and then, when her warm, loving nature looked forth from her eyes, for fear of hurting his feelings. Hand in hand they walked along, as if they still were children, and held much counsel, as they went, about the difficulties between them. But happen what would, they made up their minds about one thing; and for them henceforth both plural and singular were entirely merged in the dual. That sentence is priggish and pedantic, but I think young lovers can solve it; if not, let them put their heads together, and unriddle it in *labiates*.

Nothing ever, ever, ever, in the world of fact, or in the reach of imagination, should hold apart that faithful pair, whose all in all was to each the other. This they settled with much satisfaction, before discussing anything else.

"Except, of course, you know, darling," said the more thoughtful maiden, "if either of us should die."

Clayton shuddered at the idea, for it was a dark place of the wood, and the rustle of the ivy-leaves seemed to whisper " die." Then he insisted upon his amends for such a nasty suggestion; and she, with the tender thought moving her heart, could not refuse strict justice.

"And so you say, love, I must stay at Oxford until I take my degree. What a long time it does seem! Doesn't it?"

"Never mind, dearest, how long it is, if we are true to one another."

"Oh, that of course there's no doubt about. And you think I must tell my father?"

"Of course you must, Clayton. We are not very old, you know; he will think that he can part us, and that may make him less angry,"— here she laughed at her own subtlety,—" and putting that out of the question, neither of us could bear to be deceiving him so long. After all, you are but a younger son; and I am a lady, I hope. I have been thoroughly educated; and there is nothing but money against me."

She looked so proud in the shade of the spruce, that he was obliged to stop and admire her. At least he thought it his duty to do so, and the opinion did not offend her.

"But what will your brother Cradock say? He is so different from you. So odd, so determined and—upright."

"I don't care *that* for what he says. Only he had better be civil. He treated me very badly that time about the Ireland. I have a very great regard for Cradock; he is a very decent fellow; but I must teach him his proper place."

"And you can beat him easily in Latin; my father says you can. What a shame that he would not go in for the Hertford, that you might turn the tables upon him! He would not even have got a proxy, or whatever it was he gave you."

"I don't know that," said Clayton, who was truthful in spite of vanity; "very likely he would have beaten me. But I have cut him out in two things; for I can't help thinking that he has a hankering after you."

He looked at her with a keen, shrewd glance, for he was desperately jealous. She saw it, and smiled, and only said—"Would you believe that he could help it? But it happens that I know otherwise."

"Oh, then, you would have had him, if you could?"

"Now, Clayton, don't be childish. In your heart you know better."

Of course he did, a great deal better. Then

there was that to make up again, because she looked so hurt and so charming. But we can't stop here all day, or follow all these little doings, even if honour allowed us.

"And another thing, not so important, though, I have cut him out in, most decidedly," said Clayton, lifting his head again ; " the governor likes me long chalks better than he does Cradock, I can tell you."

"No doubt of it, I should say, dear. But I don't think you ought to talk of it."

"No, only to you. No secrets from one's wife, you know. But you won't tell your father yet, till I've opened upon Sir Cradock ?"

" Why not ? I intend to tell him directly I get home. And one thing is certain, Clayton, he will be more angry than yours will."

Clayton found it very difficult to change her determination. But at last he succeeded in doing so.

" But only for a week, mind; I will only put it off for a week, Clayton; and I would not do that, only as you say he would rush off at once to Sir Cradock; and I must give you time to take your father at the very best opportunity."

" And when will that be, my sweet prime minister, in your most sage opinion ?"

" Why, of course, on my dear love's birthday, next week, when all those rejoicings are to be at his brother becoming of age."

The young lady meant no mischief at all, but her lover did not look gracious.

"My brother! oh yes, to be sure, my brother! And I dreamed last night that I was the elder. He used to talk about giving me half; but I haven't heard much of that lately. As for my majority, as the lawyers are pleased to call it, nobody cares two straws for that. All my life I shall be a minor."

"Yes, somebody cares for it, darling; and more than all the hundreds put together who will shout and hurrah for your brother."

And she looked at him fondly from her heart. What a hot little partisan! The whole of that heart was now with Clayton, and he felt its strength by sympathy. So he lifted her hand to his lips, as a cavalier does in a picture. For the moment all selfish regrets lost their way in the great wide world of love.

"And my fealty shall be to you," he cried, kneeling half in play before her; "you are my knightly fee and fortune, my castle, my lands, and my home."

They had stopped at a point where two forest-paths met, and the bushes fell back a little, and the last of the autumn sunset glanced through the pales of a moss-grown gate, the mark whereby some royalty, or right of chase, was limited. Kneeling there, Clayton Nowell looked so courtly and gentle, with the bowered light of the west half saddening his happy, affectionate countenance, that his newly-betrothed must needs stoop graciously, and kiss his uncovered forehead.

While Clayton was admiring secretly the velvet of her lips, back she leaped, as if stung by a snake; then proudly stood confronting. Clayton sprang up to defend her; but there was no antagonist. All he saw was a man on horseback, passing silently over the turf, behind a low bank crowned with fern. Here a narrow track, scarce visible, saved the traveller some few yards, subtending as it did the angle where the two paths met. Clayton could not see the horse, for the thick brake-fern eclipsed him. But he felt that the nag was rather tired, and getting sad about supper-time. The rider seemed to be making a face, intended to express the most abstract philosophy possible, and superlunary contemplation. Any rabbit skilled in physiognomy would have come out of his hole again, quite reassured thereby. A short man he was, and apparently one meant by his mother for ruddiness; and still the brick-red of his hair proclaimed some loyalty to her intention. But his face was browned, and flaked across, like a red potato roasting, and his little eyes, sharp as a glazier's diamond, and twinkling now at the zenith, belied his absent attitude. Then as he passed by a shadowy oak, which swallowed him up in a moment, that oak (if it had been duly vocal) would have repeated these words—

"Well, if that ain't the parson's daughter, grind

me under a curry-stone. What a sly minx!—but devilish pretty. You're a deal too soft, John Rosedew."

As he passed on towards Nowelhurst the lovers felt that they had been seen, and perhaps watched ever so long; and then they felt uncomfortable. The young lady was the first to recover presence of mind. She pressed on her glossy round head the hat which had been so long in her left hand, and, drawing a long breath, looked point-blank at the wondering stare of her sweetheart.

"Well, Clayton, we may make up our minds for it now."

"For what, I should like to know? Who cares for that interloping, beetroot-coloured muff?"

"He is no muff at all, I can tell you, but an exceedingly clever man. Do you mean to say you don't know him?"

"Not I, from Esau or Ishmael. And he looks like a mixture of both."

"He is Doctor Rufus Hutton."

Clayton indulged in a very long whistle, indrawn, and not melodious. 'Twas a trick he had learned at Oxford; it has long been discarded elsewhere, but at both Universities still subsists, as the solace of newly-plucked men; the long-drawn sound seems to wind so soothingly down the horns of dilemma. Then the youth jumped up, and gathered a nut, cracked it between his white front teeth, and offered it, husk and all, without any thought of hygrometry, to his beautiful frightened

darling. She took it, as if his wife already, and
picked out the thin shell, piece by piece, anxiously
seeking the kernel. He all the while with admiration watched the delicate fingers moving, the reflex
play of the lissome joints, the spiral thread and
varying impress of the convex tips, and the faintly
flushing pink beneath the transparency of her nails.
Then she laughed and jumped, as it proved to be
a magnificent double nut—two fat kernels close
together, shaped by one another. Of course she
gave him one, and of course we know what they
did about it. I will only state that they very soon
forgot all about Dr. Rufus Hutton, and could
scarcely part where the last branch-path was quite
near to the maiden's window. Even there, where
the walks divided, when neither could see the
other, each steppped aside, very proud of love's
slyness, to steal the last of the other's footfall;
and soon, with a blush of intuition, each knew
that the other was lingering, and each felt ashamed
of himself or herself, and loved the other all the
more for it. So they broke from the bushes, detected and laughing, to put a good face upon it,
and each must go to tell the other how it came
about. They kissed once more, for they felt it
was right now that the moon was risen; then
home ran both, with a warmth of remembrance
and hope glowing in the heart.

CHAPTER XI.

WHATEVER the age, or the intellect of the passing age, may be, even if ever arise again such a galaxy of great minds as dawned upon this country three hundred years ago, though all those great minds start upon their glorious career, comprising and intensifying all the light engendered by, before, and since the time of Shakspeare, Bacon, Newton; then, though they enhance that light tenfold by their own bright genius, till a thousand waking nations gleam, like hill-tops touched with sunrise—to guide men on the human road, to lead them heaven-ward, all shall be no more than a benighted river wandering away from the stars of God. Do what we will, and think as we may, enlarging the mind in each generation, growing contemptuous of contempt, casting caste to the winds of heaven, and antiquating prejudice, nevertheless we shall never outrun, or even overtake Christianity. Science, learning, philosophy, may regard it through a telescope : they touch it no more than astronomy sets foot upon a star. To a thoughtful man, who is scandalized at all the littleness felt and done under the holy name, until he almost begins to doubt if the good outweigh the evil, it is reassurance to remember that we are not Christians yet, and comfort to confess that on earth we never can be. For nothing shows more clearly that our faith is of heaven, than the truth that we cannot rise to it until it raise us thither. And this reflection is akin to the stately writer's sentiment, that our minds conceive so much more than our bodies can perform, to give us token, ay, and earnest, of a future state.

Of all the creeds which have issued as yet from God, or man, or the devil, there is but one which is far in advance of all human civilization. True Christianity, like hope, cheers us to continual effort, exalts us to unbounded prospect, flies in front of our best success. Let us call it a worn-out garb, when we have begun to wear it ; as yet the mantle is in the skies, and we have only the skirt with the name on it.

Such thoughts as these were always stirring in the heart of a man of power, a leading character in my story, a leading character everywhere, whithersoever he went. Bull Garnet was now forty-five years old, and all who met him were surprised at his humble place in the common-wealth. A sense of power so pervaded even the air he breathed, that strong men rebelled instinctively, though he urged no supremacy; weak men caught some infection from him, and went home and astonished their families. Strong and weak alike confessed that it was a mysterious thing how a man of such motive strength, and self-reliance illimitable, could be content with no higher post than that of a common steward. But neighbourly interest in this subject met with no encouragement. Albeit his views of life expanded into universal sympathy, his practice now and then admitted some worldly-wise restrictions. And so, while really glad to advise on the doings of all around him, he never permitted brotherly inter-ference with his own.

Whoever saw Bull Garnet once was sure to know him again. If you met him in a rush to save the train, your eyes would turn and follow him. "There goes a man remarkable, whether for good or evil." Tall though he was, and large of frame, with swinging arms, and a square ex-pression, it was none of this that stopped the bystander's glance into a gaze. It was the cubic mass of the forehead, the span between the enor-mous eyes, and the depth of the thick-set jowl, which rolled with the volume of a tiger's. The rest of the face was in keeping therewith: the nose bold, broad, and patulous, the mouth large and well banked up, the chin big and heavily rounded. No shade of a hair was ever allowed to dim his healthy colouring, his head was cropped close as a Puritan's, and when beard grew fast he shaved twice in a day. High culture was a necessity to him, whether of mind, or body, or of the world external; he would no more endure a moustache on his lip than a frouzy hedgerow upon his farm. That man, if you came to think about him, more and more each time you saw how different he was from other men. Distinctness is a great merit in roses, especially when the French rosarians have so overpiled the catalogue. It is pleasant to walk up to a standard, and say, "You are 'Jules Margottin,' and your neighbour the 'Keepsake of Malmaison;' I cannot mistake you for any other, however hot the weather may be." Distinctness is also a merit in apples, pears, and even peaches; but most of all in man. And so, without knowing the reason, perhaps, we like a man whom we cannot mistake for any other of our million brethren. The same principle tells in love at first sight. But, lo! here again we are wandering.

Mr. Garnet's leading characteristic was not at first sight amiable. It was, if I may be allowed for once, upon the strength of my subject, not to mince words into *entremets*—a furious, reckless, damnable, and thoroughly devilish temper. All great qualities, loving - kindness, yearnings for Christian ideals, fell like sugar-canes to a hurricane in the outburst and rush of that temper. He was always grieved and deeply humbled, when the havoc was done; and, being a man of generous nature, would bow his soul in atonement. But in the towering of his wrath, how grand a sight he afforded! as fine as the rush of the wild Atlantic upon St. David's Head. For a time, perhaps, he would chafe and fret within the straits of reason, his body surging to and fro, and his mind making grasp at boundaries. Then some little aggravation, some trifle which no other man would notice—and out would leap all the pent-up fury of his soul. His great eyes would gather volume, and spring like a mastiff from a kennel; his mighty forehead would scarp and chine like the headland when the plough turns; and all his aspect grow four-square with more than hydraulic pressure. Whoever then could gaze unmoved at the raging fire of his eyes must be either a philosopher or a fool—and often the two are synonymous.

But touch him, even then, with a single word of softness, the thought of some one dear to him, a large and genial sentiment, or a tender memory —and the lines of his face would relax and quiver, the blazing eyes be suffused and subdued to a tremulous glow; and the man, so far beyond reason's reach, be led back, like a boy, by the feelings.

All who think they can catch and analyze that composite, subtle, volatile gas—neither body nor spirit, yet in fief to the laws of either—which men call "human nature," these, I say, will opine at once, from even this meagre description, that Mr. Bull Garnet's nature was scant of that playful element, humour. If thought be (as German philosophers have it) an electric emanation, then wit is the forked flash, gone in a moment; humour the soft summer lightning that shows us the clouds and the depth, the background and night of ourselves. No man of large humour can be in a passion, without laughing inwardly at himself. And wrath, which laughs at itself, is not of much avail in business. Mr. Garnet's wrath, on the contrary, was a fine, free-boiling, British anger, not at all amenable to reason, and therefore very valuable. By dint of it, he could score at night nearly twice as much work done in the day as a peaceable man could have reckoned. Man or woman, boy or girl, Mr. Garnet could extract from each all the cubic capacity, leaving them just enough of power to crawl home stiff, and admire him. For the truth of it is, as all know to their cost, who have had much to do with spade or plough, hod or hammer, that the British workman admires most the master who makes him sweat most. Perhaps it ought not to be so. Theoretically, we regard it thus, that a man ought to perspire, upon principle, when he is working for another man. But tell us where, and oh! where, to find the model British labourer who takes that view of the subject.

Sith it will na better be, let us out and look for him. The sky is bright blue, and the white clouds flock off it, like sheep overlapping each other. What man but loves the open air, and to walk about and think of it, with fancies flitting lazily, like fluff of dandelion? What man but loves to sit under a tree, and let the winds go wandering, and the shadows come and play with him, to let work be a pleasant memory, and hurry a storm of the morning? Everybody except Bull Garnet.

CHAPTER XII.

ALL the leaves of the New Forest, save those of
the holly and mistletoe, some evergreen spines, and
the blinder sort, that know not a wink from a nod
—all the leaves, I mean, that had sense of their
position, and when to blush and when to retire, and
how much was due to the roots that taught them—
all these leaves were beginning to feel that their
time in the world was over.   The trees had begun
to stand tier upon tier, in an amphitheatrical
fashion, and to sympathise more with the sunset;
while the sun every evening was kissing his hands,
and pretending to think them younger.   Some
outspoken trees leaned forward, well in front of
the forest-galleries, with amber sleeves, and loops
of gold, and braids of mellow abandonment, like
liberal Brazilian ladies, bowing from the balconies.
Others drew away behind them, with their mantles
folded, leaning back into unprobed depths of semi-
transparent darkness, as the forest of the sky

amasses, when the moon is rising. Some had cast off their children in parachutes, swirling as the linden berries do throughout September; some were holding their treasures grimly, and would, even when they were naked. Now the flush of the grand autumnal tide had not risen yet to its glory, but was freaking, and glancing, and morrising round the bays and the juts of the foliage. Or it ruffled, among the ferny knaps, and along the winding alleys. The sycamores truly were reddening fast, and the chestnut palms growing bronzy; the limes were yellowing here and there, and the sere leaves of the woodbine fluttered the cob of clear red berries. But the great beechen hats, which towered and darkened atop of the moorland hollows and across the track of the woodman— these, and the oaks along the rise, where the turtle-dove was cooing, had only shown their sense of the age by an undertint of olive.

It was now the fifth day of October—a day to be remembered long by all the folk of Nowelhurst. Mr. Garnet stood at the end of his garden, where a narrow pinewood gate opened to one of the forest rides. Of course he was doing something, and doing it very forcibly. His life was a fire that burned very fast, having plenty of work to poke it. But the little job which he now had in hand was quite a relaxation: there was nothing Bull Garnet enjoyed so much as cutting down a tree. He never cared what time of year it was, whether the leaves were on or off, whether the sap were up or down,

as we incorrectly express it. The sap of a tree is
ever moving, like our own life-blood; only it feels
the change of season more than we who have no
roots. Has a dormouse no circulation, when he
coils himself up in his elbowed hole? Is there no
evaporation from the frozen waters? The two
illustrations are wide apart, but the principle is the
same. Nature admits no absolute stoppage, except
as death, in her cradle of life; and then she sets
to, and transmutes it. Why Bull Garnet so
enjoyed the cutting down of a tree, none but those
who themselves enjoy it may pretend to say. Of
course, we will not refer it to the reason assigned
in the well-known epigram, which contains such a
wholesale condemnation of this arboricidal age.
In another century, London builders will perhaps
discover, when there are no trees left, that a bit of
tuck-pointing by the gate, and a dab of mud-
plaster beside it, do not content the heart of man
like the leaves, and the drooping shadowy rustle,
which is the type of himself.

Bull Garnet stood there in the October morning,
with the gate wide open, flung back by his strong
hand upon its hinges, as if it had no right to them.
The round bolt dropped from the quivering force,
dropped through the chase of the loop, and bedded
deep in the soft, wet ground. With much satisfaction the gate brought up, and felt itself anchored
safely; Bull Garnet gave the bolt a kick, which
hurled all the rusty screws out. Then he scarcely
stopped to curse the blacksmith; he wanted the

time for the woodcutters. At a glint from the side of his vast round eyes—eyes that took in everything, and made all the workmen swear and believe that he could see round a corner—he descried that the axemen were working the tree askew to the strain of the ropes. The result must be that the comely young oak, just proud of its first big crop of acorns, would swerve on the bias of the wind, stagger heavily, and fall headlong upon the smart new fence. There was no time for words—in a moment he had kicked the men right and left, torn off his coat, and caught up an axe, and dealt three thundering strokes in the laggard twist of the breach. Away went the young oak, swaying wildly, trying once to recover itself, then crashing and creaking through the brushwood, with a swish from its boughs and leaves, and a groan from its snaggy splinters. A branch took one of the men in his face, and laid him flat in a tussock of grass.

"Serve you right, you lubber; I'm devilish glad," cried Bull Garnet; "and I hope you won't move for a week."

The next moment, he went up and raised him, felt that his limbs were sound, and gave him a dram of brandy.

"All right, my fine fellow. Next time you'll know something of the way to fell a tree. Go home now, and I'll send you a bottle of wine."

But the change of his mood, the sudden softening, the glisten that broke through the flash of his eyes, was not caused this time by the inroad of

rapid Christian feeling. It was the approach of
his son that stroked the down of his heart the right
way. Bull Garnet loved nothing else in this world,
or in the world to come, with a hundredth part of
the love wherewith he loved his only son. Lo, the
word "love" thrice in a sentence—nevertheless, let
it stand so. For is there a word in our noble
tongue, or in any other language, to be compared
for power and beauty with that little word "love?"

Bob came down the path of the kitchen garden
at his utmost speed. He was like his father in one
or two things, and most unlike in others. His
nature was softer and better by far, though not so
grand and striking—Bull Garnet in the young
Adam again, ere ever the devil came. All this the
father felt, but knew not: it never occurred to
him to inquire why he adored his son.

The boy leaped the new X fence very cleverly,
through the fork of the fingers, and stood before
his father in a flame of indignation. Mr. Garnet,
with that queer expression which the face of a
middle-aged man wears when he recalls his boyhood, ere yet he begins to admire it, was looking
at his own young life with a contemplative terror.
He was saying to himself, "What cheek this boy
has got!" and he was feeling all the while that he
loved him the more for having it.

"Hurrah, Bob, my boy; you're come just in
time."

Mr. Garnet tried very hard to look as if he expected approval. Well enough all the time he knew

that he had no chance of getting it. For Bob loved nature in any form, especially as expressed in the noble eloquence of a tree. And now he saw why he had been sent to the village on a trifling errand that morning.

"Just in time for what, sir?" Bob's indignation waxed yet more. That his father should dare to chaff him!

"Just in time to tell us all about these wonderful red-combed fungi. What do you call them—some long name, as wonderful as themselves?"

Bob kicked them aside contemptuously. He could have told a long story about them, and things which men of thrice his age, who have neglected their mother, would be glad to listen to. Nature, desiring not revenge, has it in the credulous itch of the sons who have turned their backs on her.

"Oh, father," said Bob, with the tears in his eyes; "father, you can't have known that three purple emperors came to this oak, and sat upon the top of it, every morning for nearly a week, in the middle of July. And it was the most handsomest thirty-year oak till you come right to Brockenhurst bridge."

"Most handsomest, Bob!" cried Mr. Garnet, glad to lay hold of anything; "come along with me, my son; I must see to your education."

Near them stood a young spruce fir, not more than five feet high. It had thrown up a straight and tapering spire, scaled with tender green. Below were tassels, tufts, and pointlets, all in triple

order, pluming over one another in a pile of beauty.
The tips of all were touched with softer and more
glaucous tone. But all this gentle tint and form
was only as a framework now, a loom to bear the
web of heaven. For there had been a white mist
that morning—autumn's breath made visible ; and
the tree with its net of spider's webs had caught
the lucid moisture. Now, as the early sunlight
opened through the layered vapours, that little
spruce came boldly forth a dark bay of the forest,
and met all the spears of the orient. Looped and
traced with threads of gauze, the lacework of a
fairy's thought, scarcely daring to breathe upon its
veil of tremulous chastity, it kept the wings of
light on the hover, afraid to weigh down the
whiteness. A maiden with the love-dream nestling under the bridal faldetta, a child of genius
breathing softly at his own fair visions, even an
infant's angel whispering to the weeping mother—
what image of humanity can be so bright and exquisite as a common tree's apparel ?

"Father, can you make that?" Mr. Garnet
checked his rapid stride ; and for once he admired
a tree.

"No, my son; only God can do such glorious
work as that."

"But it don't take God to undo it. Smash !"

Bob dashed his fists through the whole of it, and
all the draped embroidery, all the pearly filigree,
all the festoons of silver, were but as a dream
when a yawning man stretches his scraggy arms

forth.   The little tree looked wobegone, stale, and draggled with drunken tears.

"Why, Bob, I am ashamed of you."

"And so am I of you, father."

Before the bold speech was well out of his mouth, Bob took heartily to his heels; and, for once in his life, Mr. Garnet could not make up his mind what to do.   After all, he was not so very angry, for he thought that his son had been rather clever in his mode of enforcing the moral; and a man who loves ability, and loves his boy still more, regards with a liberal shrewdness the proof of the one in the other.

Alas, it is hard to put Mr. Garnet in a clear, bold stereoscope, without breach of the third commandment.   Somehow or other, as fashion goes—and happily it is on the go always—a man, and threefold thrice a woman, may, at this especial period, in the persons of his or her characters, break the sixth· commandment lightly, and the seventh with great applause.   Indeed, no tale is much approved without lèse-majesté of them both. Then for what subterranean reason, or by what diabolical instrumentality (that language is strictly parliamentary, because it is words and water), is a writer now debarred from reporting what his people said, unless they all talked tracts and milk, or rubrics and pommel-saddles?   In a word—for sometimes any fellow must come to the point—Why do our judicious and highly-respected Sosii score out all our d—ns?

Is it not true that our generation swears almost as hard as any? And yet it will not allow a writer to hint the truth in the matter. Of course we should do it sparingly, and with due reluctance. But, unless all tales are written for women, and are so to be accepted, it is a weak attempt at imposture on our sons and grandsons to suppress entirely in our pictures any presence not indecent, however unbecoming.

Mr. Garnet was a Christian of the most advanced intelligence, so far as our ideas at the present time extend. He felt the beauty and perfection of the type which is set before us. He never sneered, as some of us do, at things which were too large for him, neither did he clip them to the shape of his own œsophagus. Only in practice, like the rest of us, he was sadly centrifugal.

Now with his nostrils widely open, and great eyes on the ground, he was pacing rapidly up and down his sheltered kitchen garden. Every square was in perfect order, every tree in its proper compass, all the edging curt and keen. The ground was cropped with that trim luxuriance which we never see except under first-rate management. All the coleworts for the winter, all, the well-earthed celery, all the buttoning Brussels sprouts, salsify just fit to dig, turnips lifting whitely forth (as some ladies love to show themselves), modest savoys just hearting in and saying "no" to the dew-beads, prickly spinach daily widening the clipped arrowhead—they all had room to eat and drink, and no man grudged his neighbour; yet Puck himself could not have skipped through with dry feet during a hoar-frost. As for weeds, Bull Garnet—well, I must not say what he *would* have done. Suddenly a small, spare man turned the corner upon him, where a hedge of hornbeam, trimmed and dressed as if with a pocket-comb, broke the south-western violence. Most men would have shown their hats above the narrow spine, but Rufus Hutton was very short, and seldom carried a chimney-pot.

"Sir, what can I do for you?" said Mr. Garnet, much suprised, but never taken aback.

"Excuse me, sir, but I called at your house, and came this way to find you. You know me well, by name, I believe; as I have the pleasure of knowing you. Rufus Hutton; ahem, sir! Delightful occupation! I, too, am a gardener. 'Dumelow Seedling,' I flatter myself. Know them well by the eye, sir. But what a difference the soil makes! Ah, yes, let them hang till the frost comes. What a plague we have had with earwigs! Get into the seat of the fruit; now just let me show you. Ah, you beggars, there you are. Never take them by the head, sir, or they'd nip my fingers. Take them under the abdomen, and they haven't room to twist upon you. There, now; what can he do?"

"Not even thank you, sir, for killing him. And now what can I do for you?"

"Mr. Garnet, I will come to the point. A man

learns that in India. Too hot, sir, for much talking. Bless my heart, I have known the thermo-
meter at 10 o'clock P.M., sir—not in the barracks,
mind me, nor in a stifling nullah——"

"Excuse me, I have read of all that. I have
an engagement, Dr. Hutton, at eight minutes past
eleven."

"Bless my heart, and I have an appointment
at 11.9 and five seconds. How singular a coin-
cidence !"

Bull Garnet looked down at the little doctor,
and thought him too small to be angry with.
Moreover, he was a practical man, and scarcely
knew what chaff meant. So he kept his temper
wonderfully, while Rufus looked up at him gravely,
with his little eyes shining like glow-worms between the brown stripes of his countenance.

"I have heard of you, Dr. Hutton, as a very
skilful gardener. Perhaps you would like to look
round my garden, while I go and despatch my
business. If so, I will be with you again in
exactly thirty-five minutes."

"Stop, stop, stop ! you'll be sorry all your life,
if you don't hear my news."

So Rufus Hutton thought. But Mr. Garnet
was sorry through all the rest of his life that he
ever stopped to hear it.

CHAPTER XIII.

BULL GARNET forgot his appointment for eight minutes after eleven; indeed it was almost twelve o'clock when he came out of the summer-house (made of scarlet-runners) to which he had led Dr. Hutton, when he saw that his tale was of interest. As he came forth, and the noonday sun fell upon his features, any one who knew him would have been surprised at their expression. A well-known artist, employed upon a fresco in the neighbourhood, had once described Mr. Garnet's face in its ordinary aspect as "violence in repose." Epigrammatic descriptions of the infinite human nature are like tweezers to catch a whale with. The man who unified so rashly all the Garnetian impress, had only met Mr. Garnet once—had never seen him after dinner, or playing with his children.

Now Rufus Hutton, however garrulous, was a kind and sensible man, and loth to make any mischief. He ran after Mr. Garnet, hotly. Bull

Garnet had quite forgotten him, and would take
no notice.   The doctor made a short cut through
a quarter of Brussels sprouts (which almost knocked
off his wide-awake hat) and stood in the arch of
trimmed yew-tree, opening at the western side
upon the forest lane.   Here he stretched his arms
to either upright, and mightily barred all exit.
He knew that the other would not go home, because he had told him so.

Presently Bull Garnet strode up : not with his
usual swing, however; not with his wonted self-
confidence.   He seemed to walk off from a staggering blow, which had dulled his brain for the
moment.   He stopped politely before Mr. Hutton
(who expected to be thrust aside), and asked as if
with new interest, and as if he had not heard the
tale out—

" Are you quite sure, Dr. Hutton, that you
described the dress correctly ? "

" As sure as I am of the pattern of my own
unmentionables.   Miss Rosedew wore, as I told
you, a lavender serge, looped at the sides with
purple—a pretty dress for Christmas, but it struck
me as warm for Michaelmas.   Perhaps it was
meant for the Michaelmas daisies ; or perhaps she
suffers from rheumatism, or flying pains in the
patella."

" And the cloak and hat, as you described them
—are you sure about them ? "

" My dear sir, I could swear to them both if I
saw them on a scarecrow.   How can I speak of

such a thing after that lovely creature? Such an exquisite fall of the shoulders—good wide shoulders too—and such a delicious waist! I assure you, my dear sir, I have seen fine women in India——"

"Dr. Hutton," said Mr. Garnet, sternly, "let me hear no more of that. You are a newly-married man, a man of my time of life. I will have no warm description of—of any young ladies."

Rufus Hutton was a peppery man, and not very easily cowed. Nevertheless, his mind was under the pressure of a stronger one. So he only relieved himself with a little brag.

"Why, Mr. Garnet, you cross-examine me as I did the natives when I acted as judge in Churramuttee, when the two chuprassies came before me, and the water-carrier. I tell you, sir, I see more in a glance than most men do in a long set stare, when they are called in to appraise a thing. I could tell every plait in your shirt-front, and the stuff and cut of your coat, before you could say 'good morning.' It was only last Thursday that Mrs. Hutton, who is a most remarkable woman, made an admirable observation about my rapid perception."

"I have not the smallest doubt of it. And I believe that you fully deserved it. You will therefore perceive at once that this matter must go no further. Did you see my—son at the house here?"

"No. Only the maid-servant, who directed me where to find you."

"Then you did not go in at all, I suppose?"

"No; but I admired greatly your mode of training that beautiful tropæolum over the porch. I must go and look at it again, with your kind permission. I never neglect the chance of a wrinkle such as that."

"Another time, Dr. Hutton, I shall hope to show it to you; though you must have seen it all at a glance, for it is simpler than my shirt-fronts. But my business takes me now to the Hall, and I shall be glad of your company."

"Hospitable fellow, with a vengeance!" thought little Rufus. "And I heard he had some wonderful sherry, and it's past my time for a snack. Serves me right for meddling with other people's business."

But while he stood hesitating, and casting fond glances towards the cottage, Mr. Garnet, without any more ado, passed his powerful long arm through the little wing of Rufus, and hurried him down the dingle.

"Excuse me, sir, but I have never much time to waste. This, as you know, is a most busy day, and all the preparations are under my sole charge. I laugh at the fuss, as a matter of course. But that question is not for me. Cradock Nowell is a noble fellow, and I have the highest respect for him."

"Well, I rather prefer young Clayton. Having

brought them both into the world, I ought to understand them.   But I hope he won't make a fool of himself in this matter we have been talking of."

Mr. Garnet jerked his companion's arm, and his face went pale as Portland stone.

"Make a d—d rogue more likely. And he won't be the first of his family."

"Yes, as you say," replied the doctor to all he could catch of the muttered words, which flew over the crown of his hat, "beyond all doubt the first family in this part of the kingdom, and so they must have their jubilee.   But I trust you will use with the utmost caution what I thought it best to confide to you, under the bond of secresy.   Of course, I could not think of telling papa, either of lady or gentleman; and knowing how you stand with the family, you seemed to me the proper person to meet this little difficulty."

"Beyond a doubt, I am."

"Pooh, sir, a boy and a girl.   I wonder you think so much about it.   Men never know their own minds in the matter until they arrive at our age.   And as for the chits on the other side— whew, they blow right and left, as the feathers on their hats do."

"That is not the case with *my* family.   We make up our minds, and stick to them."

"Then your family is the exception, which only proves my rule; and I am glad that it is not concerned in the present question."

When they came to that part of the lawn in

front of the ancient Hall where the fireworks' stage
had been reared on a gently-rising mound, Cradock
Nowell met them, with a book in his hand. To-
morrow he would be twenty-one; and a more
honest, open-hearted fellow, or a better built one,
never arrived at man's estate, whether for wealth
or poverty. He had not begun to think very
deeply; indeed, who could expect it, where trouble
had never entered? It is pain that deepens the
channel of thought, and sorrow that sweeps the bar
away. Cradock as yet was nothing more than a
clever, fine young man, an elegant and accurate
scholar, following thought more than leading it.
Nevertheless, he had the material of a grand un-
selfish character—of a nature which, when per-
fected, could feel its imperfections. Sorrow and
trial were needed for him; and God knows he
soon got enough of them.

He shoved away his Tauchnitz Herodotus in his
shooting-coat pocket. Neither of the men he met
was a scholar; neither would feel any interest in
it. Being driven forth by his father's grumbling
at the little pleasure he showed in the fuss that was
making about him, he had brought his genial, true
cosmopolite to show him a thing which his heart
would have loved. Cradock had doubled down the
leaf whereon was described the building of the
boat-bridge over the Hellespont. Neither had he
forgotten the interment of the Scythian kings. It
was not that he purposed to instruct the carpenters
thence, or to shed any light on their doings; but

that he hoped to learn from them some words to jot down on the margin. He had discovered already, being helped thereto by the tongue of Ytene, that hundreds of forcible Saxon words still lurk in the crafts to which the beaten race betook itself—words which are wanted sadly, and pieced out very unpleasantly by roundabout foreign fanglements.

Even the gratitude now due to the good-will of all the neighbourhood, had failed to reconcile his mind to the turgid part before him. At Oxford he had been dubbed already "Caradoc the Philosopher;" and the more he learned, the less he thought of his own importance. He had never regarded the poor around him as dogs made for him to whistle to; he even knew that he owed them some duties, and wondered how to discharge them. Though bred of high Tory lineage, and corded into it by the twists of habit and education, he never could hang by neck and gullet; he never could show basement only, as a well-roped onion does. Encased as he was by strict surroundings, he never could grow quite straight and even, without a seed inside him, as a prize cucumber does in the cylinder of an old chimney-glass.

Some of this dereliction sprang, no doubt, from his granulation, and some from the free trade of his mind with the great heart called "John Rosedew."

Now he came up, and smiled, like a boy of fourteen, in Mr. Garnet's face; for he liked Bull Garnet's larger qualities, and had no fear of his

smaller ones.   Mr. Garnet never liked; he always
loved or hated.   He loved Cradock Nowell
heartily, and heartily hated Clayton.

"Behind my time, you see, Cradock.   I am glad
you are doing my duty.—Ha, there! *I see you,
my man.*"

The man was skulking his work, in rigging out
with coloured lamps an old oak fifty yards off.
That ancient oak, the pride of the chase, was to
represent, to-morrow night, a rainbow reflecting
"Cradock Nowell."   Young Crad, who regarded
it all as ill-taste, if it were not positive sin, had
lifted his voice especially against that oak's bedizenment.   "It will laugh at us from every acorn," he
had said to his father.   But Sir Cradock was now
a man of sixty; and threescore resents being
budded.   The incision results in gum only.

At the sound of that tremendous voice, the man
ran recklessly out on the branch, the creaking of
which had alarmed him.   Snap went the branch at
a cankered part, and the poor fellow dropped from
a height of nearly forty feet.   But the crashing
wood caught in the bough beneath, which was
sound and strong, and there hung the man, un-
injured as yet, clinging only by one arm, and
struggling to throw his feet up.   In a moment
Cradock had seized a ladder, reared, and fixed, and
mounted it, and helped the poor fellow to slide off
upon it, and stayed him there gasping and quivering.   Bull Garnet set foot on the lowest rung, and
Rufus Hutton added his weight, which was not

very considerable. A dozen workmen came running up, and the man, whose nerves had quite failed him, was carefully eased to the ground.

"Mr. Garnet," said Cradock, with flashing eyes, "would you have walked on that branch yourself?"

"To be sure I would, after I had looked at it."

"But you gave this poor man no time to look. Is it brave to make another do what you yourself would fear?"

"Give me your hand, my boy. I was wrong, and you are right. I wish every man to hear me. Jem, come to my house this evening. You owe your life to Mr. Cradock."

Nature itself is better than the knowledge of human nature. Mr. Garnet, by generosity quicker than quickest perception, had turned to his credit an incident which would have disgraced a tyrant. A powerful man's confession of wrong always increases his power. While the men were falling to work again, every one under the steward's eyes, Sir Cradock Nowell and Clayton his son came cantering up from the stables. The dry leaves crackled or skirred away crisply from their horses' feet, for the day was fine and breezy; the nags were arching their necks and pricking their ears with enjoyment; but neither of the riders seemed to be in high spirits. The workmen touched their hats to them in a manner very different from that with which they received Mr. Garnet or Cradock Nowell. There was more of distant respect in it, and less of real interest.

Sir Cradock now was a perfect specimen of the
well-bred Englishman at threescore years of age.
Part of his life had been touched by sorrow, but
in the main he had prospered. A man of ability
and high culture, who has not suffered deeply, is
apt, after passing middle age, to substitute tact for
feeling, and common sense for sympathy. Mellow
and blest is the age of the man who soberly can do
otherwise.

Sir Cradock Nowell knew his age, and dressed
himself accordingly. Neither stiffness nor laxity,
neither sporting air nor austerity, could be perceived
in his garb or manner. He respected himself and
all whom he met, until he had cause to the contrary.
But his heart, instead of expanding, had narrowed
in the loneliness of his life; and he really loved
only one in the world—the son who rode beside
him. He had loved John Rosedew well and truly
for many an honest year; of late, admiration was
uppermost, and love grown a thing to be thought
about. The cause of the change was his own
behaviour, and John's thorough hate of injustice.
That old friend of the family could not keep
silence always at the preference of Clayton, and
the disparagement of Cradock. The father himself could not have told whence arose this preference. Year by year it had been growing, for a long
time unsuspected; suspected then and fought with,
then smothered at once and justified; allowed at
last to spread and thrive on the right of its own
existence. And yet any one, to look at Sir Cradock, would have thought him justice personified.

And so he was, as Chairman of the Quarter Sessions. Clear intelligence, quick analysis, keen perception of motive in others, combined with power to dispense (when nature so does) with reason, and used with high sense of honour—all these things made him an oracle to every one but himself. Although he had never been in the army, he looked like a veteran soldier; and his seat on horseback was stiff and firm, rather than easy and graceful. Tall, spare figure, and grey moustache, Roman nose, and clear, bright eyes, thin lips, and broad white forehead—the expression of the whole bespoke an active, resolute, upright man, not easily pleased or displeased.

As every one was to keep holiday, the farmers had challenged the Ringwood club to play them a game of cricket, and few having seen a bat till now, some practice seemed indispensable. Accordingly, while Bull Garnet was busy among the working men, the farmers, being up for play, were at it in hard earnest, labouring with much applause and merriment, threshing or churning, mowing or ploughing, and some making kicks at the ball. Rufus Hutton looked on in a spirited manner, and Cradock was bowling with all his might at the legs of a petty tyrant, when his father and brother rode up between the marquees and awnings. The tyrannical farmer received a smart crack on the shin, and thought (though he feared to say) " d—n."

"Hurrah, Crad! more jerk to your elbow!" cried Clayton, who also disliked the man;

"Blackers, you mustn't break the ball, it's against the laws of cricket."

Grinning sympathy and bad wit deepened the bruise of the tibia, till Farmer Blackers forgot all prudence in the deep jar of the marrow.

"Boul awai, meester, and be honged to you. I carries one again *you*, mind."

To the great surprise of all present there, Sir Cradock did not look at the speaker, but turned on his son with anger.

" Sir, you ought to know better. Your sense of justice will lead you, I hope, to apologise to that man."

He did not wait to see the effect of this public reproof, which was heard by a hundred people, but struck his mare hastily on the shoulder, called Clayton, and rode away. Cradock, who now had the ball in his hands, threw it a hundred feet high.

"Catch it who will," he said; "I shall bowl no more to-day. Farmer Blackers, I apologise to you; I did not know you were so tender."

Feeling far more tender himself (for all that was the youth's bravado), he went away, doubting right and wrong, to his own little room on the ground floor. There he would smoke his pipe, and meditate, and condemn himself, if the verdict were true. That young fellow's sense of justice was larger, softer, more deeply fibred, than any Sir Cradock Nowell's.

CHAPTER XIV.

MEN of high culture and sensitive justice, who
have much to do with ill-taught workmen, lie
under a terrible disadvantage. They fear to presume upon the mere accident of their own position,
they dread to extract more dues from another than
they in his place would render, they shrink from
saying what may recall the difference betwixt
them, they cannot bear to be stiff and dogmatic,
yet they know that any light word may be taken
in heavy earnest. True sympathy is the only
thing to bring master and man together; and
sympathy is a subtle vein, direct when nature hits
it, but crooked and ungrammatical to the syntax
of education. Cradock Nowell often touched it,
without knowing how; and hence his popularity
among the "lower classes." Clayton hit upon it
only in the softer sex. Bull Garnet knew how to
move it deeply, and owed his power to that knowledge, even more than to his energy.

Cradock was pondering these things in the pipe of contemplation, when a pair of keen eyes twinkled in at the window, and a shrewd, shrill voice made entry.

"Pray let me in, Mr. Cradock Nowell; I want to inquire about the grapes."

"What a wonderful man that is!" said Cradock to himself, as he came from his corner reluctantly to open the French window; "there is nothing he doesn't inquire about. Erotetic philosopher! He has only been here some three or four days, and he knows all our polity better than we do! I wish his wife would come; though I believe he is an honest fellow."

Unconscious of any satirical antithesis, he opened the window, and admitted the polypragmonic doctor; and, knowing that homœopathic treatment is the wisest for garrulous subjects, he began upon him at once. Nor omitted a spice of domesticity, which he thought would be sovereign.

"Now, Dr. Hutton, it is too bad of you to wander about like a bachelor. How long before we have the pleasure of seeing Mrs. Hutton?"

"My dear boy, you know the reason; I hope you know the reason. Your roads are very rough for ladies, especially when in delicate health, and our four-wheel is being mended. So I rode over alone; and what a lovely ride it is! Ah, Clayton —yes, I saw Clayton somewhere. But your father has promised most kindly to send a carriage to-morrow to Geopharmacy Lodge—the name of our little place, sir."

At the thought of his home, the little doctor pulled up both his shirt-collars, and looked round the room disparagingly.

"Oh, I am very glad to hear it. Meanwhile, you would like to see our grapes. Let me show you the way to the vinery; though I cannot take you without misgivings. Your gardening fame has frightened us. Our old man, Snip, is quite afraid of your new lights and experience."

"Sensible lad," muttered Rufus Hutton, who was pleasantly conceited—"uncommonly sensible lad! I am not at all sure that he isn't a finer fellow than Clayton. But I must take my opportunity now, while he has his stock off. There is something wrong : I am sure of it."

"Excuse me a moment," said Cradock; "I am sorry to keep you waiting, but I must just put on my neckerchief, if I can only find it. How very odd! I could have declared I put it on that table."

"What's that I see on the floor there, by the corner of the bookcase?" Rufus pointed his cane at the tie, which lay where himself had thrown it.

"Oh, thank you; I must be getting blind, for I am sure I looked there just now."

While the young man stooped forward, the little doctor, who had posted himself for the pur-

pose, secured a quick glimpse at the back of his
neck, where the curling hair fell sideways. That
glance increased his surprise, and confirmed his
strange suspicions. The surprise and suspicion
had broken upon him, as he stood by the farmer's
wicket, and Cradock sprang up to the bowling
crease; now, in his excitement and curiosity, he
forgot all scruples. It was strange that he had
felt any, for he was not very sensitive; but
Cradock, with all his good nature, had a certain
unconscious dignity, from which Dr. Hutton retreated.

"The grapes I came to inquire about," said
Rufus, with much solemnity, "are not those in the
vinery, which I have seen often enough, but those
on your neck, Mr. Nowell."

Cradock looked rather amazed, but more at the
inquirer's manner than at his seeming imper-
tinence.

"I really cannot see how the 'grapes,' as some
people call the blue lines on my neck, can interest
you, sir, or are important enough to be spoken of."

"Then I do, Cradock Nowell. Do you refuse
to let me see them?"

"Certainly not; though I should refuse it to
almost any one else. Not that I am sensitive
about such a trifle. You, as a medical man, and
an old friend of my father, are welcome to your
autopsy. Is not that what you call it, sir?"

Nevertheless, from the tone of his voice, Rufus
Hutton knew that he liked it not—for it was a

familiarity, and seemed to the youth a childish one.

"Sit down, young man, sit down," said the doctor, very pompously, and waiving further discussion. "I am not—I mean to say you are taller than when I first—ah, yes, manipulated you."

As the doctor warmed to his subject, he grew more and more professional, and perhaps less gentlemanly, until his good feelings came into play, for his heart, after all, was right. All the terms which he used shall not be repeated, because of their being so medical. Only this, that he said at last, after a long inspection—

"Sir, this confirms to a nicety my metrostigmatic theory."

"Dr. Hutton, I know not what you mean, neither do I wish to know."

Cradock put on his neckerchief anyhow, and walked to his chair by the mantelpiece, although no fire was burning. The medical man said nothing, but gravely looked out of the window. Presently the young gentleman felt that he was not acting hospitably.

"Excuse me, sir, if I have seemed rude; but you do not know how these things——I mean, when I think of my mother. Let me ring for some sherry and sandwiches; you have had no lunch."

"Ring for some brandy, my boy; and give me a cheroot. Fine property! Look at the sweep of the land—and to think of losing it all!"

Instead of ringing, Cradock went and fetched the cognac himself, and took down a glass from a cupboard.

"Two glasses, my dear boy, two."

"No, sir; I never touch it."

"Then take it now, for the first time. Here, let me feel your pulse."

"Once for all, I beg you to tell me what is all this mystery? Do you think I am a child?"

"Fill your pipe again, while I light a cigar."

Cradock did as he was told, although with trembling hands. Rufus Hutton went for a wine-glass, filled it with brandy, and pushed it across, then gulped down half a tumblerful; but Cradock did not taste his.

"Now, my boy, can you bear some very bad news indeed?"

"Anything better than this suspense. I have heard some bad news lately, which has seasoned me for anything."

He referred to Amy Rosedew.

"It is this. You are not your father's heir; you are only the younger son."

"Is that all?"

"All! Isn't that enough? Good God! What more would you have?—you don't deserve brandy."

"My father will be glad, and so will Clayton, and—perhaps one other. But I don't mean to say that I am."

" I should rather fancy not. But you take it most philosophically ! "

Dr. Hutton gazed at the poor young fellow in surprise and admiration, trying vainly to make him out. Then he reached over to Cradock's elbow, took his glass of cognac, and swallowed it.

" This has upset me, my boy, more than you. How miserable I felt about it! But perhaps you place no faith in the assertion I have made ? "

" Indeed, it has quite amazed me; and I have had no time to think of it. My head seems spinning round. Please to say no more just for a minute or two, unless you find it uncomfortable."

He leaned back in his chair, and tried to think, but could not.

Rufus Hutton said nothing. In spite of all his experience, the scene was very strange to him ; and he watched it out with interest, which deepened into strong feeling.

" Now, Dr. Hutton," said the youth, trying to look as he thought he ought, though he could not keep the tears back, " I beg you to think of me no more. Let us have the strictest justice. I have not known you so long—so long as you have known me—but I feel that you would not say what you have said, without the strongest evidence."

" Confound me for a meddlesome fool ! My dear boy, no one has heard us. Let us sink the matter entirely. Least said, soonest mended."

"What do you mean? Do you think for a moment that I would be a blackguard?"

"Hush!—don't get so excited. Why, you look as fierce as Bull Garnet. All I mean is—you know the old saying—'Quieta non movere.'"

"The motto of fools and dastards. 'Have it out,' is an Englishman's rule. No sneaking tricks for me, sir. Oh, what a fool I am! I beg your pardon with all my heart; you will make allowances for me. Instead of being rude, I ought to be grateful for kindness which even involves your honour."

And he held out his hand to the doctor.

"Crad, my dear boy," exclaimed Mr. Hutton, with a big tear twinkling in each little eye, "the finest thing I ever did was showing you to the daylight. If I rob you of what has appeared your birthright, curse all memorandum-books, and even my metrostigmatic treatise, which I fully meant to immortalize me."

"And so I hope it may do. I am not so calm as I ought to be. Somehow a fellow can't be, when he is taken off the hooks so. I know you will allow for this; I beg you to allow for nothing else, except a gentleman's delicacy. Give me your reasons, or not, as you like. The matter will be for my father."

Cradock looked proud and beautiful. But the depth of his eyes was troubled. A thousand

thoughts were moving there, like the springs that
feed a lake.

"Hah, ho, very hard work!" said Rufus Hutton,
puffing; "I vote that we adjourn. I do love the
open air so, ever since I took to gardening."

Rufus Hutton hated "sentiment," but he could
not always get rid of it.

CHAPTER XV.

ON the morning of that same day, our Amy at her father's side, in the pretty porch of the Rectory, uttered the following wisdom: "Darling Papples, Papelikidion—is there any other diminutivicle half good enough for you, or stupid enough for me?—my own father (that's best of all), you must not ride Corœbus to-day."

"Amy amata, peramata a me, aim of my life, amicula, in the name of sweet sense, why not?"

"Because, pa, he has had ten great long carrots, and my best hat full of new oats; and. I know he will throw you off."

"Scrupulum injecisti. I shouldn't like to come off to-day. And it rained the night before last." So said the rector, proudly contemplating a pair of new kerseymeres, which Channing the clerk had made upon trial. "Nevertheless, I think that I have read enough on the subject to hold on by his mane, if he does not kick unreasonably. And if he gives me time to soothe him—that horse is fond of Greek—and, after all, the ground is soft."

"No, dad, I don't think it is prudent. And you won't have me there, you know."

"My own pet, that is too true. And with all your knowledge of riding! Why, my own seems quite theoretical by the side of yours. And yet I have kept my seat under very trying circumstances. You remember the time when Coraebus met the trahea?"

"Yes, pa; but he hadn't had any oats; and I was there to advise you."

"True, my child, quite true. But I threw my equilibrium just as a hunter does. And I think I could do it again. I bore in mind what Xenophon says——"

"Pa, here he is! And he does look so fat, I know he will be restive."

"Prepare your Aunt Doxy's mind, my dear, not to scold more than she can help, in case of the worst—I mean, if the legs of my trousers want rubbing. How rash of me, to be sure, to have put them on to-day! Prius dementat. I trust sincerely—and old Channing is so proud of them, and he says the cut is so fashionable. Nevertheless, I heard our Clayton, as he went down the gravel-walk, treating, with what he himself would have called 'colores orationis,' upon Uncle John's new bags; θύλακοι, I suppose he meant, as opposed to ἀναξυρίδες. I was glad that the subject possessed so lively an interest for him; notwithstanding which,

I was very glad Mr. Channing did not hear him."

"The impudence! Well, I am astonished. And to see the things he brought back from Oxford—quince-coloured, with a stripe that wide, like one of my fancy gourds. I'll be sure to have it out with him. No, I can't, though; I forgot." And Amy looked down with a rosy smile, remembering the delicacy of the subject. "But I am quite sure of one thing, pa: Mr. Cradock would never have done it. Ræbus, don't kick up the gravel. Do you suppose we can roll every day? Oh, you are so fat, you darling!"

"When the sides are deep," said the rector, quoting from Xenophon, "and somewhat protuberant at the stomach, the horse is generally more easy to ride. What a comfort, Amy! Stronger, moreover, and more capable of enjoying food."

"He has enjoyed a rare lot this morning. At least I hope you have, you sweetest. Why, pa, I declare you are whistling!"

"It also behoves a horseman to know that it is a time-honoured precept to soothe the steed by whistling, and rouse him by a sharp sound made between the tongue and the palate."

"Oh, father, don't do that. Promise me now, dear, won't you?"

"I will promise you, my child, because I don't know how to do it. I tried very hard last Wednesday, and only produced a guttural. But I think I shall understand it, after six or seven visiting days. At least, if the air is sharp."

"No, pa, I hope you won't. It would be so reckless of you; and I know you will get a sore throat."

"Sweet of my world, cor cordium, you have wrapped me with three involucres tighter than any hazel-nut. They will all go into my pocket the moment I am round the corner."

"No, daddy, you won't be so cruel. And after the rime this morning! Ræbus will tell if you do. Won't you now, my pretty?"

Coræbus was a handsome pony, but not a handsome doer. He could go at a rare pace when he liked, but he did not often like it. His wind was short, and so was his temper, and he looked at things unpleasantly. Perhaps he had been disappointed in love in the tenderness of his youth. Nevertheless he had many good points, and next to himself loved Amy. He would roll his black eyes, put his nose to her lips, and almost leave oats to look at her. His colour varied sensitively according to the season. In the height of summer, a dappled bay; towards the autumnal equinox, a tendency to nuttiness; then a husky bristle of deepest brown flaked with hairs of ginger; after the clips a fine mouse-colour, with a spirited sense of nakedness, fierce whiskers, and a love of buck jumps. Then ere the blessed Christmas-tide, nature began to blanket him with a nap the colour of black frost; and so through the grizzle of spring he came round to his proper bay once more. Amy declared she could tell every month by the special hue of Coræbus; but, albeit she was the most truthful of girls, her heart was many degrees too warm for her lips to be always at dew-point.

Both in the stable and out of it, that pony had a bluff way with his heels, which none but himself thought humorous. He never meant any harm, however—it was only his mode of expressing himself; and he liked to make a point when he felt his new shoes tingling. But as for kicking his Amy, he was not quite so low as that. He would not even jump about, when she was on his back, more than was just the proper thing to display her skill and figure. "Oh, you sad Coræby," always brought him to sadness; and he expected a pat from her little gloved hand, and cocked his tail with dignity the moment he received it. Nevertheless, for her father, the rector of the parish, he entertained, when the oats were plentiful, nonconformist sentiments, verging almost upon scepticism. He liked him indeed, as the whole world must; he even admired his learning, and turned up his eyes at the Greek; but he was not impressed, as he should have been, by the sacerdotal office. Fatal defect of all, he knew that the rector could not ride. John Rosedew was a reasoning man, and uncommonly strong in the legs, but a great deal too philosophical to fit himself over a horse well. He had written a treatise upon the Pele-

thronian Lapiths (which he could never be
brought to read before a learned society), he knew
all about the Olympics and Pythics, and Xenophon gave him a text-book; but, for all that, he
never put his feet the right way into the stirrups.

"Look at him now," said John, as the boy led
the pony up and down, while Amy was knotting
the mufflers so that they never might come undone
again; "how beautifully Xenophon describes
him! 'When the horse is excited to assume that
artificial air which he adopts when he is proud, he
then delights in riding, becomes magnificent, ter-
rific, and attracts attention!' And again, 'persons
beholding such a horse pronounce him generous,
free in his motions, fit for military exercise, high-
mettled, haughty, and both pleasant and terrible
to look on.' Pleasant, I suppose, for other people,
and terrible for the rider. But why our author
insists so much upon the horse being taught to
'rear gracefully,' I am not horseman enough as
yet to understand. It has always appeared to me
that Coræbus rears too much already. And then
the direction—'but if after riding, and copious
perspiration, and when he has reared gracefully,
he be relieved immediately both of the rider and
reins, there is little doubt that he will spontaneously
advance to rear when necessary.' What does that
mean, I ask you? I never find it necessary, except, indeed, when the little girls jump up and
pull my coat-tails, in their inquisition for apples,
and then I am always afraid that they may suffer

some detriment. But let us not overtask his patience; here he comes again. Jem, my boy, lead him up to the chair."

"Any jam in your pocket, father?"

"No, my child, not any. Your excellent Aunt Eudoxia has it all under lock and key. Now I will mount according to Xenophon, though I do not find that he anywhere prescribes a Windsor chair. 'When he has well prepared himself for the ascent, let him support his body with his left hand, and stretching forth his right hand let him leap on horseback, and when he mounts thus he will not present an uncomely spectacle to those behind. There, I am up, most accurately; excellent horse, and great writer! And now for the next direction: 'We do not approve of the same bearing a man has in a carriage, but that an upright posture be observed, with the legs apart.'"

"How could they be otherwise, pa, when the horse is between them?"

"Your criticisms are rash, my child. Jem, how dare you laugh, sir? I will buy a pair of spurs, I declare, the next time I go to Ringwood. Good-bye, darling; Aunt Doxy will take you up to the park, when the sun comes out, to see all the wonderful doings. I shall be home in time to dress for the dinner at the Hall."

Sweet Amy kissed her hand, and curtseyed—as she loved to do to her father; and, after two or three wayward sallies (repressed by Jem with the gardening broom), Coræbus pricked his little ears, and shook himself into a fair jog-trot. So with his elbows well stuck out, and shaking merrily to and fro, his right hand ready to grasp the pommel in case of consternation, and one leg projected beyond the other, after the manner of a fowl's side-bone, away rode John Rosedew in excellent spirits, to begin his Wednesday parochial tour.

Being duly victualled, and thoroughly found, for a voyage of long duration and considerable hazard, the good ship "John Rosedew" set sail every Wednesday for commerce with the neighbourhood. This expedition was partly social, partly ministerial, in a great measure eleemosynary, and entirely loving and amicable. There was no bombardment of dissenters, no firing of red-hot shot at Papists, no up with the helm and run him down, if any man launched on the mare magnum, or any frail vessel missed stays. And yet there was no compromise, no grand circle sailing, no luffing to a trade-wind; straight was the course, and the chart most clear, and the good ship bound, with favour of God, for a haven beyond the horizon. Barnacles and vile teredoes, algæ and desmidious trailers:—I doubt if there be more sins in our hearts to stop us from loving each other than parasites and leeching weeds to clog a stout ship's bottom. Nevertheless she bears them on, beautifies and cleanses them, until they come to temperate waters, where the harm has failed

them.   So a good man carries with him those who
carp and fasten on him; content to take their little
stings, if the utterance purify them.

The parish of Nowelhurst straggles away far
into the depths of the forest. To the southward
indeed it has moorland and heather, with ridges,
and spinnets, and views of the sea, and fir-trees
naked and worn to the deal by the chafing of the
salt winds. But all away to the west, north, and
east, the dark woods hold dominion, and you seem
to step from the parish churchyard into the grave
of ages. The village and the village warren, the
chase, and the Hall above them, are scooped from
out the forest shadow, in the shape of a hunting
boot. Lay the boot on its side with the heel to
the east, and the top towards the north, and we get
pretty near the topography. The village scattered
along the warren forms the foot and instep, the
chase descending at right angles is the leg and
ancle, the top will serve to represent the house
with its lawns and gardens, the back seam may
run as the little river which flows under Nowelhurst bridge. The shank of the spur is the bridge
and road, the rowel the church and rectory. Away
to the west beyond the toe, some quarter of a mile
on the Ringwood-road, stands the smithy kept by
the well-known Roger Sweetland, who can out-
swear any man in the parish, and fears no one
except Bull Garnet. Our sketchy boot will leave
unshown the whereabouts of the Garnet cottage,
unless we suppose the huntsman to insert just his

toe in the stirrup.   Then the top of the iron rung
will mark the house of the steward, a furlong or so
north-west of the village, with its back to the lane
which leads from the smithy to the Hall.   And
this lane is the short cut from Nowelhurst Hall to
Ringwood.   It saves three-quarters of a mile, and
risks a little more than three-quarters of the neck.
Large and important as the house is, it has no high
road to Ringwood, and gets away with some difficulty even towards Lyndhurst or Lymington.
Bull Garnet was always down upon the barbarity
of the approaches, but Sir Cradock never felt sore
on the subject, save perhaps for a week at Christmas-tide.   He had never been given to broad in-
discriminate hospitality, but loved his books and
his easy-chair, and his friend of ancient standing.

The sun came out and touched the trees with
every kind of gilding, as John Rosedew having
done the village, and learned every gammer's
alloverishness, and every gaffer's rheumatics, drew
the snaffle upon Coræbus longside of Job Smith's
pigsty, and plunged southward into the country.
He saw how every tree was leaning forth its green
with yellowness ; even proud of the novelty, like a
child who has lost his grandmother.   And though
he could not see very far, he observed a little thing
which he had never noticed before.   It was that
while the other trees took their autumn evenly,
the elm was brushed with a flaw of gold while the
rest of the tree was verdure.   A single branch
would stand forth from the others, mellow against

their freshness, like a harvest-sheaf set up perhaps on the foreground of a grass-plot. The rector thought immediately of the golden spray of Æneas, and how the Brazilian manga glistens in the tropic moonlight. Then soothing his pony with novel sounds, emulous of equestrianism, he struck into a moorland track leading to distant cottages. Thence he would bear to the eastward, arrive at his hostel by one o'clock, visit the woodmen, and home through the forest, with the evening shadows falling.

CHAPTER XVI.

BESIDE the embowered stream that forms the eastern verge of the chase, young Cradock Nowell sat and gazed, every now and then, into the water. Through a break in the trees beyond it, he could see one chimney-top and a streak of the thatch of the Rectory. In vain he hoped that Dr. Hutton would leave him to himself; for he did not wish to go into the proofs, but to meditate on the consequences. Some bitterness, no doubt, there was in the corner of his heart, when he thought of all that Clayton now had to offer Amy Rosedew. He had lately been told, as a mighty secret, something which grieved and angered him; and the more, that he must not speak of it, as his straight-forward nature urged him. The secret was that innocent Amy met his brother Clayton, more than once, in the dusk of the forest, and met him by appointment. It grieved poor Cradock, because he loved Amy with all his unchangeable heart; it

angered him, because he thought it very mean of
Clayton to take advantage of one so young and
ignorant of the world. But never until the present moment, as he looked at the homely thatch in
the distance, and the thin smoke curling over it,
had it occurred to his honest mind, that his brother
might not be like himself—that Clayton might
mean ill by the maiden.

And now for the moment it seemed more likely,
as he glanced back at the lordly house, commanding the country for miles around, and all that
country its fief and its thrall, and now the whole
destined for Clayton. He thought of the mean-
ness about the Ireland, and two or three other
little things, proofs of a little nature. Then he
gazed at the Rectory thatch again, and the smoke
from the kitchen chimney, and seemed to see pure
playful Amy making something nice for her
father.

"Good God! I would shoot him if he did; or
strike him dead into this water."

In the hot haste of youth he had spoken aloud,
with his fist gathered up, and his eyes flashing
fire. Rufus Hutton saw and heard him, and
thought of it many times after that day.

"Oh, you are thinking of Caldo, because he
snapped at me. There are no signs of hydro-
phobia. You must not think of shooting him."

"I was not thinking of Caldo. I hope I did
not mean it. God knows, I am very wicked."

"So we are all, my boy. I should like to see a

fellow that wasn't. I'd pay fifty pounds for his body, and dissect him into an angel."

Cradock Nowell smiled a little at such a reward for excellence, and then renewed his gaze of dreary bewilderment at the water.

"Now let me show you my tracings, Cradock. Three times I have pulled them out, and you won't condescend to glance at them. You have made up your mind to abdicate upon my *ipse dixi*. Now look at the bend sinister, that is yours ; the bend dexter is for the elder brother."

"Dr. Hutton, it may be, and is, I believe, false shame on my part; but I wish to hear nothing about it. Perhaps, if my mother were living, I might not have been so particular. But giving, as she did, her life for mine, I cannot regard it medically. The question is now for my father. I will not enter into it."

"Oh the subjectiveness of the age !" said Rufus Hutton, rising, then walking to and fro on the bank, as he held discourse with himself; "here is a youth who ought to be proud, although at the cost of his inheritance, of illustrating, in the most remarkable manner, indeed I may say of originating, my metrostigmatic theory. He carries upon the cervical column a clear impression of grapes, and they say that before the show at Romsey the gardener was very cross indeed about his choice Black Hamburgs. His brother carries the identical impress, only with the direction inverted — dexter in fact, and dexter was the

mark of the elder son. This I can prove by the
tracing made at the time, not with any view to
future identification, but from the interest I felt,
at an early stage of my experience, in a question
then under controversy. If I prove this, what
happens? Why, that he loses everything—the
importance, the house, the lands, the title; and
becomes the laughing-stock of the county as the
sham Sir Cradock. What ought he to do at
once, then? Why, perhaps to toss me into that
hole, where I should never get out again. By
Gad, I am rash to trust myself with him, and no
other soul in the secret!" Here Dr. Hutton shuddered to think how little water it would take to
drown him, and the river so dark and so taciturn!
"At any rate, he ought to fall upon me with
forceps, and probe, and scalpel, and tear my evidence to atoms. For, after all, what is it, without
corroboration? But instead of that, he only says,
'Dr. Hutton, no more of this, if you please, no
more of this! The question is now for my father.'
And he must know well enough to which side his
father will lean in the inquiry. Confound the
boy! If he had only coaxed me with those great
eyes, I would have kept it all snug till Doomsday.
Oh what will my Rosa say to me? She has
always loved this boy, and admired him so im-
mensely."

Perhaps it was his pretty young wife's high
approval of Cradock which first had made the testy
Rufus a partisan of Clayton. The cause of his

having settled at "Geopharmacy Lodge" was, that upon his return from India he fell in love with a Hampshire maiden, whom he met "above bar" at Southampton. How he contrived to get introduced to her, he alone can tell; but he was a most persevering fellow, and little hampered with diffidence. She proved to be the eldest daughter of Sir Cradock's largest tenant, a man of good standing and education, who lived near Fordingbridge. As Rufus had brought home tidy pickings from his appointment in India, the only thing he had to do was to secure the lady's heart. And this he was not long about, for many ladies like high colour even more than hairiness. First she laughed at his dancing ways, incessant mobility, and sharp eyes; but very soon she began to like him, and now she thought him a wonderful man. This opinion (with proper change of gender) was heartily reciprocated, and the result was that a happier couple never yet made fools of themselves, in the judgment of the world; never yet enjoyed themselves, in the sterling wisdom of home. They suited each other admirably in their very differences; they laughed at each other and themselves, and any one else who laughed at them.

"Well, I shall be off," said Dr. Hutton at last, in feigned disgust; "you will stare at the water all day, Mr. Cradock, and take no notice of me."

"I beg your pardon, I forgot myself ; I did not mean to be rude, I assure you."

"I know you did not. I know you would never

be rude to any one. Good-bye, I have business
on hand."

"You will be back, Dr. Hutton, when my father
returns from his ride? It is very foolish of me,
but I cannot bear this suspense."

"Trust me. I will see to it. But he will not
be back, they tell me, till nearly four o'clock."

"Oh, what a time to wait! Don't send for me
if you can help it. But, if he wants me, I will
come."

"Good-bye, my lad. Keep your pecker up.
There are hundreds of men in the world with
harder lines than yours."

"I should rather think so. I only wish there
were not."

Cradock attempted a lively smile, and executed
a pleasant one, as Rufus Hutton shook his hand,
and set off upon his business. And his business
was to ride at once as far as the "Jolly Foresters,"
that lonely inn on the Beaulieu-road, at the eastern
end of the parish, whereat John Rosedew baited
Coræbus at the turn of the pastoral tour. The
little doctor knew well enough, though he seldom
passed that way, how the smart Miss Penny of
former days, Mrs. O'Gaghan's assistant, was now
the important Mrs. George Cripps, hostess of the
"Jolly Foresters," where the four roads met.

Meanwhile, the scaffolds went on merrily under
Mr. Garnet's care, and so did the awnings, marquees, &c., and the terraces for the ladies. The
lamps in the old oak being fixed, the boughs were

manned, like a frigate's yards, with dexterous fellows hoisting flags, devices, and transparencies, all prepared to express in fire the mighty name of Cradock. All the men must finish that night, lest any one lose his legitimate chance of being ancestrally drunk on the morrow. Cradock Nowell, wandering about, could not bear to go near them. Those two hours seemed longer to him than any year of his previous life. He went and told Caldo all about it; and that helped him on a little.

Caldo was a noble setter, pure of breed, and high of soul, and heavily feathered on legs and tail. His colour was such a lily white, that you grieved for him on a wet fallow; and the bright red spots he was endowed with were like the cheeks of Helen. Delicate carmine, enriched with scarlet, mapped his back with islands; and the pink of his cheeks, where the whiskers grew, made all the young ladies kiss him. His nostrils were black as a double-lined tunnel leading into a pencil-mine; and his gums were starred with violet, and his teeth as white as new mushrooms. In all the county of Hants there was no dog to compare with him; for he came of a glorious strain, made perfect at Kingston, in Berkshire. Lift but a finger, and down he went, in the height of his hottest excitement; wave the finger, and off he dashed, his great eyes looking back for repression. For style of ranging, all dogs were rats to him, anywhere in the New Forest; so freely he went, so buoyant, so careful, and yet all the while so hilarious. Only one fault he had, and I never knew dog without one; he was jealous to the backbone.

Cradock was dreadfully proud of him. Anything else he had in the world he would have given to Clayton, but he could not quite give Caldo; even though Clayton had begged, instead of backing his Wena against him. Wena was a very nice creature, anxious to please, and elegant; but of a different order entirely from the high-minded Caldo. Dogs differ as widely as we do. Who shall blame either of us?

Cradock now leaned over Caldo, with the hot tears in his eyes, and gently titillating the sensitive part of his ears, and looking straight into his heart, begged to inform him of the trouble they were both involved in. "Have they taken the shooting from us?" was Caldo's first inquiry; and his eyes felt rather sore in his head that he should have to ask the question. "No, my boy, they haven't. But we must not go shooting any more, until the whole matter is settled." "I hate putting off things till to-morrow," Caldo replied, impatiently; "the cock-pheasants come almost up to my kennel. What the deuce is to come of it?" "Caldo, please to be frigido. You shall come to my room by-and-by. I shall be able then to smoke a pipe, and we will talk about it together. You know that I have never cared about the title and all that stuff."

"I know that well enough," said Caldo; "nevertheless, I do. It gives me a status as a dog, which I thoroughly appreciate. Am I to come down from goodly paunches to liver and lights and horses' heads and hounds' food? I don't think I could stand it. But I would live on a crust a day, if you would only come and live with me." And he nuzzled up to his master, in a way that made his tears come.

Cradock was sent for suddenly. Old Hogstaff trotted across the yard (wherein he seldom ventured) to say that Sir Cradock Nowell wished to see his son. Cradock following hastily, with all his heart in his mouth, wondered at the penny-wort, the wall-rue, and the snap-dragons, which he had never seen before. Hogstaff tottered along before him, picking uneasily over the stones, bobbing his chin, and muttering.

Sir Cradock sat in the long heavy room known as the "justice-hall," where he and his brother magistrates held oyer of many a culprit. The great oak table was dabbed with ink, and the grey walls with mop-shaped blotches, where sullen prisoners had thrown their heads back, and refused to answer. At the lower end was Rufus Hutton, jerky, dogmatical, keenly important; while the old man sat at the head of the table, with his back to the pointed window, and looked (perhaps from local usage) more like a magistrate than a father. Straight up the long room Cradock walked, as calmly as if he were going to see where his quoit was stuck; then he made salutation to his father, as his custom was, for many bygone fashions were retained in the ancient family. Sir Cradock was

proud of his son's self-command and dignified
manly carriage, and if Dr. Hutton had not been
there, he would have arisen to comfort him. As
it was, he only said, with a faint and doubtful
smile—

"So, sir, I find that, after all, you are but an
impostor."

Young Cradock was a proud man—man from
that day forth, I shall call him " lad" no longer—
ay, a prouder man, pile upon pile, than the father
who once had spoiled him. But his pride was of
the right sort—self-respect, not self-esteem. So
he did not appeal, by word or look, to the sympathy lurking, and no doubt working, in the pith
of his father's heart, but answered calmly and
coldly, though his soul was hot with sorrow—

"Sir, I believe it is so." His eyes were on his
father's. He longed to look him down, and felt
the power to do it; but dropped them as should
a good son. Although the white-haired man was
glad at the promotion of his favourite, his heart
was yearning towards the child more worthy to
succeed him. But his notions of filial duty—which
himself had been called upon to practise chiefly in
memory, having seen very little of his father, and
having lost him early—were of the stern, cold order
now, the buckle and buckram style; though much
relaxed at intervals in Master Clayton's favour.
Finding no compunction, no humility in his son's
look, for a mistake which was wholly of others,
and receiving no expression of grief at the loss of

heirship, Sir Cradock hardened back again into his proper dignity, and resumed his air of inquiry. "I wish John Rosedew were here," he thought, and then it repented him of the wish, for he knew how stubborn the parson was, and how he would have Craddy the foremost.

Rufus Hutton, all this time, was in the agony of holding his tongue. He tried to think of his Rosa, and so to abstract himself airily from the present scene. He had ridden over to see her yesterday, and now dwelt upon their doings. Rosa was to come to-morrow, and he would go to fetch his wife in a carriage that would amaze her. Then he met Cradock Nowell's eyes, and wondered what he was thinking of.

"Now, Sir Cradock Nowell, this won't do at all. How long are we to play fast and loose with a finer fellow than either of us?" Oh, that hot-headed Rufus, what mischief he did then! "Although I have not the honour, sir, of being in the commission of peace for this little county, I have taken magisterial duty in a district rather larger than Ireland thrown into Great Britain. And I can grow, per acre, thrice the amount of corn that any of your farmers can." His colour deepened with self-assertion, like the central quills of a dahlia.

"We must have you to teach us, Dr. Hutton. It is a thing to be thought about. But at present you are kindly interested in—in giving your evidence."

Even then, if Dr. Hutton, with all his practised

acumen, had mixed one grain of the knowledge of
men, he might have done what he liked with Sir
Cradock, and re-established the dynasty; unless,
indeed, young Cradock were bent upon going
through with everything. But the only mode
Rufus Hutton knew of meeting the world was
antagonism.

"Yes, sir, you may think nothing of it. But
I have hunted a thing for three hundred leagues,
and got at it through the biggest liars that ever
stole a white man's galligaskins."

"Thank you, Dr. Hutton," said Cradock, divert-
ing the contest; "λωποδύτης is the word you mean.
And I fear it applies to me also."

"Perhaps, young man," cried Rufus Hutton,
"you know more Hindustani than I do. Trans-
late——," and he poured out a sentence which I
dare not try to write down. "But, my good fellow, you forget it is we who are stealing yours."

"I think," said Sir Cradock, slowly, and seriously
displeased — Good Heavens! to joke about the
succession to the Nowelhurst title and lands!—"I
think, sir, this can hardly be looked upon as
evidence. I always cut short the depositions, sir.
As Chairman of the Quarter Sessions, I always cut
short the depositions."

"And so you wish to cut short, sir, the deposition
of your son." Rufus laughed at his own bad
joke, and expected the others to laugh with him.
It made things worse than ever. Sir Cradock was
afraid to speak, lest he might say anything un-

seemly to a visitor. The young man saw his opportunity, and took advantage of it.

"Father, I beg you to let me go. You would not wish me, I am sure, to be here; only you think it my right to be. If you please, I will waive that right; I can wholly trust your decision."

He bowed to his father with cold respect, being hurt at his rapid conviction, to Rufus Hutton with some contempt and a smile at the situation. Then he marched down the long room placidly, and whistled when he was out of it. The next moment he bolted away to his bedroom, and wept there very heavily.

"Glorious fellow!" cried Dr. Hutton. "But we don't at all appreciate him. Requires a man of mind to do that. And now for Mrs. O'Gaghan!" Leaving Sir Cradock this speech to digest, he arose and rang the bell sharply. He felt himself fully invested now with supreme judicial authority, and he longed to be at the Irishwoman, who had called him a "red gossoon."

CHAPTER XVII.

BIDDY O'GAGHAN was hard at work, boiling down herbs and blessing them, drying and bottling cleverly, scraping, and picking the cloves out. She had turned the still-room of the house into her private laboratory; and she saved all the parish and half of the hundred from "them pisoners, as called theirselves doctors." Now, she was one of those powerful women—common enough, by-the-by—who can work all the better for talking; and, between her sniffs at the saucepan-lids, and her tests upon the drying-pans, she had learned that something strange was up, and had made fifty guesses about it. Blowing the scum and the pearly beads from a pot of pellitory of the wall (one of her staunch panaceas), she received a command most peremptory to present herself in the justice-room.

"Thin was that the way as they said it, Dick? No sinse nor manners but that! An' every bit of the blessed while they knowed it for my bilin'-day! Muckstraw, thin, is Bridget O'Gaghan no more count than a pisonin' doctor? Hould that handle there, Dick. If iver you stirs it the bridth of one on your carroty whiskers from that smut on the firebar, till such time as you sees me agin, I'll down with it arl in your crooked back bilin', and your chilthers shall disinherit it."

Leaving Dick rooted in trepidation, for she was now considered a witch, she hurried into her little bedroom; for she had the strongest sense of propriety, and would not "make herself common." Then she dashed her apron aside, and softened the fire-glow from her nose, and smoothed the creases of her jet-black hair, which curled in bars like crochet-work. This last she did, with some lubricous staple of her own discovery, applying it with the ball of her thumb. "The hairs of me head," as she always called them, were thick of number and strong of fibre, and went zig-zag on their road to her ears, like a string of jockey's horses shying, or a flight of jack-snipes. Then a final glance at her fungous looking-glass, just to know if she were all right; the glass gave her back a fine, warm-hearted face, still young in its rapid expression, Irish in every line of it, glazed with lies for hatred, and beaming with truth for love. So Biddy gave two or three nods thereat, and knew herself match for fifty cross-examiners, if she could only keep her temper.

As she marched up to the table, with her head

thrown back, her portly shape made the most of, and the front of her strong arms glistening, then dropped a crisp curtsey to Sir Cradock without deigning to notice his visitor, the little doctor's experience told him that he had caught a thorough Tartar. All his solemn preparations were thrown away upon her, though the biggest Testament in the house lay on the table before him; and a most impressive desk was covered with pens, and paper, and sealing-wax.

· Dr. Hutton would not yet open his mouth, because he wished to begin augustly. Meanwhile, Sir Cradock kept waiting for him, till Biddy could wait no longer. Turning her broad back full upon Rufus, who appreciated the compliment, she made another short scrape to her master, and asked, with an ogle suppressed to a mince—

"And what wud your honour be pleased to want with the poor widow, Bridget O'Gaghan, then?"

"Bridget, that gentleman, Dr. Hutton, has made an extremely important discovery, affecting most nearly my honour and that of the family. And now I rely upon you, Bridget, as a faithful and valued dependent of ours, to answer, without reservation or attempt at equivocation, all the questions he may put to you."

"Quistions, your honour?" and Biddy looked stupid in the cleverest way imaginable.

"Yes, questions, Bridget O'Gaghan. Inquiries, interrogations—ah! that quite explains what I mean."

"Is it axing any harm, thin, any ondacency of a poor lone widder woman, your honour wud be afther?" She took to her brogue as a tower of refuge. Bilingual races are up to the tactics of rats with a double hole.

"Sir Cradock Nowell," said Rufus, from the bottom of his chest, "you, I believe, are a magistrate for this county of Hants, Vice-Lieutenant, Colonel of Yeomanry, the representative of the sovereign. I call upon you now, in all these capacities, to administer the oath to this prevaricating woman."

The penultimate word rather terrified Bridget, for she never had heard it before; but the last word of all reassured her.

She turned round suddenly on little Rufus, who had jumped from his chair in excitement, and standing by head and shoulders above him, she opened her great eyes down upon him, like the port-holes of a frigate.

"Faix, thin, and I niver seen this young man at all at all. It's between the airms of the cheer he were, and me niver to look so low for him! 'Tis the black measles as he've tuk, and I've seen as bad a case brought through with. The luck o' the blessed saints in glory! I've been bilin' up for the same. If it's narse him I can to the toorn of it, I'm intirely at your sairvice, Sir Craduck. I likes to narse a base little chap, sin' there's no call to fear for his beauty."

This last was uttered gently, and quite as a

private reflection; but it told more than all the
rest.   For ever since Dr. Hutton had married a
woman half his age, he had grown exceedingly sensitive as to his personal appearance.   By a very
great effort he kept silent, but his face was almost
black with wrath, as he handed the great book to
Sir Cradock.   The magistrate presented it very
solemnly to Bridget, who took it as patly as if it
had been a flat iron.   A score of times she had
sworn according to what was thought good for her,
years ago, in Ireland.   At the right moment of
dictation, she gave the book a loud smack that
required good binding to stand it, and then crossed
herself very devoutly, to take the taste away.   Of
a heretic oath she had little fear, though she would
not have told a big lie to her priest.   Then she
dropped her eyes, and chastened her aspect, as if
overcome by the sense of solemn responsibility.

"Bridget O'Geoghegan," began the worthy
doctor, emphasising slowly every syllable of her
name, and prepared to write down her replies,
"you are now upon your solemn oath, to declare
the truth, the whole truth, and nothing but the
truth.   And if you fail in this, remember, you
will place your precious soul in the power of the
evil one."

"Amin to that same, thin.   And more power
to yer."

"Bridget, do you remember the night when
your master's children were born?"

" Sure an' I do, thin. Unless it wur the mornin'. How wud I help remimber it ? "

" And do you remember the medical gentleman who was suddenly called in ? "

" And if I wur ten times on my oath, I don't remimber no gintleman. A bit of a red-haired gossoon there was, as wor on the way to be transported."

" Do you remember his name ? "

" Remimber it ? Let me see, thin. It wor hardly worth the throuble of forgittin. Button, or Mutton ; no, faix I b'lieve it wor Rubus Rotten."

" Well, never mind his name——"

" My faith, and I niver did, thin, nor the little spalpin ayther. But to my heart I was sorry for the dear, good, beautiful lady—glory be to her sowl—along o' that ignorant, carroty, sprawlin', big-knuckled omadhawn. Small chance for her to git over it."

" Silence, woman, how dare you? " said Sir Cradock, very angrily.

" And I thought it was arl the truth as yer honour said I was to tell." Here Biddy looked hurt and amazed. " Have the little clerk got it all in black and white? " With a sigh for his incapacity, she peered over the desk at his paper.

" Now, Mrs. O'Gaghan, no trifling! " Her master spoke sternly and sharply. But Rufus could not speak at all. He was in such a choking passion.

"If so be I have said any harm, sir, for the best of us is errowneous, I axes a humble pardon. Iver since I lose my good husband—and a better husband there cudn't be, barrin only the bellises, and I wudn't deny upon my oath but what I desarved the spout now and thin——"

"Mrs. O'Gaghan," said Dr. Hutton, trying very hard to look amiable, "do your best for once, I entreat you, to prove yourself, if there is such a thing, *a respectable Irishwoman.*"

From that moment the tables were turned. Her temper boiled up like a cauldron. It is quite of a piece with a thing that is all pieces—the genuine Irish nature—that, proud as they are of their country, they cannot bear to be told of their citizenship.

"Irish, thin, is it? Irish indade! Well, and I knows I'm Irish. And if I ain't, what do I care who knows I am?"

She flung up her head superbly, and great tears ran from her eyes. Rufus Hutton perceived his advantage, and, though not at all a mean fellow, he was smarting far too sharply from the many attacks on his vanity, to forego his sweet revenge.

"You remember, then, when the doctor gave you the first-born child, that he made some odd remark, and told you to keep it separate?"

"And how can a poor Irishwoman remimber anything at all?"

"Come, you know very well that you remember that. Now, can you deny it?"

" Is it likely you'll catch me deny anything as is a lie, then, Irish or not, as you plases ? " Her bosom still was heaving with the ground-swell of her injury.

" Well, now, for the honour of old Ireland, tell us the truth for once. What were the words he said ? "

" Save me if evir a bit of me can tell. Mayhap I might call to mind, if I heer'd them words agin."

" Were they not these—' Left to right over the shoulder, and a strapping boy he is ? ' "

" Bedad thin, and they might have been."

" I want to know what they were."

" How can I tell what they were ? I only know what they was."

" Well, and what was that ? "

" Thim very same words as you've said." She turned towards the door with a sullen air, while he looked at Sir Cradock in triumph. Nevertheless, he still wanted her evidence as to the subsequent mistake. He had been, as I said, to the " Jolly Foresters" and seen the Miss Penny of old; who now, as the mother of nine or ten children, was kindly communicative upon all questions of infancy.

" So then, Mrs. O'Gaghan, with the best intentions in the world, you marked the elder child with a rosette, as I saw on the following day."

" Thrue for you as the Gospel. And what more wud you have me do ? "

" Nothing. Only take a needle and thread to
it; instead of crimping it into the cap."

Poor Biddy started from where she stood, and
pressed one hand to her heart. " It's the divil
himself," she muttered, " as turns me inside out so.
And sure that same is the reason he does be so
black red." Then aloud, with a final rally—

" And who say they iver see me take a needle
and thread? And if I did, what odds to them?"

" No, that was the very thing you omitted to
do, until it was too late. But when you sent to
Mrs. Toaster for her large butter-scales, what was
it you put on each side?"

" What was it? No lining at all. Fair play
for the both of them, as I hope to be weighed in
purgatory."

Sir Cradock was looking on, all this while, with
the deepest amazement and interest. He had not
received any hint beforehand of this confirmative
evidence. " And, pray, what was the reason that
you wanted to weigh them at all? You know that
it is considered unlucky among nurses to weigh
infants."

" Why else wud I weigh them, except to see
which wur the heaviest?"

" And pray, Bridget, which was the heavier?"
asked Sir Cradock, almost smiling.

" Mr. Cradock, as is now, your honour. I'd
swear it on my dying bed. Did you think, then,
I'd iver wrong him, the innocents as they was?"

" And did you weigh them with rosettes on ?"
Rufus Hutton had not finished yet.

" How cud I, and only one got it ?"

" Oh, then, you had fastened it on again ?"

" Do you think they was born with ribbons on ?"

This was poor Biddy's last repartee. She lost
heart and told everything afterwards. How she
had heard that there was some difference in the
marks of the infants, though what it was she knew
not justly; having, like most Irishwomen, the
clearest perception that right and left are only relative terms, and come wrong in the looking-glass,
as they do in heraldry. How, when she found the
rosette adrift, she had done the very best she
could, according to her lights, to work even-handed
justice, and up to this very day believed that the
heft of the scales was the true one. Then she fell
to a-crying bitterly that her darling Crad should
be ousted, and then she laughed as heartily that
her dear boy Clayton was in for it.

With timid glances at Mrs. O'Gaghan, like a
boy's at his schoolmaster, Jane Cripps came in,
and told all she knew, saying " please sir," at every
sentence. She had seen at the time Dr. Hutton's
sketch, which was made without Biddy's knowledge, because she never would have allowed it, on
account of the bad luck to follow. And Mrs.
Cripps was very clever now everything was known.
She had felt all along that things went queerly on
the third day after the babes were born. She had

made up her mind to speak at the time, only Mrs.
O'Gaghan was such—excuse her—such a dis-
ciplinarian, that—that—and then Lady Nowell
died, and everything was at sixes and sevens, and
no one cried more violent, let them say what they
like about it, than she, Jane Penny as had been.

"If Sir Cradock thought further evidence need-
ful, there was Mrs. Bowyer, a most respectable
woman, who washed thirty shilling a week, Mrs.
Cripps' first cousin and comate, who had heard at
the time all about the drawing, and had not been
easy about the scales, and had dreamed of it many
times afterwards, as indeed her Aunt Betsy know;
and her husband was no man, or he never would
have said to her——"

By this time the shadows came over the room,
and the trees outside were rustling, and you could
see them against the amber sunset, like a child's
scrawling on his horn-book. Volunteers throughout the household longed to give their evidence.
Their self-respect for a week would be hostile, if
it were not accepted. But Sir Cradock kept the
door fastened, till Mrs. O'Gaghan slipped out, and
put all the wenches down the steps backwards.
Mrs. Toaster alone she durst not touch; but Mrs.
Toaster will never forgive her, and never believe
the case tried on its merits, because she was not
summoned to depose to the loan of the scales.

Ha, so it is in our country, and among the
niggers also. When wealth, position, title, even
bastardom from princes, even the notoriety which

a first-rate murderer stabs for—when any of these are in question, how we crowd into the witness-box, how we feel the reek of the court an aureola on our temples. But let any poor fellow, noble unknown, an upright man now on the bend with trouble, let him go in to face his creditors, after the uphill fight of years, let him gaze around with work-worn eyes—which of his friends will be there to back him, who will give him testimony?

After all, what matters it except in the score against us? We are bitter with the world, we make a fuss, and feel it fester, we explode in small misanthropy, only because we have not in our heart-sore the true balm of humanity. No longer let our watchword be, "Every man for himself, and God for us all," but "Every man for God, and so for himself and all." So may we do away with all illicit process, and return to the primal axiom that "the greater contains the less."

CHAPTER XVIII.

THE rays of the level sun were nestling in the brown bosom of the beech-clump, and the fugitive light went undulating through the grey-arched portico, like a reedy river; when Cradock and Clayton Nowell met in the old hall of their child-hood. With its deep embrasures, and fluted piers, high-corniced mantel of oak relieved with alabaster figures, and the stern array of pike, and steel-cap, battle-axe, and arquebus, which kept the stag-heads over against them nodding in perpetual fear, this old hall was so impressed upon their earliest memories, that they looked upon it, in some sort, as the entrance to their lives.

As the twins drew near from opposite doors, each hung back for a moment: knowing all that had passed that day, how would his brother receive him? But in that moment each perceived how the other's heart was; Cradock cried, "Hurrah, all right!" and Clayton's arms were round his neck. Clayton sobbed hysterically—for he had always been woman-hearted — while Cradock coaxed him with his hand, as if he were ten years the elder. It was as though the days of childhood had returned once more, the days when the world came not between them, but they were the world to each other.

"Crad, I won't have a bit of it. Did you think I would be such a robber, Crad? And I don't believe one syllable of their humbugging nursery stories. Why, every fellow knows that you *must* be the eldest brother."

"Viley, my boy, I am so glad that it has turned out so. You know that I have always longed to fight my way in the world, and I am fitter for it than you are. And you are more the fellow for a baronet, and a big house, and all that sort of thing; and in the holidays I shall come every year to shoot with you, and to break your dogs, and all that; for you haven't got the least idea, Viley, of breaking a dog."

"Well, no, I suppose I haven't," said Clayton, very submissively; at any other time he would have said, "Oh, haven't I?" for it was a moot point between them. "But, Craddy, you *shall* have half, at any rate. I won't touch it, unless you take half."

"Then the estates must go to the Queen, or to Mr. Nowell Corklemore, your especial friend, Viley."

Clayton was famed for his mimicry of the pom-

pous Mr. Corklemore, and he could not resist it
now, though the tears were still in his eyes.

"Haw, yes; I estimate so, sir. A mutually
agreeable and unobjectionable arrangement, sir.
Is that your opinion? Haw!" and Clayton
stroked an imaginary beard, and closed one eye at
the ceiling. Cradock laughed from habit; and
Clayton laughed because Cradock did.

Oh that somebody had come by to see them
thus on the very best terms, as loving as when
they whipped tops together, or practised Sir Roger
de Coverley! They agreed to slip away that
evening from the noise of the guests and the wine-
bibbing, and have a quiet jug of ale in Cradock's
little snuggery. There they would smoke their
pipes together, and consider the laws of inheritance.
Already they were beginning to laugh and joke
about the matter; what odds about the change of
position, if they only maintained the brotherhood?
Unluckily no one came near them. The servants
were gathered in their own hall, discussing the
great discovery; Sir Cradock was gone to the
Rectory to meet John Rosedew upon his return,
and counsel how to manage things. Even the
ubiquitous Dr. Hutton had his especial *alibi.* He
had rushed away to catch Mr. Garnet and the
illumination folk, that the necessary changes might
be made in the bedizenment of the oak-tree.

Suddenly Clayton exclaimed, "Oh, what a fool
I am, Craddy! I forgot a most important thing,
until it is nearly too late for it."

"What?" asked Cradock, eagerly, for he saw there was great news coming.

"When I was out with the governor to-day, what do you think I saw?"

"What, what, my boy? Out with it."

"Can't stop to make you guess. A woodcock, sir; a woodcock."

"A woodcock so early? Nonsense, man; it must have been a hawk or a night-jar."

"Think I don't know a woodcock yet? And I'll tell you who saw it, too. Glorious old Mark Stote; his eyes are as sharp as ever. We marked him down to a T, sir, just beyond the hoar-witheys at the head of Coffin Wood; and I should have been after him two hours ago if it had not been for this rumpus. I meant to have had such a laugh at you, for I would not have told you a word of it; but now you shall go snacks in him. Even the governor does not know it."

"Fancy killing a woodcock in the first week of October!" said Cradock, with equal excitement; "why, they'll put us in the paper, Viley."

"Not unless you look sharp. He's sure to be off at dusk. He's a traveller, as Mark Stote said: sailed on from the Wight, most likely, last night; he'll be off for Dorset, this evening. Run for your gun, Crad, your pet Purday; I'll meet you here with my Lancaster in just two minutes' time. Don't say a word to a soul. Mind, we'll go quite alone."

"Yes; but you bring your little Wena, and I'll

take my Caldo, and work him as close as possible.
I promised him a run this afternoon."

Away they ran, out of different doors, to get
their guns and accoutre themselves; while the poor
tired woodcock sitting on one leg, under a holly
bush, was drawing up the thin quivering coverlet
over his great black eyes.

Cradock came back to the main hall first, with
his gun on his arm, and his shot-belt across him,
his broad chest shown by the shooting-jacket, and
the light of hope and enterprise in his clear strong
glance. Before you could have counted ten, Clayton was there to meet him; and none but a very
ill-natured man could have helped admiring the
pair of them. Honest, affectionate, simple fellows,
true West Saxons as could be seen, of the same
height and figure as nearly as could be, each with
the pure bright Nowell complexion, and the straight-
forward Nowell gaze. The wide forehead, pointed
chin, arched eyebrows, and delicate mouth of each
boy resembled the other's exactly, as two slices cut
from one fern-root. Nevertheless, the expression—
if I may say it without affectation, the mind—of
the face was different. Clayton, too, was beginning
to nurse a very short moustache, a silky bright
brown tasselet; while Cradock exulted rationally
in a narrow fringe of young whiskers. And Viley's
head was borne slightly on one side, Cradock's
almost imperceptibly on the other.

With a race to get to the door first, the twins
went out together, and their merry laugh rang

round the hall, and leaped along the passages. That hall shall not hear such a laugh, nor the passages repeat it, for many a winter night, I fear, unless the dead bear chorus.

The moment they got to the kennel, which they did by a way of their own, avoiding all grooms and young lumbermen, fourteen dogs, of different races and a dozen languages, thundered, yelled, and yelped at the guns, some leaping madly and cracking their staples, some sitting up and begging dearly, with the muscles of their chest all quivering, some drawing along on their stomachs, as if they were thoroughly callous, and yawning for a bit of acti-vity; but each in his several way entreating to be the chosen one, each protesting that he was truly the best dog for the purpose—whatever that might be—and swearing stoutly that he would "down-charge" without a hand being lifted, never run in upon any temptation, never bolt after a hare. All the while Caldo sat grimly apart; having trust in human nature, he knew that merit must make its way, and needed no self-assertion. As his master came to him he stood upon his hind-legs calmly, balanced by the chain-stretch, and bent his fore-arms as a mermaid or a kangaroo does. Then, suddenly, Cradock Nowell dropped the butt of his gun on his boot, and said, with his face quite altered:

"Viley, I am very sorry; but, after all, I can't go with you."

"Not come with me, Craddy, and a woodcock

marked to a nicety! And you with your vamplets on, and all! What the deuce do you mean?"

"I mean just what I say. Don't ask me the reason, my dear fellow; I'll tell you by-and-by, when we smoke our pipes together. Now I beg you, as an especial favour, don't lose a moment in arguing. Go direct to the mark yourself, and straight powder to you! I'll come and meet you in an hour's time in the spire-bed by the covert."

"Crad, it's no good to argue with you; that I have known for ages. Mind, the big-wigs don't dine till seven o'clock, so you have plenty of time to come for me. But I am so sorry I shan't have you there to wipe my eye as usual. Nevertheless, I'll bring home Bill Woodcock; and what will you say to me then, my boy? Ta, ta; come along, Wena, won't we astonish the natives? But I wish you were coming with me, Crad."

The brothers went out at the little gate, and there Cradock stopped and watched the light figure hurrying westward over the chase, taking a short cut for the coverts. Clayton would just carry down the spinney, where the head of the spring was, because the woodcock might have gone on there; and if ever a snipe was come back to his home yet, that was the place to meet him. Thence he would follow the runnel, for about a third of a mile, down to the spot in the Coffin Wood, where the hollies grew, and the hoar-witheys. When quit of that coppice, the little stream stole away down the valley, and so past Mr. Garnet's cottage to the Nowelhurst water beyond the church bridge. Now whether this were the self-same brook on whose marge we observed Master Clayton last week walking, not wholly in solitude, is a question of which I will say no more, except that it does not matter much. There are so many brooks in the New Forest; and after all, if you come to that, how can the most consistent of brooks be identical with the special brook which we heard talking yesterday? Isn't it running, running on, even as our love does? Join hands and keep your fingers tight; still it will slip through them.

When Clayton was gone but a little way over the heather and hare-runs, his brother made off, with his gun uncharged, for the group still at work in the house-front. Bull Garnet was there, with Rufus Hutton sticking like a leech to him; no man ever was bored more sharply, or more bluntly expressed it. The veins of his temples and close-cropped head stood out like a beech-tree's stay roots; he was steaming all over with indignation, and could not find a vent for it. When Cradock came up, Bull saw in a glimpse that he was expected to say something; in fact, that he ought, as a gentleman, to show his interest, not his surprise. Nevertheless he would not do it, though he loved and admired Cradock; and for many reasons was cut to the heart by his paulo-postponement. So he left Craddy to begin, and presented no notch in his swearing. His swearing was tremendous, for he hated change of orders.

" Mr. Garnet," said Cradock, at last, " I have heard a great deal of bad language, especially among the bargees at Oxford and the piermen at Southampton; and I don't pretend to split hairs myself, nor am I mealy-mouthed; but I trust you will excuse my observing, that up to the present moment I have never heard such blackguardly language as you are now employing."

Bull Garnet turned round and looked at him. If Cradock had shown any sign of fear, he would have gone to the earth at once, for his unripe strength would have had no chance with Garnet's prime in its fury. The eyes of each felt hot in the other's, as in reciprocal crucibles; then Mr. Garnet's rolled away in a perfect blaze of tears. He dashed out his hand and shook Cradock's mightily, quite at the back of the oak-tree; then he patted him on the shoulders, to resume his superiority; and said:

" My boy, I thank you."

"Well," thought Cradock, " of all the extraordinary fellows I ever came across, you are the most extraordinary. And yet it is quite impossible to doubt your perfect sincerity, and almost impossible to call in question your sanity."

These reflections of Master Cradock were not so lucid as usual. At least he made a false antithesis. If it had been possible to doubt Mr. Garnet's sincerity, he would not have been by any means so extraordinary as he was.

" Not much trouble, after all," cried Rufus Hutton, rollicking up like a man of thrice his true cubic capacity; " ah, these things are simple enough for a man with a little νοῦς. I shall explain the whole process to Mrs. Hutton, she is so fond of information. Never saw a firework before, sir—at least, I mean the machinery of them—and now I understand it thoroughly; much better, indeed, than the foreman does. Did not I hear you say so, George ?"

" Eh, my mon, I deed so "—the foreman was a shrewd, dry Scotchman—"in your own opeenion mainly. But ye havena peyed us yet, my mon, for the dustin' o' your shoon."

Rufus Hutton began, amid some laughter, to hunt his French purse for the siller, when the foreman leaped up as if he were shot, and dashed behind the oak-tree. " Awa, mon, awa, if ye value your life! Dinna ye see the glue-pot burstin'?"

Rufus dropped the purse, and fled for his life, and threw himself flat, fifty yards away, that the explosion might pass over him. Even then, when the laugh was out, and Mr. Garnet had said to him, " Perhaps, sir, you will explain that process for the benefit of Mrs. Hutton," instead of being disconcerted he was busier than ever, and took Mr. Garnet aside some little way down the chase.

" They want to make a job of it, I can see that

well enough. To charge for it, sir; to charge
for it."

"Thank you for your advice, Dr. Hutton," replied Bull Garnet, crustily; he was very morose
that afternoon, and surly betwixt his violence;
"but perhaps you had better leave them to me, for
fear of the glue-pot bursting."

"Ah, I suppose I shall never hear the last of
that most vulgar pleasantry. But I tell you they
can't see it, or else it is they won't. They are determined to do it all over again, and they need
only change four letters, and the fixings all come
in again. For the R they should put an L, for
the D a Y——Bless my soul, Mr. Garnet, what is
it you see there?"

No wonder Rufus Hutton asked what Mr.
Garnet saw, for the steward's eyes were fixed
intently, wrathfully, ferociously, upon something
not very far from the place where his home lay
among the trees. His forehead·rolled in three
heavy furrows, deep and red at the bottom, his
teeth were set hard, and the muscles of his
shoulders swelled as he clenched his hands fast.
Dr. Hutton, gazing in the same direction, could
see only trees and heather. "What is it you see
there, Mr. Garnet?" Rufus Hutton by this time
was quivering with curiosity.

"I'd advise you, sir, not to ask me:" then he
added, in a different tone, "the most dastardly
scoundrel poacher that ever wanted an ounce of

lead, sir. Let us go back to the men, for I have
little time to waste."

"Cool fellow," thought Rufus; "waste of time
to talk to me, is it? But what eyes the man must
have!"

And so he had, and ears too. Bull Garnet saw
and heard every single thing that passed within
the rim of his presence. No matter what he was
doing, or to whom he was talking, no matter what
was afoot, or what temper he was in, he saw and
heard as clearly as if his whole attention were on
it, every moving, breathing, speaking, or spoken
thing, within the range of human antennæ. So a
spider knows if even a midge or a brother spider's
gossamer floats in the dewy unwoven air beyond
his octagonal subtlety. From this extraordinary
gift of Bull Garnet, as well as from his appearance, and the force of his character, the sons of
the forest were quite convinced that he was under
league to the devil.

In half an hour's time or less, when the dusk
come down like wool, Cradock cast loose his favourite Caldo, and set out for the Coffin Wood.
From habit more than forethought, and to give
his dog some pleasure, there by the kennel he
loaded his double-barrelled gun. He had made
up his mind to shoot no more upon his father's
land, until he had express permission from Sir
Cradock Nowell. This was a whim, no doubt,
and a piece of pride on his part; but the scene of

that afternoon, and his father's bearing towards him, had left some bitter feeling, and a sense of alienation. This was the reason why he would not go with Clayton, much as he longed to do so. Now, with some dull uncertainty and vague depression clouding him, he loaded his gun in an absent manner; putting loose shot, No. 6, in one barrel, and a cartridge in the other. "Hie away, boy!" he cried to Caldo, who had crouched at his feet the while; then he struck off hot foot for the westward, with the gun upon his shoulder. But just as he started, one of the lads, who was often employed as a beater, ran up, and said, with his cap in his hand, in a manner most insinuating—

"Take I 'long of 'ee, Meestur Craduck. I'll be rare and keerful, sir."

"No, thank you, Charley, not this time. I am not even going shooting, and I mean to go quite alone."

Poor Cradock, unlucky to the last. Almost everything he had done that day had been a great mistake; and now there was only one more to come, the deadliest error of all.

Whistling a dreamy old tune, he hurried over the brown and tufted land, sometimes leaping a tussock of bed-furze, sometimes following a narrow hare-run, a soft green thread through the heather.

The sun had been down for at least half an hour, and under the trees there was twilight; but here, in the open, a tempered brightness flowed from some yellow clouds still lingering in the west. You might still know a rabbit from a hare at fifty or sixty yards off. And, in truth both bunnies and hares were about; the former hopping, and stopping, and peeping, and pricking their ears as the fern waved, and some sitting gravely upon, a hillock, with their backs like a home-made loaf; the hares, on the other hand, lopping along, with their great ears drooping warily, and the spring of their haunches gathered up for a dash away any whither: but all alike come abroad to look for the great and kind God who feeds them. Then, from either side of the path, or the sandy brows of the gravel-pit, the diphthong cry of the partridge arose, the call that tells they are feeding. Convivial and good-hearted bird, who cannot eat without conversation, nor without it be duly eaten; no marvel that the Paphlagonians assign you a brace of hearts. The pheasants were flown to the coverts long ago (they are fearful of losing the way to bed), two or three brown owls were mousing about, and a horned fellow came sailing smoothly from the deep settlements of the thicket, as Cradock Nowell leaped up the hedge, a hedge overleaning, overtwisting, stubby, and crowded with ash, rose, and hazel, the fence of the Coffin Wood. Though Caldo had stood picturesquely at least a dozen times, and looked back at his master reproachfully, turning the white of his eye, and champing his under lip, and then dropped as if he himself

were shot, when the game sped away with a whirr,
Cradock, true to his resolution, had not pulled
trigger yet. And though the repression was not
entirely based upon motives humane, our Cradock
felt a new delight in sparing the lives of those poor
things who have no other life to look to. At
least so we dare to restrict them. So merry and
harmless to him they seemed, so glad that the
dangerous day was done, so thankful for having
been fed and saved by the great unknown, but
felt, Feeder, Father, and Saviour.

CHAPTER XIX.

MEANWHILE Sir Cradock Nowell had found, at the peaceful Rectory, a tumult nearly as bad as that which he had left in his own household. In a room which was called by others the book-room, by herself "the library," Miss Eudoxia sat half choked, in a violent fit of hysterics, Amy and fat Jemima doing their utmost to console her and bring her round. Sir Cradock had little experience of women, and did the worst thing he could have done—that is to say, he stood gazing.

"Amy," groaned Miss Eudoxia—"Amy, if you don't want to kill me, get him out of the room, my child."

"Go, go, go!" cried Amy, in desperation. "Can't you see, godpapa, that we shall do better without you; oh, ever, ever so much?"

Sir Cradock Nowell felt a longing to box pretty Amy's ears; he had always loved his godchild, Amy, and chastened her accordingly. He now

loved Amy best in the world, next to his pet son,
Clayton.   To tell the truth, he had bathed himself
in the sunset-glow of match-making, all the way
down the chase.   Clayton, proclaimed the heir and
all that, should marry Amy Rosedew; what could
it matter to him about money, and where else
would he find such a maiden?   Then, in the
course of a few more years—so soon as ever there
were five, or, say at the most six children—he, Sir
Cradock, would make over the management of the
property; that is, if he felt tired of it, and they
were both very steady.   And what of Cradock,
you planning father, what of your other son,
Cradock?   In faith, he must do for a parson.

Sir Cradock retired in no small flurry, and went
to the garden to look for Jem.   Miss Eudoxia
became at once unconscious, as she ought to have
been long ago; and thenceforth she would never
acknowledge that she had seen the intruder at all;
or, indeed, that there had been one.   However, it
cured her, for a very long time, of those sad
attacks of hysteria.

This present attack was the natural result of a
violent conflict with Amy, who was not going to
be trampled upon, even by Aunt Doxy.   It appears
that, early in the afternoon, the good aunt began
to wonder what on earth was become of her niece.
Of course she could not be at the school, because
Wednesday was a half-holiday; she was not in the
library, nor in the back-kitchen, nor even out at
Pincher's kennel.   No, nor even in the garden,

although she had a magnificent lot of bulbs to plant, for which she had saved up ever so much of her little pocket-money. "Well," said Miss Eudoxia, who was thirsting for her gossip, which 'she always held after lunch—"well, I must say this is *most* inconsiderate of her. And I promised John to take her to the park, and how am I to get ready? Girls are not what they used to be, though Amy is such a good girl. They read all sorts of trashy books, and then they go eloping."

That last idea sent the good aunt in hot haste to Amy's bedroom; and who should be there, sitting by the window, with a small book in her hand, but beautiful Amy herself.

"Well!" cried Miss Eudoxia, heavily offended; "indeed, I *am* surprised. So this is what you prefer, is it, to your own aunt's conversation? And, I declare, what a colour you have! And panting, as if you had asthma! Let me see that book this moment, miss!"

"To be sure, Aunt Eudoxia," said Amy, rather indignantly; "but you need not be in a pet, you know."

"Oh, needn't I, indeed, when you read such books as this! Oh, what will your poor father say? And *you* to have a class in the Sunday-school!"

Of all the grisly horrors produced to make the traveller's hair creep, one of the most repulsive and glaring was in Amy's delicate hand. A hideous ape, with an open razor, was about to cut a young lady's throat. Chuckling, he drew her fair neck to the blade by her dishevelled hair.   At her feet lay an elderly woman, dead; while a man with a red cap was gazing complacently in at the window. The back of the volume was relieved by a ghost, a death's head, and a pair of cross-bones.

"Well!" said Miss Eudoxia.   Her breath was gone for a long while, and she could say nothing more.

"I know the cover is ugly, aunt, but the inside is so beautiful.   Oh, and so very wonderful!   I can't think how any one ever could imagine such splendid horrible things.   Oh, so clever, Aunt Doxy; and full of things that make me tingle, as if my brain were gone to sleep.   And I want to ask papa particularly about galvanizing the mummy."

"Indeed; yes, galvanizing! and pray does your father know of your having this horrible book?"

"No; but I mean to tell him, the moment I have got to the end of it."

"Good child, and most dutiful!   When you have swallowed the poison, you'll tell us."

"Poison indeed, Aunt Eudoxia!   How dare you talk to me like that?   Do you dare to suppose that I would read a thing that was unfit for me?"

"No, I don't think you would, knowingly.   But you are not the proper judge.   Why did you not ask your father or me, before you began this book?"

"Because I thought you wouldn't let me read it."

"Well, that does beat everything.   Candid im-

pudence, I call that, perfectly candid insolence!"
Aunt Doxy's throat began to swell; there was weak
gorge in the family. Meanwhile, Miss Amy, who
all the time had been jerking her shoulders and
standing upright, in a manner peculiarly her own
—Amy felt that her last words required some
explanation. She had her father's strong sense of
justice, though often pulled crooked by womanhood.

"You know well enough what I mean, aunt,
though you love to misrepresent me so. I mean
that you would not let me read it, not because it
was wrong (which it isn't), but for fear of making
me nervous. And upon that subject, at least, I
think I have a right to judge for myself."

"Oh, I dare say; you, indeed! And pray who
lent you that book? Unless, indeed, in your self-
assertion, you went to a railway and bought it."

"That is just the sort of thing I would rather
die than tell, after all the fuss you have made
about it."

"Thank you; I quite perceive. A young
gentléman—not to be betrayed—*scamp*, whoever
he is." It was Clayton Nowell who had lent the
book.

"Is he indeed? I wish you were only half as
upright and honourable."

Hereupon Miss Eudoxia, who had dragged her
niece down to the book-room, with dialogue all down
the stairs, muttered something about her will, that
she had a little to leave, though not much, but

honestly her own—God knew—and down she went
upon the chair, with both hands to her side. At
the sequel, as we have seen, Sir Cradock Nowell
assisted, and took little for his pains.

After this, of course, there was a great recon-
ciliation. For they loved each other thoroughly;
and each was sure to be wild with herself for
having been harsh to the other. They agreed that
their eyes were much too red now to go and see
the nascent fireworks.

"A gentleman's party to-night; my own sweet
love, how glad I am! I ought to know better, Amy
dearest; and they have never sent the goulard.
I ought to know, my own lovey pet, that we can
trust you in everything."

"No, aunty dear, you oughtn't. I am as obstinate as a pig sometimes; and I wish you would
box my ears, aunt. I hope my hair won't be right
for a month, dearest aunt, where you pulled it;
and as for the book, I have thrown it into the
kitchen-fire long ago, though I do wish, darling
aunt, you could have read about the descent into
the Mäelstrom. I declare my head goes round ever
since! What amazing command of language!
And he knows a great deal about cooking."

James Pottles, groom and gardener, who even
aspired to the hand, or at any rate, to the lips, of
the plump and gaudy Jemima, was not at all the
sort of fellow you would appreciate at the first
interview. His wits were slow and mild, and had

never yet been hurried, for his parents were un-
ambitious. It took him a long time to consider,
and a long time again to express himself, which he
did with a roll of his tongue. None the less for
that, Jem Pottles was quoted all over the village as
a sayer of good things. No conclusion was thought
quite safe, at least by the orthodox women, until it
had been asked with a knowing look—"And what
do Jem Pottles say of it?" Feeling thus his
responsibility, and the gravity of his opinion, Jem
grew slower than ever, and had lately contracted a
habit of shutting one eye as he cogitated. As
cause and effect always act and react, this added
enormously to his repute, until Mark Stote the
gamekeeper, and Reuben Cuff the constable, ached
and itched with jealousy of that "cock-eyed, cock-
headed boy."

Sir Cradock found Jem quite at his leisure,
sweeping up some of the leaves in the shrubbery,
and pleasantly cracking the filberts which he discovered among them. These he peeled very carefully, and put them in the pocket of his stable
waistcoat, ready for Jemima by-and-by. He swished
away very hard with the broom the moment he saw
the old gentleman, and touched his hat in a way
that showed he could scarcely spare time to do it.

"What way, my lad, do you think it likely your
master will come home to-day?"

This was just the sort of question upon which
Jem might commit himself, and lose a deal of

prestige; so he pretended not to hear it, and brushed the very ground up. These tactics, however, availed him not, for Sir Cradock repeated his inquiry in a tone of irritation. Jem leaned his chin on the broom-handle, and closed one eye deliberately.

"Well, he maight perhaps come the haigher road, and again a maight come the lower wai, and I've a knowed him crass the chase, sir, same as might be fram alongside of Meester Garnet's house. There never be no telling the wai, any more than the time of un. But it's never no odds to me."

"And which way do you think the most likely now?"

"Not to say 'now,' but bumbai laike. If so be a cooms arly, a maight come long of the haigher road as goes to the 'Jolly Foresters;' and if a com'th middlin' arly, you maight rackon may be on the town wai; but if he cometh unoosial late, and a heap of folks be sickenin, or hisself hath pulled a book out, a maight goo round by Westacot, and come home by Squire Garnet's wai." Rich in alternatives, Jem Pottles opened the closed eye, and shut the open one.

"What a fool the fellow is!" said Sir Cradock to himself; "I'll try the first way, at any rate. For if John is so late, I could not stop for him, with all those people coming. How I wish we were free from strangers to-night, with all these events in the family! But perhaps, if we manage it well, it will carry it off all the better."

Sir Cradock Nowell was in high spirits as he started leisurely for a saunter along the higher road. This was the road which ran eastward, both from the Hall and the Rectory, into the depth of the forest. In all England there is no lovelier lane, if there be one to compare with it. Many of the forest roads are in fault, because they are too open. You see too far, you see too much, and you are not truly embowered. In a forest we do not want long views, except to rejoice in the amplitude. And a few of those, just here and there, enlarge the great enjoyment. What we want, as the main thing of all, as the staple feeling, is the deep, mysterious, wondering sense of being swallowed up, and knowing it: swallowed up, not as we are in catacombs, or wine-vaults, or any railway tunnel; but in our own mother's love, with God around us everywhere. To many of us, perhaps to most, so placed at fall of evening, there is a certain awe, a dread which overshades enjoyment. If so, it springs in part at least from our unnatural nature; that is to say, the education which teaches us so very little of the things around us.

How the arches spring overhead, and the brown leaves flutter among them! In and out, and through and through, across and across, with delicacy, veining the very shadows. For miles we may wander beneath them, and see no two alike. How, for fear of wearying us, after infinite twists and turns—but none of them contortions—after playing across the heavens, and sweeping away the sunshine, now in this evening light they hover, and rustle like the skirts of death. Is there one of them with its lichen-mantle copied from its neighbour's? Is there one that has borrowed a line, a character, even a cast of complexion from its own brother rubbing against it? Their arms bend over us as we walk, we are in their odour and influence, we know that, like the Magi of old, they adore only God and His sun; and, when we come out from under them, we never ask why we are sad.

CHAPTER XX.

THERE is a long, mysterious thrill, a murmur rather felt than heard, a shudder of profundity, which traverses the woodland hollows at the sun's departure. In autumn most especially, when the glory of trees is saddening, and winter storms are in prospect, this dark disquietude moves the wood, this horror at the nightfall, and doubt of the coming hours. Touched as with a subtle stream, the pointlets of the oak-leaves rise, the crimped fans of the beech are fluttered, and lift their glossy ovals, the pendulous chains of the sycamore swing; while the poplar flickers its silver skirts, the tippets and ruffs of the ivy are ruffling, and even the three-lobed bramble-leaf cannot repress a shiver.

Touched with a stream at least as subtle, we, who are wandering among the dark giants, shiver and shrink, we know not why; and our hearts beat faster, to feel how they beat. The cause is the same both for tree and for man. Earthly

o 2

nature has not learned to count upon immortality. Therefore all her works, unaided, loathe to be undone.

Whether it were this, or his craving for his dinner, that made Sir Cradock Nowell feel chilled, as he waited under the shuddering trees for his friend John Rosedew—far be it from me to say, be cause it may have been both, sir. And the other cause to which he always ascribed it—after the event—to wit, a divine afflatus of diabolical presentiment, is one we have no faith in, until we own to nightmare. Anyhow, there he was, for upwards of an hour; and no John Rosedew came up the hill, which Sir Cradock did not feel it at all his duty to descend, on the very safe presentiment of the distress *revocare gradum*.

Meanwhile John Rosedew was speeding merrily, according to his ideas of speed (which were relative to the last degree), along a narrow bridle-way, some two miles to the westward. It would be a serious insult—so the parson argued—to the understanding of any man who understood a horse, and now John Rosedew had owned Coræbus very nearly nine months, and though he had never owned a horse before, surely by this time he could set papers in the *barbara celarent* of the most recondite horse-logic—or was it dialectics?—an insult it would be to that Hippicus who felt himself fit now to go to a fair and discuss many points with the jockeys, if anybody suggested to him that Coræbus ought to trot.

" Trot, sir !" cried John Rosedew, to an imaginary Hippodamas, " hasn't he been trotting for
nearly an hour to-day, sir ? Quite an *equus tolu-*
tarius. And upon my word, I only hope he is not
so sore as I am." Then he threw the reins over
the pony's neck, and let him crop some cytisus.

" Coræbus, have no fear, my horse, you shall not
be overworked. Or if Epirus or Mycenæ be thy
home and birthplace—*incertus ibidem sudor*—thrice
I have wiped it off, and no oaten particles in it;
urit avenœ, so I suppose oats must dry the skin.
' Ad terramque fluit devexo pondere cervix,' a line
not to be rendered in English, even by my Cradock.
How fine that whole description, but made up from
alien sources ! Oh how Lucretius would have
done it ! Most sad that he was not a Christian."

A believer was what John Rosedew meant. But
by this time he was beginning to look upon all his
classical friends as in some sort Christians, if they
only believed in their own gods. Wherein, I fear,
he was far astray from the text of one of the
Articles.

Cob Coræbus by this time knew his master
thoroughly ; and exercising his knowledge cleverly,
made his shoes last longer. If the weather felt
muggy and " trying"—from an equine view of probation—if the road was rough and against the
grain, even if the forest-fly came abroad upon
business, Coræbus used (in sporting parlance) to
" shut up" immediately. This he did, not in a
defiant tone, not in a mode to provoke antagonism;

he was far too clever a horse for that; but with every appearance of a sad conviction that his master had no regard for him. At this earnest appeal to his feelings, John Rosedew would dismount in haste, and reflect with admiration upon the weeping steeds of Achilles, or the mourning horse of Mezentius, while he condemned with acrimony the moral conveyed by a song he had heard concerning the "donkey wot wouldn't go." Then he would loosen the girths, and, remonstrating with Coræbus for his want of self-regard, carefully wipe with his yellow silk pocket-handkerchief first all the accessible parts of the cob that looked at all uncomfortable, and then his own capacious forehead. This being done, he would search around for a juicy mouthful of grass, or dive for an apple or slice of carrot—Coræbus at the same time diving nasally—into the depths of his black coat pocket, where he usually discovered his lunch, which he had altogether forgotten. While the horse was discussing this little refreshment, John would put his head on one side, and look at him very knowingly, revolving in his mind a question which very often presented itself, whether Coræbus were descended from Corytha or Hirpinus.

However this may have been—and from his "staying qualities" one would have thought him rather a chip from the old block of Troy—he was the first horse good John Rosedew had ever called his own; and he loved and admired him none the

less for certain calumnies spread by the envious
about seedy-toes, splints, and spavins. Of these
crimes, whatever they might be, the parson found
no mention in Xenophon, Pliny, or Virgil, and he
was more than half inclined to believe them clumsy
modern figments. As for the incontestable fact
that Coræbus began to whistle when irrationally
stimulated beyond his six miles an hour, why, that
John Rosedew looked upon as a classical accomplishment, and quoted a line from Theocritus.
Very swift horses were gifted with this peculiar
power, for the safety of those who would otherwise
be the victims of their velocity, even as the express
train always whistled past Brockenhurst station.

After contemplating the animal till admiration
was exhausted, and wondering why some horses
have hairy, while others have smooth ankles, he
would refresh himself with a reverie about the
Numidian cavalry; then declaring that Jem Pottles was "impolitiæ notandus," he would pass his
arm through the bridle, and calling to mind the
Pæon young lady who unduly astonished Darius,
pull an old book from some inner pocket, and
stroll on, with Coræbus sniffing now and then at
his hat-brim.

To any one who bears in mind what a punctual
body Time is, this account of the rector's doings
will make it not incredible that he was often late
for dinner. But he never lost reckoning altogether
in his circumnavigation, because his leisure did not
begin till he had passed the "Jolly Foresters;" for

there he must be by a certain hour, or Coræbus would feel aggrieved, and so would Mrs. Cripps, who always looked for him at or about 1.30 P.M. For some mighty fine company was to be had by a horse who could behave himself, in the stable of the " Jolly Foresters," about middle-day on a Wednesday. Several high-stepping buggy-mares, one or two satirical Broughamites, even some nags who gave a decided tone to the neighbourhood, silver-hamed Clevelands, and champ-the-bit Clydesdales : even these were not too proud—that they left for vulgarian horses—to snort and blow hard at the " Foresters'" oats, and then eat them up like winking. To this select circle our own Coræbus had been admitted already, and his conversational powers admired, when he had produced an affidavit that his master was in no way connected with trade.

Coræbus now bade fair to be spoiled by all this grand society. Every Wednesday he came home less natural, more coxcombical. He turned up his nose at many good horses, whom he had once respected, fellows who wandered about in the forest, and hung down their chins when the rain came ! And then he became so affected and false, with an interesting languor, when Amy jumped out to caress him ! Verily, friend Coræbus, thou shalt pay out for this ! What call, pray, hast thou to become a humbug, from seeing how men do flourish ?

John Rosedew awoke quite suddenly to the laws

of time and season, as the hazel branches came over his head, and he could see to read no longer. The grey wood closed about him, to the right hand and to the left; the thick shoots of the alder, the dappled ash, and the osier, hustled among the taller trees whose tops had seen the sunset; tufts of grass, and blackberry-tangles, hipped dog-roses leaning over them, stubby clumps of buckthorn, brake-fern waving six feet high where the ground held moisture—who, but an absent man, would have wandered at dusk into such a labyrinth?

" ' Actum est' with my dinner," exclaimed the parson aloud, when he awoke to the situation; " and what, perhaps, is more important to thee, at least, Coræbus, thine also is ' pessum datum.' And there is no room to turn the horse round without scratching his eyes and his tail so. Nevertheless, this *is* a path, or at one time must have been so; ' semita, callis, trames '—that last word is the one for it, if it be derived from ' traho' (which, however, I do not believe)—for, lo! there has been a log of wood dragged here even during a post-diluvial period : we will follow this track to the uttermost; what says the cheerful philosopher :— ' παντοίην βιότοιο τάμοις ὁδόν.' Surely a gun, nay, two, or, more accurately, two explosions; now for some one to show us the way. Coræbus, be of good cheer, there is supper yet in thy φάτνῃ, not εὐξέστῳ; advance then thy best foot. Why not?—seest thou an εἴδωλον? Come on, I say, mine horse— Great God!——" And he was silent.

Tired as he was, Coræbus had leaped back from the leading rein, then cast up his head and snorted, and with a glare of terror stood trembling. What John Rosedew saw at that moment was stamped on his heart for ever. Across his narrow homeward path, clear in the grey light, and seeming to creep, was the corpse of Clayton Nowell, laid upon its left side, with one hand to the heart, the wan face stark and spread on the ground, the body stretched by the final throe. The pale light wandered over it, and showed it only a shadow. John Rosedew's nerves were stout and strong, as of a man who has injured none; he had buried hundreds of fellow-men, after seeing them die; but, for the moment, he was struck with a mortal horror. Back he fell, and drove back his horse; he could not look at the dead man's eyes fixed intently upon him. One minute he stood shivering, and the ash-leaves shivered over him. He was conscious somehow of another presence which he could not perceive. Then he ran up, like a son of God, to what God had left of his brother. The glaze (as of ground glass) in the eyes, the smile that has swooned for ever, the scarlet of the lips turned out with the chalky rim of death, the bulge of the broad breast, never again to rise or fall in breathing—is there one of these changes we do not know, having seen them in our own dearest ones?

But a worse sight than of any dead man—dead, and gone home to his Father—met John Rosedew's quailing eyes, as he turned towards the opening. It was the sight of Cradock Nowell, clutching his gun with one hand, and clinging hard with the other, while he hung from the bank (which he had been leaping) as a winding-sheet hangs from a candle. The impulse of his leap had failed him, smitten back by horror; it was not in him to go back, nor to come one foot forward. The parson called him by his name, but he could not answer; only a shiver and a moan showed that he knew his baptism. The living was more startled, and more startling, than the dead.

CHAPTER XXI.

THERE was a little dog that crept and moaned
by Clayton's body, a little dog that knew no
better, never having been taught much. It was
a small black Swedish spaniel, skilful only in
woodcocks, and pretty well up to a snipe or two,
but actually afraid of a pheasant on account of
the dreadful noise he made. She knew not any
more than the others why her name was " Wena,"
and she was perfectly contented with it, though it
must have been a corruption. The men said it
ought to be " Winifred ;" the maids, more roman-
tic, " Rowena ;" but very likely John Rosedew
was right, being so strong in philology, when he
maintained that the name was a syncopated form
of " Wadstena," and indicated her origin.

However, she knew her master's name better
than her own. You had only to say " Clayton,"
anywhere or anywhen, and she would lift her
tangled ears in a moment, jerk her little whisk of

a tail, till you feared for its continuity, and trot about with a sprightly air, seeking all around for him. Now she was cuddled close into his bosom, moaning, and shivering, and licking him, staring wistfully at his eyes and the wound where the blood was welling. She would not let John Rosedew touch him, but snapped as he leaned over; and then she began to whimper softly, and nuzzle her head in closer. "Wena," he said, in a very low voice—"pretty Wena, let me." And then she understood that he meant well, and stood up, and watched him intently.

John knew in a moment that all was over between this world and Clayton Nowell. He had felt it from the first glance indeed, but could not keep hope from fluttering. Afterwards he had no idea what he did, or how he did it, but the impression left by that short gaze was as stern as the death it noted. Full in the throat was the ghastly wound, and the charge had passed out at the back of the neck, through the fatal grape-cluster. Though the bright hair flowed in a pool of blood, and the wreck of life was pitiful, the face looked calm and unwrung by anguish, yet firm and staunch, with the courage summoned to ward death rather than meet it.

John Rosedew, shy and diffident in so many little matters, was not a man to be dismayed when the soul is moving vehemently. Now he leaped straight to the one conclusion, fearful as it was.

"Holy God, have mercy on those we love

so much! No accident is this, but a savage murder."

He fell upon his knees one moment, and prayed with a dead hand in his own. He knew, of course, that the soul was gone, a distance thought can never gaze; but prayer flies best in darkness.

Then, with the tears all down his cheeks, he looked round once, as if to mark the things he would have to tell of. In front of the corpse lay the favourite gun, with the muzzle plunged into the bushes, as if the owner had fallen with the piece raised to his shoulder. The hammer of one barrel was cocked, of the other on half-cock only; both the nipples were capped, and, of course, both barrels loaded. The line of its fire was not towards Cradock, but commanded a little by-path leading into the heart of the wood.

Meanwhile, Cradock had fallen forward from the steep brow of the hedge-bank; the branch to which he clung in that staggering way had broken. Slowly he rose from the ground, and still intent and horror-struck, unable to come nearer, looked more like one of the smitten trees which they call in the forest "dead men," than a living and breathing body. John Rosedew, not knowing what he did, ran to the wretched fellow, and tried to take his hand, but the offer was quite unnoticed. With his eyes still fixed on his twin-brother's corpse, the youth began fumbling clumsily in the pocket of his shooting-coat; he pulled out a powder-flask, and rapidly, never once look-

ing at it, dropped a charge into either barrel.
John heard the click of the spring—one, two, as
quick as he could have said it. Then the young
man drew from his waistcoat-pocket two thick
patent wads, and squeezed one into either cylinder.
All at once it struck poor "Uncle John" what he
was going to do. Preparing to shoot himself!

"Cradock, my boy, is this all the fear of God
I have taught you?"

Cradock looked at him curiously, and nodded
his head in acknowledgment. It was plain that
his wits were wandering. The parson immediately
seized the gun, and sowed the powder broadcast,
then wrenched the flask away from him with a
hand there was no resisting. Then for the first
time he observed Caldo in the hedge, "down-
charging;" the well-trained dog had never moved
from the moment his master fired.

"Come with me at once, come home, Cradock;
boy, you *shall* come home with me!"

But the man of threescore was not quick enough
for the young despair. Cradock was out of sight
in the thicket, and Caldo galloped after him.
Wild with himself for his slowness of wit, John
Rosedew ran to poor Clayton's gun, for fear of his
brother finding it. Then he took from the dead
boy's pocket his new and burnished powder-flask,
though it went to his heart to do it, and leaped
upon the back of Coræbus, without a thought of
Xenophon. Only Wena was left to keep her
poor master company.

How the rector got to the Hall I know not, neither has he any recollection; but he must have sat his horse like a Nimrod, and taken a hedge and two ditches. All we know is that he did get there, with Coræbus as frightened as he was, and returned to the place of disaster and death, with three men, of whom Dr. Hutton was one. Sir Cradock was not yet come back to his home, and the servants received proper orders.

As the four men, walking in awe and sorrow, cast the light of a lamp through the bushes, they heard a quick rustle of underwood, and crackle of the dead twigs, but saw no one moving.

" Some one has been here since I left," exclaimed John Rosedew, trembling; " some one has lain beside the body, and put marks of blood on the forehead."

Each of the men knew, of course, what it was —Cradock embracing his brother!

" A good job you took the gun away; wonder you had the sense, though," said Rufus Hutton, sharply, to pretend he wasn't crying; "I only know what I should have done, if I had shot my brother so—blown out the remains of my brains, sir ! "

" Hush !" said John Rosedew, solemnly, and his deep voice made their hearts thrill; " it is not our own life to will or to do with. In the hands of the Lord are our life and our death."

They knelt around the pale corpse tenderly, shading the lamp from the eyes of it; even Rufus could not handle it in a medical manner. One of the men, who always declared that he had saved Clayton's life in his childhood, fell flat on the ground, and sobbed fearfully. I cannot dwell on it any more; it makes a fellow cry to think of it. Only, thank God, that I am not bound to tell how they met his father.

CHAPTER XXII.

MARK STOTE, the head-gamekeeper on the
Nowelhurst estate, was a true and honest specimen
of the West Saxon peasant—slow, tenacious, and
dogged, faithful and affectionate, with too much
deference, perhaps, to all who seemed "his betters."
He was now about fifty years old, but sturdy and
active as ever, with a weather-beaten face and
eyes always in quest of something. His home was
a lonely cottage in one of the plantations, and
there he had a tidy and very intelligent wife, and
a host of little anxieties. His children, the sparrow-
hawks, the weasels, the young fellows who "called
theirselves under-keepers, and all they kept was
theirselves, sir,"—what with these troubles, and
(worst, perhaps, of all) that nest of charcoal-
burners by the bustle-headed oak, with Black Will
at the head of them, sometimes, Mark Stote would

assure us, his head was gone "all wivvery* like," and he could get no sleep of night-time.

A mizzly, drizzly rain set in before the poor people got home that evening with the body of Clayton Nowell. Long mournful soughs of wind ensued, the boughs of the trees went heavily, and it blew half a gale before morning; but it takes a real storm to penetrate some parts of the forest. Once, however, let the storm get in, and it makes the most of the opportunity, raging with triple fury, as a lion does in a compound—the rage of the imperious blast, when it finds no exit.

In the grey of the morning, two men met, face to face, in the overhanging of the Coffin Wood. Which was the more scared of the two, neither could have said; although each felt a little pleased at the terror of the other. The one of strong nerves was superstitious; the other, though free from much superstition, was nervous under the circumstances. The tall and big man was Mark Stote, the little fellow who frightened him Dr. Rufus Hutton. The latter, of course was the first to recover presence of mind, for Mark Stote's mental locomotion was of ponderous metal.

"What brings you here, Mr. Stote, at this time of the morning?"

"And what brings *you* here, Dr. Hutton?"

* "Wivvery," *i. e.* giddy and dizzy.—[?] "Weavery," from the clack and thrum of the loom; or, more probably, a softer form of "quivery:" the West Saxon loves to soften words.

Mark might have asked with equal reason. He wondered afterwards why he did not; the wonder would have been if he had. As it was, he only said—

"To see the rights o' my young meester, sir."

"The wrongs, you mean," said Rufus; "Mark Stote, there is more in this matter than any man yet has guessed at."

"You be down upon the truth of it, my word for it but you be, sir. I've a shot along o' both of 'em, since 'em wor that haigh, and see'd how they thought of their guns, sir; Meester Clayton wor laike enough to shoot Meester Cradock 'xidentually; but never wicey warse, sir, as the parson sayeth, never wicey warse, sir, for I niver see no one so cartious laike."

"Mark Stote, do you mean to say that Cradock shot his brother on purpose?"

Mark stared at Rufus for several moments, then he thrust forth his broad brown hand and seized him by the collar. Dr. Hutton felt that he was nothing in that big man's grasp, but he would not play the coward.

"Stote, let me go this instant. I'll have you discharged this very day unless you beg my pardon."

"That you moy then, if you can, meester. A leetle chap coom fram Ingy, an' we bin two hunner and feefty year 'long o' the squire and his foregoers!" Nevertheless he let Rufus go, and looked over his hat indignantly.

"You are an honest fellow," cried Hutton, when he got his breath again; "an uncommonly honest fellow, although in great need of enlightenment. It is not in my nature, my man," here he felt like a patron, getting over his shaking, so elastic was his spirit; "I assure you, Luke—ah no, your name is Matthew; upon my word, I beg your pardon, I am almost sure it is Mark—Mr. Mark, I shall do my utmost for your benefit. Now talk no more, but act, Mark."

"I oodn't a talked nothing, but for mating with your honour."

"Then resume your taciturnity, which I see is habitual with you, and perhaps constitutional."

Mark Stote felt sore all over. Dr. Hutton now was the collarer. Mark, in his early childhood, had been to school for a fortnight, and ran away with a sense of rawness, which any big word renewed.

"Mr. Stote, I will thank you to search in that direction, while I investigate this way."

Mark Stote longed to suggest that possibly Dr. Hutton, being (as you might say) a foreigner, was not so well skilled in examining ground as a woodman of thirty years' standing; and therefore that he, old Mark, should have the new part assigned to him, before it was trampled by Rufus. But the gamekeeper knew not how to express it; sure though he was (as all of us are, when truth hits the heart like a hammer) that something evil would come of slurring the matter so feebly.

But who are we to blame him?—we who transport
a poor ignorant girl for trying to hide her igno-
miny, while we throttle, before she can cry, babe
Truth, who should be received in society with a
" Welcome, little stranger!"

With the heavy rain-drops hanging like leeches,
or running together, as they do, at every thorn or
scale of the bark, seeking provocation to come
down the nape of the neck of any man, Rufus
Hutton went creeping under, trying not to irritate
them, pretending that he was quite at home, and
understood them like a jungle. Nevertheless he
repented, and did not thoroughly search more
than ten square yards. The things would knock
him so in the face, and the stumps would stick in
his trousers so, and the drops were so bad for his
rheumatism ; and, as it was quite impossible for
any man to make way there, what on earth was
there to look for?

In spite of all this, he did find something, and
stowed it away in his waistcoat pocket, to be
spoken of, or otherwise, according to the turn of
events. And by this he meant no dishonesty, at
least in his own opinion, only he pitied young
Cradock most deeply, and would do all he could
in his favour. At the side of the narrow by-path
leading from that woodman's track (by which John
Rosedew had approached) into the far depth of
the thicket, Dr. Hutton found, under a black-
berry-bush, a little empty tube, unlike any tube
he had seen before. It was about two inches and
a half in length, and three-fourths of an inch in

diameter. Sodden as it was with the rain, and opened partway along the seam, it still retained, unmistakably, the smell of exploded powder. It seemed to be made of mill-board, or some other form of paper, with a glaze upon the outside and some metal foil at the butt of it. What puzzled Rufus most of all was a little cylinder passing into and across the bottom, something like a boot-tag.

Dr. Hutton was not at this time skilled in modern gunnery. He knew how to load a fowling-piece, and what the difference was between a flint-gun and a percussion-gun; moreover, he had been out shooting once or twice in India, not from any love of the sport, but to oblige his neighbours. So he thought himself both acute and learned in arriving at the conclusion that this was a cartridge-case.

"Mark, does Mr. Cradock Nowell generally shoot with cartridges?"

"He laiketh mostways to be with a curtreege in his toard barryel, sir."

"Oh, keeps a cartridge in his left barrel, does he; and fires first the right, I suppose?"

Leaving Mark to continue the search, Rufus returned to the Hall, after carefully taking the distances between certain important points. He was bound, as he felt, to lose no time in making the strictest examination of the poor youth's body. For now, in this great calamity, the management of everything seemed to fall upon Rufus Hutton. Sir Cradock, of course, was overwhelmed; John

Rosedew, although so deeply distressed, for the
boys were like his own to him, was ready to do his
utmost; but, as every one knew, except himself, he
was not a man of the world.   Unluckily, too, Mr.
Garnet, always the leading spirit wherever he
appeared, had not yet presented himself in this
keen emergency.   But his son came up, in the
course of the day, to ask how Sir Cradock Nowell
was, and to say that his father was quite laid up
with a violent bilious attack.

Dr. Hutton worked very hard, kept his mind
on the stretch continually, ordered every one
right and left.   He even contrived to repulse
all the kindred, to the twentieth collateral, who
were flocking in, that day, to rejoice at the
manhood of the heir.   From old Hog-staff, who
knew all the family, kith and kin, and friends
and enemies, he learned the names of the guests
expected, and met them with laconic missives
handed through the closed gates at the lodges.   In
many cases, it is to be feared, indignation overcame sympathy; " upstart insolence ! " was heard
through the clatter of carriage-windows, very
nearly as often as, " most sad occurrence ! "   However, most of them were consoled by the prospect
of learning everything at the inquest on the morrow.
What could be clearer than that Cradock must be
hanged for Clayton's murder ?   The disgrace would
kill the old baronet.   " And then, it would be very
painful, but my wife would be bound, sir, for the
sake of her poor children, to prove her direct

descent from that well-known Sir Cradock Nowell, who shot a man in the New Forest. Ah, I fear it runs in the family."

But their wrath was most unphilosophical, unworthy of any moralists, when they found that Rufus had cheated them all as to the time of the inquest. In every direction he spread a report that the coroner could not attend until three o'clock on Friday, while he had arranged very quietly to begin the proceedings at noon. And he had taken good care to secure the presence of all the chief men in the neighbourhood—the magistrates, the old friends of the family, all who were interested in its honour rather than in its possessions. As none of the baffled cousins could solace themselves with outcry that the matter had been hushed up, they discovered that kind feeling had made the scene too sad for them.

The coroner sat in the principal room at the "Nowell Arms;" the jury had been to see the body lying at the Hall, and now were to hear the evidence. Six or seven of the county magistrates sat behind the coroner, and their clerk was with them. Of course they did not attend officially, their jurisdiction being entirely several from that of the present court. But there could be little doubt that their action would depend, in a great measure, upon what should now transpire.

The jury was chosen carefully to preclude, so far as might be, the charge of private influence. They were known, for the most part, as men of

independencé and probity, and two of them as consistent enemies to the influence of the Hall. As
for general spectators, only a few of the village-
folk allowed their curiosity to conquer their good
feeling, or, perhaps, I should say their discretion;
for all were tenants under Sir Cradock; and,
though it was known by this time that Bull Garnet
was ill and in bed, prostrated by one of his old
attacks, everybody felt certain that he would find
out who dared to be present, and visit them pretty
smartly.

It would be waste of time to recount all the evidence given; for we know nearly all that Dr.
Hutton and the clergyman would depose. Another
medical man, Dr. Gall, had also examined poor
Clayton's remains; and the healing profession,
who cure us (like bacon) after they have killed
us, are remarkable for agreeing in public, and
quarrelling sadly in private life. So Dr. Gall
deposed exactly as *Mr.* Hutton had done. He was
very emphatic towards Rufus, in the use of the
proper prefix; but we who know the skill displayed
presuppose the game certificate.

One part, however, of the medical evidence
ought to be repeated. Poor Clayton had not died
from an ordinary small-shot wound or wounds, but
from a ghastly hole through his throat, cut as if by
a bullet. As Dr. Gall, who knew something of
guns, very concisely put it, the hole was like the
hole in a door, when boys have fired, as they sometimes do, a tallow-candle through it. And yet it

was fluted at the exit, in the fleshy part of the neck, as no bullet could have marked it. That was caused by the shot diverging, beginning to radiate, perhaps from the opposition encountered.

"In two words," said Dr. Gall, when they had badgered him in his evidence, "the deceased was killed either by a balled cartridge, or by a charge of loose shot fired within six feet of him."

"Very good," thought Rufus Hutton, who heard all Dr. Gall said; "I'll keep my cartridge-case to myself. Poor Crad shan't have that against him."

Hereupon, lest any mist (which goddesses abound in, *vide* Homer *passim*) descend upon the eyes or mind of any gentle follower of my poor Craddy's fortunes, let me endeavour to explain Dr. Gall's obscurities.

Cartridges, as used by sportsmen with guns which load at the muzzle, are packages of shot compact, and rammed down in a body. Some of them have spiral cases of the finest wire, covered round with paper; others, used for shorter distance, have only cylinders of paper to enclose the shot. The interstices between the shots are solidified with sawdust. The only use of these things is— for they save little time in loading—to kill our brother bipeds, or quadrupeds, if such we are, at a longer distance. The shots are prevented from scattering so widely as they love to do, when freed from the barrel's repression. They fly in a closer body, their expansive instincts being checked, when first they leave the muzzle, by the constraint of

the case and the tightness of their brotherhood.
But it sometimes happens, mainly with *wire*-car-
tridges, that the shot can never burst its cerements,
and flies in the compass of a slug, until it meets an
obstacle. When this is so, the quarry escapes;
unless a bullet so aimed would have hit it. This
non-expansion is called, in good English, the
" balling" of the cartridge. And those which are
used for the longest distance, and for wild-fowl
shooting—green cartridges, as they are called, containing larger shot—are especially apt to ball.

Dr. Gall was aware, of course, that no one beat-
ing for a woodcock would think of putting a green
cartridge into his gun at all; but it seemed very
likely indeed that Cradock might have used a blue
one, for a longer shot with his left barrel; and the
blue ones, having wire round them, sometimes ball,
though not so often as their verdant brothers. It
only remains to be said that when a cartridge balls,
it flies with the force, as well as in the compass, of
a bullet. With three drachms of powder behind
it, it will cut a hole at forty yards through a two-
inch deal.

Whether it were a balled cartridge or a charge
of loose shot at six feet distance, was the mo-
mentous issue. In the former case, there would be
fair reason to set it down as an accident; for the
place where Cradock had first been seen was
thirty yards from Clayton; and he might so have
shot him thence, in the dusk, and through the
thick of the covert. But if that poor boy had

died from a common charge of shot, "Murder" was the only verdict true men could return on the evidence set before them. For Cradock must have fired wilfully at the open throat of his brother, then flown to the hedge and acted horror when he saw John Rosedew. Where was Cradock? The jury trembled, and so did Rufus Hutton. The coroner repeated the question, although he had no right to do it, at that stage of the evidence.

"Since it occurred he has not been seen," whispered Rufus Hutton at last, knowing how men grow impatient and evil when unanswered.

"Let us proceed with the rest of the evidence," said his honour, grandly; "if the young man cares for his reputation, he will be here by-and-by. But I have ridden far to-day. Let us have some refreshment, gentlemen. Justice must not be hurried."

CHAPTER XXIII.

It will have been perceived already that the coroner was by no means "the right man in the right place." The legal firm, "Cole, Cole, and Son," had been known in Southampton for many years, as doing a large and very respectable business. The present Mr. Cole, the coroner, who had been the "Son" in the partnership, became sole owner suddenly by the death of his father and uncle. Having brains enough to know that he was far from having too much, he took at once into partnership with him an uncommonly wide-awake, wary fellow, who had been head-clerk to the old firm, ever biding his time for this inevitable result. So now the firm was thriving under the style and title of "Cole, Chope, and Co.," Mr. Chope being known far and wide by the nickname of "Cole's brains." Mr. Cole being appointed coroner, not many months ago, and knowing very little about his duties, took good care for a time not to attempt their discharge without having " Cole's brains" with him. But this had been found to interfere so sadly with private practice, that little by little Cole plucked up courage, as the novelty of the thing wore off, and now was accustomed to play the coroner without the assistance of brains. Nevertheless, upon an occasion so important as this, he would have come with full cerebrum, but that Chope was gone for his holiday. Mr. Cole, however, was an honest man—which could scarcely be said of his partner—and meant to do his duty, so far as he could see it. In the present inquiry he had less chance of seeing it than usual, for he stood in great awe of Mr. Brockwood, a man of ability and high standing, who, as Sir Cradock Nowell's solicitor, attended to watch the case, at the suggestion of Rufus Hutton.

Both the guns were produced to the coroner, in the condition in which they were found, except that John Rosedew, for safety's sake, had lowered the right hammer of Clayton's to the half-cock, before he concealed it from Cradock. Cradock's own unlucky piece had been found, on the following morning, in a rushy pool, where he had cast it, as he fled so wildly. Both the barrels had been discharged, while both of Clayton's were loaded. It went to the heart of every man there who could not think Cradock a murderer, when in reply to a juryman's question, what was the meaning of certain lines marked with a watch-spring file on the trigger-plate of his gun, it was explained that the twins so registered the number and kind of the season's game.

After this, Mark Stote was called, and came forward very awkwardly with a deal of wet on his velveteen cuffs, which he tried to keep from notice. His eyes were fixed upon the coroner, with a kind of defiance, but even while he was kissing the book, he was glad to sniff behind it.

"Mr. Mark Stote," said the coroner, duly prompted, "you have, I believe, been employed to examine the scene of this lamentable occurrence?"

Mark Stote took a minute to understand this, and a minute to consider his answer.

"Yees, my lard, I throwed a squoyle at 'un."

The representative of the Crown looked at Mark with amazement equal at least to that with which Mark was regarding him.

"Gentlemen," asked Mr. Cole, addressing the court in general, "what language does this man talk?"

"West Saxon," replied Mr. Brockwood, speaking apart to the coroner; "West Saxon of the forest. He can talk plain English generally, but whenever these people are nervous, they fall back unconsciously upon their native idiom. You will never be able to understand him: shall I act as interpreter?"

"With all my heart; that is to say, with the consent of the jury. But what—I mean to say, how——"

"How am I to be checked, you mean, unless I

am put upon oath; and how can you enter it as evidence? Simply thus—let your clerk take down the original answers. All the jury will understand them, and so, perhaps, will he."

The clerk, who was a fine young gentleman, strongly pronounced in attire, nodded a distinct disclaimer. It would be so unaristocratic to understand any peasant-tongue.

"At any rate, most of the magistrates do. There are plenty of checks upon me. But I am not ambitious of the office. Appoint any one you please."

"Gentlemen of the jury," said the coroner, glad to shift from himself the smallest responsibility, "are you content that Mr. Brockwood should do as he has offered?"

"Certain, and most kind of him," replied the jury, all speaking at once, "if his honour was unable to understand old English."

"Very good," said Mr. Brockwood; "don't let us make a fuss about nothing. Mr. Stote says he 'throwed a squoyle;' that is to say, he looked at it."

"And in what state did you find the ground?" was the coroner's next question.

"Twearable, twearable. Dwont 'e ax ov me vor gude now, dwont 'e." And he put up his broad hand before his broad face.

"Terrible, terrible," said the coroner, going by the light of nature in his interpretation; "but I do not mean the exact spot only where the body was found. I mean, how was the ground as regards dry and wet, for the purpose of retaining footmarks?"

"Thar a bin zome rick-rack wather, 'bout a sannit back. But most peart on it ave a droud up agin. 'Twur starky, my lard, moor nor stoachy." Here Mark felt that he had described things lucidly and powerfully, and looked round the room for approval.

"Stiff rather than muddy, he means," explained Mr. Brockwood, smiling at the coroner's dismay.

"Were there any footprints upon it, in the part where the ground could retain them?"

"'Twur dounted and full of stabbles, in the pearts whur the mulloch wur, but the main of 'un tuffets and stramots."

"That is to say," Mr. Brockwood translated, "the ground was full of impressions and footmarks, where there was any dirt to retain them; but most of the ground was hillocky and grassy, and so would take no footprints."

"When you were searching, did you find anything that seemed to have been overlooked?"

"Yees, my lard, I vound thissom"—producing Crad's stubby meerschaum—"and thissom"—a burnt felt-wad—"and a whaile vurther, ai vound thissom." Here he slowly drew from his pocket a very fine woodcock, though not over fat, with its long bill tucked most carefully under its wing. He stroked the dead bird softly, and set its feathers professionally, but did not hand it about, as the court seemed to anticipate.

"In what part, and from what direction, has that bird been shot?"

"Ramhard of the head, my lard, as clane athert shat, and as vaine a bird as iver I wish to zee. But, ah's me, her be a wosebird, a wosebird, if iver wur wan."

Mark could scarcely control his tears, as he thought of the bird's evil omen, and yet he could not help admiring him. He turned him over and over again, and dropped a tear into his tail coverts. Mr. Brockwood saw it and gave him time; he knew that for many generations the Stotes had lived under the Nowells.

"Oh, the bird was shot, you say, on the right side of the head, and clean through the head."

"Thank you," proceeded the coroner. "Now, do you think that he could have moved after he touched the ground?"

"Nivir a hinch, I allow, my lard. A vell as dead as a stwoun."

"Now inform the court, as nearly as you can, of the precise spot where you found it."

It took a long time to discover this, for Mr. Stote had not been taught the rudiments of topography. Nevertheless, they made out at last that the woodcock had been found, dead on his back, with his bill up, eight or ten yards beyond the place where Clayton Nowell fell dead, and in a direct line over his body from the gap in the hedge

where Cradock stood.   Dr. Hutton must have
found the bird, if he had searched a little further.

"Now," said the coroner, forcibly, "Mr. Stote,
I will ask you a question which is, perhaps, a little
beyond the rules of ordinary evidence, I mean, at
least, as permitted in a court of record"—here he
glanced at the magistrates, who could not claim the
rank of record—"which of these two unfortunate
brothers caused, in your opinion, the death of—of
that woodcock ?"

Mr. Brockwood glanced at the coroner sharply,
and so did his own clerk.   Even the jury knew,
by intuition, that he had no right to tout for
opinions.

"Them crink-crank words is beyand me.   Moy
head be awl wivvery wi' 'em, zame as if my old
ooman was patchy."

"His honour asks you," said Mr. Brockwood,
with a glance not lost on the justices—for it meant,
You see how we court inquiry, though the question
is quite inadmissible—"which of the brothers in
your opinion shot the bird which you found ?"

"Why, Meester Cradock, o' course.   Meester
Cleaton 'ud needs a blowed un awl to hame, where
a stwooud."

"Mr. Clayton must have blown him to pieces, if
he shot him from the place where he stood, at
least from the place where Mr. Clayton fell.   And
poor Mr. Clayton lay directly between his brother
and the woodcock ?"

Mr. Brockwood in his excitement forgot that he

had no right to put this question, nor, indeed, any other, except as formally representing some one formally implicated. But the coroner did not check him.

"By whur the blude wor, a moost a been naigh as cud be atwane the vern-patch and the wosebird."

"Very good. That fern-patch was the place where Mr. Cradock dropped from the gap in the hedge. Mr. Rosedew has proved that. Now let us have all you know, Mark Stote. Did you see any *other* marks, stabbles you call them, not, I mean, in the path Mr. Rosedew came along, nor yet in the patches of thicket through which poor Cradock fled, but in some other direction?"

This was the very question the coroner ought to have put long ago. Thus much he knew when Brockwood put it, and now he was angry accordingly.

"Mr. Brockwood, I will thank you—consider, sir, this is a court of record!"

"Then don't let it record stupid humbug!" Mr. Brockwood was a passionate man, and his blood was up. "I will take the responsibility of anything I do. All we want to elicit the truth is a little skill and patience; and for want of that the finest young fellow I have ever known may be blasted for life, for this world and the other. Excuse me, Mr. Coroner, I have spoken precipitately; I have much reverence for your court, but far more for truth.

Here Mr. Brockwood sat down again, and all
the magistrates looked at him with nods of approbation. Human passions and human warmth are
sure to have their way, even in Areopagus. At
last the question was put by the coroner himself.
Of course it was a proper one.

"Yees, I zeed wan," said Mark Stote, scratching
the back of his head (where at least the memory
ought to be); "but a wadn't of no 'count much."

"Now tell us where that one was."

"Homezide of the rue, avore you coams to
them hoar-witheys, naigh whur the bower-stone
stanneth. 'Twur zumbawdy yaping about mebbe
after nuts as had lanced fro' the rue auver the
water-tabble."

Before this could be translated, a great stir was
heard in the outer-room, a number of people
crying "Don't 'ee-now!" and a hoarse voice utter-
ing "I will." The coroner was just dismissing
Mr. Stote with deep relief to both of them, and
each the more respecting because he could not
understand the other.

"Mark Stote, you have given your evidence in a
most lucid manner. There are few people more
to be respected than the thorough Saxon gamekeeper."

"Moy un goo, my lard?" asked the patient
Mark, with his neck quite stiff, as he at first had
stuck it, and one eye cocked at the coroner, as
along the bridge of a fowling-piece.

"Mr. Stote, you may now depart. Your evidence does you the greatest credit, both as the father of a family, and as—as a conservator of game, and I may say—ah, yes—as a faithful family retainer."

"Thank 'ee, my lard, and vor my peart I dwoan't b'leeve now as you manes all the 'arm as most volks says of 'ee."

Mark was louting low, trying to remember the fashion they taught him forty years since in the Sunday-school, when the door flew back, and the cold wind entered, and in walked Cradock Nowell.

As regards the outer man, one may change in fifty ways in half of fifty hours. Villanous ague, want of sleep, violent attacks of bile, inferior claret, love rejected, scarlet fever, small-pox, any of these may make a man lose memory in the looking-glass; but all combined could not have wrought such havoc, such appalment, such drought in the fountains of the blood, as that young face now told of. There was not one line of it like the face of Cradock Nowell. It struck the people with dismay, as they made room and let him pass; it would have struck the Roman senate, even with Cato speaking. Times there are when we forget even our sense of humour, absorbed in the power of passion, and the rush of our souls along with it. No one in that room could have laughed at the best joke ever was made, while he looked at Cradock Nowell.

Utterly unconscious what any fellow thought of him (except perhaps in some under-current of electric sympathy, whose wires never can be cut, up

to the drop of the gallows), Cradock crossed the
chairs and benches, feeling them no more than the
wind feels the hills it crosses. Yet with the inbred
courtesy of nature's thorough gentleman, though
he forgot all the people there as thinking of himself, he did not yet forget himself as bound to think
of them.   He touched no man on leg or elbow, be
he baronet or cobbler, without apologizing to him.
Then he stood in the foremost place, looking at
the coroner, saying nothing, but ready to be
arraigned of anything.

Mr. Cole had never yet so acutely felt the loss
of his "brains;" and yet it is likely that even
Chope would have doubted how to manage it.
The time a man of the world might pass in a dozen
common-places, passed over many shrewd heads
there, and none knew what to say.   Cradock's deep
grey eyes, grown lighter by the change of health,
and larger from the misery, seemed to take in
every one who had any feeling for him.

"Here I am, and cannot be hurt, more than my
own soul has hurt me.   Charge me with murder if
you please, I never can disprove it.   Reputation
is a thing my God thinks needless for me ; and so
it is, in the despair which He has sent upon me."

Not a word of this he spoke, but his eyes said
every word of it, to those who have looked on men
in trouble, and heard the labouring heart.   As
usual, the shallowest man there was the first to
speak.

"Mr. Nowell," asked the coroner, blandly, as of a wealthy client, "am I to understand, sir, that you come to tender your evidence?"

"Yes," replied Cradock. His throat was tight, and he could not manage to say much.

"Then, sir, I am bound to administer to you the caution usual on these occasions. Excuse me; in fact, I know you will; but your present deposition may be—I mean it is possible——"

"Sir, I care for nothing now. I am here to speak the truth."

"Very laudable. Admirable! Gentlemen of the jury—Mr. Brockwood, perhaps you will oblige the court by examining in chief?"

"No, your honour, I cannot do that; it would be a confusion of duties.".

"I will not be examined," said Cradock, with a low hoarse voice; he had been in the woods for a day and two nights, and of course had taken cold, —"I don't think I could stand it. A woman who gave me some bread this morning told me what you were doing, and I came here as fast as I could, to tell you all I know. Let me do it, if you please, in the best way I can; and then do what you like with me."

The utter despair of those last words went cold to the heart of every one, and Mark Stote burst out crying so loud that a woman lent him her handkerchief. But Cradock's eyes were hard as flint, and the variety of their gaze was gone.

The coroner hesitated a little, and whispered to his clerk. Then he said with some relief, and a look of kindness—

"The court is ready, Mr. Nowell, to receive your statement. Only you must make it upon oath."

Cradock, being duly sworn, told all he knew, as follows:

"It had been agreed between us, that my—my dear brother should go alone to look for a woodcock, which he had seen that day. I was to follow in about an hour, and meet him in the spirebed just outside the covert. For reasons of my own, I did not mean to shoot at all, only to meet my brother, hear how he had got on, and come home with him. However, I took my gun, because my dog was going with me, and I loaded it from habit. Things had happened that afternoon which had rather upset me, and my thoughts were running upon them. When I got to the spirebed, there was no one there, although it was quite dusk; but I thought I heard my brother shooting inside the Coffin Wood. So I climbed the hedge, with my gun half-cocked, and called him by his name."

Here Cradock broke down fairly, as the thought came over him that henceforth he might call and call, but none would ever answer.

"By what name did you call him?" Mr. Brockwood looked at the coroner angrily. What difference could it make?

"I called, 'Viley, Viley, my boy!' three times, at the top of my voice. I used to call him so in the nursery, and he always liked it. I can't make out why he did not answer, for he must have been close by—though the bushes were very thick, certainly. At that instant, before I had time to jump down into the covert, a woodcock, flushed, perhaps, by the sound of my voice, crossed a little clearing not thirty yards in front of me. I forgot all about my determination not to shoot that day, cocked both barrels in a moment, but missed him clean with the first, because a branch of the hedge flew back and jerked the muzzle sharply. But the bird was flying rather slowly, and I got a second shot at him, as he crossed a little path in the copse, too narrow to be called a ride. I felt quite sure that I shot straight at him, and I thought I saw him fall; but the light was very bad, and the trees were very thick, and he gave one of those flapping jerks at the moment I pulled the trigger, so perhaps I missed him."

"That 'ee doedn't, Meester Craydock. Ai'se larned 'ee a bit too much for thic. What do 'ee call thissom?" Here he held up the woodcock. "Meester Craydock, my lard, be the sprackest shat anywhur round these pearts."

Poor Mark knew not that in his anxiety to vindicate his favourite's skill, he was making the case more black for him.

"Mark Stote, no more interruptions, if you

please," exclaimed the coroner; "Mr. Nowell, pray proceed."

"Dwoan't 'ee be haish upon un, my lard, dwoan't 'ee vaind un guilty. A coodn't no how 'ave doed it. A wor that naice and pertiklar, a woodn't shat iven toard a gipsy bwoy. And his oyes be as sprack as a merlin's. A cood zee droo a mokpie's neestie."

Cradock's face, so pale and haggard but a minute before, was now of a burning red. The jury looked at him with astonishment, and each, according to his bias, put his construction upon the change. Two of them thought it was conscious guilt; the rest believed it to be indignation at the idea of being found guilty. It was neither; it was hope. The flash and flush of sudden hope, leaping across the heart, like a rocket over the sea of despair. He could not speak, but gasped in vain, then glutched (to use a forest word, which means gulped down a sob), and fell back into John Rosedew's arms, faint, and stark, and rigid.

The process of his mind which led him to the shores of light—but only for a little glimpse, a glimpse and then all dark again—was somewhat on this wise: "Only a bullet, or balled cartridge, at the distance I was from him, could have killed my darling Viley on the spot, as I saw him dead, with the hole cut through him. I am *almost* sure that my cartridge was in the left barrel of the gun, where I always put it. And now it is clear that the left barrel killed that unlucky bird, and killed him with shot flying separate, so the cartridge must have opened. Viley, too, was ten feet under the height the bird was flying. I don't believe *that I hit him at all.* I had loose shot in my right barrel; the one that sent so random, on account of the branch that struck it. I am *almost* sure I had, and I fired quite straight with the left barrel. God is good, the great God is merciful, after all I thought of Him." No wonder that he fainted away, in the sudden reaction.

There is no need to dwell any longer on the misery of that inquest. The principal evidence has been given. The place where Cradock stood in the hedge, and the place where Clayton fell and died; how poor Cradock saw him first, in the very act of jumping, and hung like a nut-shuck, paralysed; how he ran back to his dead twin-brother and could not believe in his death, and went through the woods like a madman, with nothing warm about him except his brother's blood,—all this, I think, is clear enough, as it had long been to the jury, and now was to the coroner. Only Cradock awoke from his hope—what did he care for their verdict? He awoke from his hope not in his moral—that there could be no doubt of—but in his manual innocence; when, to face all circumstances, he had nothing but weak habit. He could not swear, he could not even feel confident (and we want three times three for swearing, that barbarous institution) that he had rammed the cartridge down the left barrel, and the charge of shot down the right. All he could say was this, that it was a very odd thing if he had not.

The oddity of a thing is seldom enough to establish its contrary, in the teeth of all evidence. So the jury found that "Violet Clayton Nowell had died from a gunshot wound, inflicted accidentally by his brother Cradock Nowell, whom, after careful consideration, they absolved from all blame."

CHAPTER XXIV.

RUFUS HUTTON rode home that night to Geo-pharmacy Lodge. He had worked unusually hard, even for a man of his activity, during the last three days, and he wanted to see his Rosa again, and talk it all over with her. Of course he had cancelled her invitation, as well as that of all others, under the wretched circumstances. But before he went, he saw Cradock Nowell safe in the hands of the rector, for he could not induce him to go to the Hall, and did not think it fair towards his wife, now in her delicate health, to invite him to the Lodge. And even if he had done so, Cradock would not have gone with him.

. If we strike the average of mankind, we shall find Rufus Hutton above it. He had his many little-nesses—and which of us has few?—his oddities of mind and manner, even his want of charity, and his practical faith in selfishness; none the less for all of that there were many people who loved him.

And those of us who are loved of any—save parents, wife, or daughter—loved, I mean, as the word is felt and not interpreted,—with warmth of heart, and moistened eyes (when good or ill befalls us); any such may have no doubt of being loved by God.

All this while, Sir Cradock Nowell had been alone; and, as Homer has it, "feeding on his heart." Ever since that fearful time, when, going home to his happy dinner with a few choice friends, he had overtaken some dark thing, which he would not let them hide from him—ever since that awful moment when he saw what it was, the father had not taken food, nor comfort of God or man.

All they did—well-meaning people—was of no avail. It was not of disgrace he thought, of one son being murdered, and the other son his murderer; he did not count his generations, score the number of baronets, and weep for the slur upon them; rave of his painted scutcheon, and howl because this was a dab on it. He simply groaned and could not eat, because he had lost his son—his own, his sweet, his best-beloved son.

As for Cradock, the father hoped—for he had not now the energy to care very much about it—that he might not *happen* henceforth to meet him (for all things now were of luck) more than once a month, perhaps; and then they need not say much. He never could care for him any more; of that he felt as sure as if his heart were become a tombstone.

Young Cradock, though they coaxed and petted, wept before him at the parson's, and still more behind him, and felt for him so truly deeply that at last he burst out crying (which did him Heaven's own good)—Cradock, on his part, would not go to his father, until he should be asked for. He felt that he could fall on his knees, and crawl along in abasement, for having robbed the old grey man of all he loved on earth. Only his father must ask for him, or at least give him leave to come.

Perhaps he was wrong. Let others say. But in the depths of his grief he felt the need of a father's love; and so his agony was embittered because he got no signs of it. Let us turn to luckier people.

"Rufus, why, my darling Rufus, how much more —— are you going to put on that little piece of ground, no bigger than my work-table?"

Mrs. Hutton had been brought up to "call a spade a spade;" and she extended this wise nomenclature to the contents of the spade as well.

"Rosa, why, my darling Rosa, that bed contains one hundred, and twenty-five feet. Now, according to the great Justus Liebig, and his mineral theory——"

"One hundred and twenty-five feet, Rue! And I could jump across it! I am sure it is not half so long as my silk measure in the shell, dear!"

"Dearest Rosa, just consider: my pet, get out your tablets, for you are nothing at mental arithmetic."

"Indeed!   Well, you never used to tell me things like that, Rufus!"

"Well, perhaps I didn't, Roe.   I would have forsworn to any extent, when I saw you among the candytuft.   But now, my darling, I have got you; and from a lofty feeling, I am bound to tell the truth.   Consider the interests, Rosa——"

"Go along with your nonsense, Rue.   You talk below your great understanding, because you think it suits *me*."

"Perhaps I do," said Rufus, "perhaps I do now and then, my dear: you always hit the truth so. But is it not better to do that than to talk Greek to my Rosa?"

"I am sure I don't know; and I am sure I don't care either.   When have I heard you say anything, Rufus, so wonderful, and so out of the way, that I, *poor I*, couldn't understand it?   Please to tell me that, Rufus."

"My darling, consider.   You are exciting yourself so fearfully.   You make me shake all over."

"Then you should not say such things to me, Rufus.   Why, Rue, you are quite pale!"—What an impossibility!   She might have boiled him in soda without bringing him to a shrimp-colour.— "Come into the house this moment, I insist upon it, and have two glasses of sherry.   And you *do* say very wonderful things, much too clever for me, Rufus; and indeed, I believe, too clever for any woman in the world, even the one that wrote Homer."

Rosa Hutton ran into the house, and sought for the keys high and low; then got the decanter at last out of the cellaret, and brought out a bumper of wine. Crafty Rufus stopped outside, thoroughly absorbed in an autumn rose; knowing that she liked to do it for him, and glad to have it done for him.

" Not a drop, unless you drink first, dear. Rosa, here under the weeping elm: you are not afraid of the girls who are making the bed, I hope!"

" I should rather hope not, indeed! Rue, dear, my best love to you. Do you think I'd keep a girl in the house I was afraid to see through the window?"

To prove her spirit, Mrs. Hutton tossed a glass of wine off, although she seldom took it, and it was not twelve o'clock yet. Rufus looked on with some dismay, till he saw she had got the decanter.

" Well done, Rosa! What good it does me to see you take a mere drop of wine! You are bound now to obey me. Roe, my love, your very best health, and that involves my own. You're not heavy on my shoulder, love."

" No, dear, I know that: you are so very strong. But don't you see the boy coming? And that hole among the branches! And the leaves coming off too! Oh, do let me go in a moment, Rue!——"

" Confound that boy! I'm blest if he isn't always after me."

The boy, however, or man as he called himself,

was far too important a personage in their domestic economy to be confounded audibly. Gardener, groom, page, footman, knife-boy, and coachman, all in one; a long, loose, knock-kneed, big-footed, what they would call in the forest a " yaping, shammocking gally-bagger." His name was Jonah, and he came from Buckinghamshire, and had a fine drawl of his own, quite different from that of Ytene, which he looked upon as a barbarism.

"Plase, sir, Maister Reevers ave a zent them traases as us hardered." Jonah's eyes, throughout this speech, which occupied him at least a minute, were fixed upon the decanter, with ineffable admiration at the glow of the wine now the sun was upon it.

"Then, Jonah, my boy," cried Rufus Hutton, all animation in a moment, "I have a great mind to give you sixpence. Rosa, give me another glass of sherry. Here's to the health of the great horticulturist, Rivers! Most obliging of him to send my trees so early, and before the leaves are off. Come along, Roe, you love to see trees unpacked, and eat the fruit by anticipation. I believe you'll expect them to blossom and bear by Christmas, as St. Anthony made the vines do."

"Well, darling, and so they ought, with such a gardener as you to manage them.—Jonah, you shall have a glass of wine, to drink the health of the trees. He has never taken his eyes off the decanter, ever since he came up, poor boy."

Rosa was very good-natured, and accustomed

to farm-house geniality. Rufus laughed and whispered, "My love, my Indian sherry!"

"Can't help it," said Mrs. Hutton; "less chance of its disagreeing with him. Here, Jonah, you won't mind drinking after your master."

"Here be vaine health to all on us," said Jonah, scraping the gravel and putting up one finger as he had seen the militia men do (in imitation of the regulars); "and may us nayver know no taime warse than the prasent mawment."

"Hear, hear!" cried Rufus Hutton; "now, come along, and cut the cords, boy."

Dr. Hutton set off sharply, with Rosa on his arm, for he did not feel at all sure but what Jonah's exalted sentiment might elicit, at any rate, half a glass more of sherry. They found the trees packed beautifully; a long cone, like a giant lobster-pot, weighing nearly two hundred-weight, thatched with straw, and wattled round, and corded over that.

"Out with your knife and cut the cords, boy."

"Well, Rufus, you *are* extravagant!"—"Rather fine, that," thought Dr. Hutton, "after playing such pranks with my sherry!"—"Jonah, I won't have a bit of the string cut. I want every atom of it. What's the good of your having hands if you can't untie it?"

At last they got the great parcel open, and strewed all the lawn with litter. There were trees of every sort, as tight as sardines in a case, with many leaves still hanging on them, and the roots tied up in moss. Half a dozen standard apples;

half a hundred pyramid pears, the prettiest things imaginable, furnished all round like a cypress, and thick with blossom-spurs; then young wall-trees, two years' trained, tied to crossed sticks, and drawn up with bast, like the frame of a schoolboy's kite; around the roots and in among them were little roses in pots No. 60, wrapped in moss, and webbed with bast; and the smell of the whole was glorious.

"Hurrah!" cried Rufus, dancing, "no nurseries in the kingdom, nor in the world, except Sawbridge-worth, could send out such a lot of trees, perfect in shape, every one of them, and every one of them true to sort. What a bore that I've got to go again to Nowelhurst to-day! Rosa, dear; every one of these trees ought to be planted to-day. The very essence of early planting (which in my opinion saves a twelvemonth) is never to let the roots get dry. These peach-trees in a fortnight will have got hold of the ground, and be thinking of growing again; and the leaves, if properly treated, will never have flagged at all. Oh, I wish you could see to it, Rosa."

"Well, dear Rufus, and so I can. To please you, I don't mind at all throwing aside my banner-screen, and leaving my letter to cousin Magnolia."

"No, no. I don't mean that. I mean, how I wish you understood it."

"Understood it, Rue! Well, I'm sure! As if anybody couldn't plant a tree! And I, who had a pair of gardening gloves when I was only that high ! "

" Roe, now listen to me. Not one in a hundred even of professional gardeners, who have been at it all their lives, knows how to plant a tree."

" Well, then, Rufus, if that is the case, I think it very absurd of you to expect that I should. But Jonah will teach me, I dare say. I'll begin to learn this afternoon."

" No, indeed, you won't. At any rate, you must not practise on *my* trees; nor in among them, either. But you may plant the mop, dear, as often as you like, in that empty piece of ground where the cauliflowers were."

" Plant the mop, indeed ! Well, Dr. Hutton, you had better ride back to Nowelhurst, where all the grand people are, if you only come home for the purpose of insulting your poor wife. It is there, no doubt, that you learn to despise any one who is not quite so fine as they are. And what are they, I should like to know? What a poor weak thing I am, to be sure; no wonder no one cares for me. I can have no self-respect. I am only fit to plant the mop."

Hereupon the blue founts welled, the carmine of the cheeks grew scarlet, the cherry lips turned bigarreaux, and a very becoming fur-edged jacket lifted, as if with a zephyr stealing it.

Rufus felt immediately that he had been the lowest of all low brutes; and almost made up his

mind on the spot that it would be decidedly wrong
of him to go to Nowelhurst that, evening. We will
not enter into the scene of strong self-condemnation,
reciprocal collaudation, extraordinary admiration,
because all married people know it; and as for
those who are single, let them get married and
learn it. Only in the last act of it, Jonah, from
whom they had retreated, came up again, looking
rather sheepish—for he had begun to keep a
sweetheart—and spake these winged words :

"Plase, sir, if you be so good, it baint no vault
o' maine nohow."

"Get all those trees at once laid in by the heels.
What is no fault of yours, pray ? Are you always
at your dinner ? "

"Baint no vault o' maine, sir; but there coom
two genelmen chaps, as zays they musten zee
you."

"Must see me, indeed, whether I choose it or
no! And with all those trees to plant, and the
mare to be ready at three o'clock ! "

"Zo I tould un, sir; but they zays as they *must*
zee you."

"In the name of the devil and all his works,
but I'll give them a bitter reception. Let them
come this way, Jonah."

"Oh dear, if you are going to be violent ! You
know what you are sometimes, Rue—enough to
frighten any man."

"Never, my darling, never. You never find

Rufus Hutton formidable to any one who means rightly."

"No, no, to be sure, dear. But then, perhaps, they may not. And after all that has occurred to-day, I feel so much upset. Very foolish of me, I know. But promise me not to be rash, dear."

"Have no fear, my darling Rosa. I will never injure any man who does not insult you, dear."

While Rufus was looking ten feet high, and Mrs. Rufus tripping away, after a little sob and a whisper, Jonah came pelting down the walk with his great feet on either side of it, as if he had a barrow between them. At the same time a voice came round the corner past the arbutus-tree, now quivering red with strawberries, and the words thereof were these:

"Perfect Paradise, my good sir! I knew it must be, from what I heard of him. Exactly like my friend the Dook's, but laid out still more taste-fully. Bless me, why, his Grace must have copied it! Won't I give him a poke in the ribs when he dines with me next Toosday! Sly bird, a sly bird, I say, though he is such a capital fellow. Knew where to come, I'm blest if he didn't, for taste, true science, and landscape."

"Haw! Yes; I quite agree with you. But his Grace has nothing so chaste, so perfect as this, in me opeenion, sir. Haw!"

The cockles of the Rufine heart swelled warmly; for of course he heard every word of it, though, of course, not intended to do so. "Now Rosa ought to have heard all that," was passing in his mind, when two gentlemen stood before him, and were wholly amazed to see him. One of them was a short stout man, not much taller than Rufus, but of double his cubic contents; the other a tall and portly signor, fitted upon spindle shins, with a slouch in his back, grey eyebrows, long heavy eyes, and large dewlaps.

The short gentleman, evidently chief spokesman and proud of his elocution, waved his hat most gracefully, when he recovered from his surprise, drew back for a yard or so, in his horror at intruding, and spoke with a certain flourish, and the air of a man above humbug.

"Mr. Nowell Corklemore, I have the honour of making you known to the gentleman whose scientific fame has roused such a spirit among us. Dr. Hutton, sir, excuse me, the temptation was too great for us. My excellent friend, Lord Thorley, who has, I believe, the honour of being related to Mrs. Hutton, pressed his services upon us, when he knew what we desired. But, sir, no. 'My lord,' said I, 'we prefer to intrude without the commonplace of society; we prefer to intrude upon the footing of common tastes, my lord, and warm, though far more rudimental and vague pursuit of science.' Bless me, all this time my unworthy self, sir! I am too prone to forget myself, at least my wife declares so. Bailey Kettledrum, sir, is my name, of Kettledrum Hall, in Dorset. And

I have the enlightenment, sir, to aspire to the
honour of your acquaintance."

Rufus Hutton bowed rather queerly to Mr.
Nowell Corklemore and Mr. Bailey Kettledrum;
for he had seen a good deal of the world, and had
tasted sugar-candy. Moreover, the Kettledrum
pattern was known to him long ago; and he had
never found them half such good fellows as they
pretend to think other people. Being, however,
most hospitable, as are nearly all men from India,
he invited them to come in at once, and have some
lunch after their journey. They accepted very
warmly; and Mrs. Hutton, having now appeared
and been duly introduced, Bailey Kettledrum set
off with her round the curve of the grass-plot, as
if he had known her for fifty years, and had not
seen her for twenty-five. He engrossed her whole
attention by the pace at which he talked, and
by appeals to her opinion, praising all things,
taking notes, red-hot with admiration, impressively
confidential about his wife and children, and, in a
word, regardless of expense to make himself agreeable. Notwithstanding all this, he did not get on
much, because he made one great mistake. He
rattled and flashed along the high road leading to
fifty other places, but missed the quiet and pleasant
path which leads to a woman's good graces—the
path, I mean, which follows the little brook called
"sympathy," a winding but not a shallow brook,
over the meadow of soft listening.

Mr. Nowell Corklemore, walking with Rufus

Hutton, was, as he was forced to be by a feeble nature enfeebled, a dry and pompous man.

"Haw! I am given to understand you have made all this yourself, sir. In me 'umble opeenion, it does you the greatest credit, sir; credit, sir, no less to your heart than to your head. Haw!"

Here he pointed with his yellow bamboo at nothing at all in particular.

"Everything is in its infancy yet. Wait till the trees grow up a little. I have planted nearly all of them. All except that, and that, and the weeping elm over yonder, where I sit with my wife sometimes. Everything is in its infancy."

"Excuse me; haw! If you will allow me, I would also say, with the exception of something else." And he looked profoundly mystic.

"Oh, the house you mean," said Rufus. "No, the house is not quite new; built some seven years back."

"Sir, I do not mean the house—but the edifice, haw!—the tenement of the human being. Sir, I mean, except just *this*."

He shut one eye, like a sleepy owl, and tapped the side of his head most sagely; and then he said "Haw!" and looked for approval.

And he might have looked a very long time, in his stupidly confident manner, without a chance of getting it; for Rufus Hutton disliked allusions even to age intellectual, when you came to remember that his Rosa was more than twenty years younger.

" Ah, yes, now it strikes me," continued Mr.
Corklemore, as they stood in front of the house,
" that little bow-window—nay, I am given to understand, that bay-window is the more correct—
haw! I mean the more architectural term—I
think I should have felt inclined to make that nice
bay-window give to the little grass-plot. A mere
question, perhaps, of idiosyncrasy, haw!"

" Give what?" asked Rufus, now on the foam.
That his own pet lawn, which he rolled every day,
his lawn endowed with manifold curves and sweeps
of his own inventing, with the Wellingtonia upon
it, and the plantain dug out with a cheese-knife—
that all this should be called a " little grass-plot,"
by a fellow who had no two ideas, except in his in-
tonation of " Haw !"

" Haw! It does not signify. But the term, I
am given to understand, is now the correct and re-
cognised one."

" I wish you were given to understand anything
except your own importance," Rufus muttered
savagely, and eyed the yellow bamboo.

" Have you—haw! excuse my asking, for you
are a great luminary here; have you as yet made
trial of the Spergula pilifera?"

" Yes; and found it the biggest humbug that
ever aped God's grass."

Dr. Hutton was always very sorry when he had
used strong language; but being a thin-skinned,
irritable, cut-the-corner man, he could not be expected to stand Nowell Corklemore's " haws."

And Mr. Corklemore had of "haw" no less than seven intonations. First, and most common of all, the haw of self-approval. Second, the haw of contemplation. Third, the haw of doubt and inquiry. Fourth, that of admiration. Fifth, that of interlude and hiatus, when words or ideas lingered. Sixth, the haw of accident and short-winded astonishment; *e.g.* he had once fallen off a hayrick, and cried "Haw!" at the bottom. Seventh, the haw of indignation and powerful remonstrance, in a totally different key from the rest; and this last he now adopted.

"Haw—then!—haw!—I have been given to understand that the Spergula pilifera succeeds most admirably with people who have—haw!—have studied it."

"Very likely it does," said Rufus, though he knew much better, but now he was on his own door-step, and felt ashamed of his rudeness; "but come in, Mr. Corklemore; our ways are rough in these forest outskirts, and we are behind you in civilization. Nevertheless, we are heartily glad to welcome our more intelligent neighbours."

At lunch he gave them home-brewed ale and pale sherry of no especial character. But afterwards, being a genial soul, and feeling still guilty of rudeness, he went to the cellar himself and fetched a bottle of the richest Indian gold. Mrs. Hutton withdrew very prettily; and the three gentlemen, all good judges of wine, began to warm over it luminously, more softly indeed than they would have done after a heavy dinner. Surely, noble wine deserves not to be the mere operculum to a stupidly mixed hot meal.

"Have another bottle, gentlemen; now do have another bottle."

"Not one drop more for the world," exclaimed they both, with their hands up. None the less for that, they did; and, what was very unwise of them, another after that, until I can scarcely write straight in trying to follow their doings. Meanwhile Jonah had prigged three glassfuls out of the decanter left under the elm-tree.

"Now," said Rufus, who alone was *almost* in a state of sobriety, "suppose we take a turn in the garden and my little orchard-house? I believe I am indebted to that for the pleasure of your very disagreeable—ahem, most agreeable company to-day."

Bailey Kettledrum sprang up with a flourish. "No, sir, no, sir! Permit me to defend myself and this most marketable—I—I mean remarkable gentleman here present, Mr. Nowell Corklemore, from any such dis—dish—sparagus, disparagizing imputations, sir. An orchard, sir, is very well, and the trees in it are very well, and the fruit of it is very good, sir; but an orchard can never appear, sir, to a man of exalted sentiments, and temporal—I mean, sir, strictly intemperate judgment, in the light of an elephant—irrelevant—no, sir, I mean of course an equilevant—for a man, sir, for a man!" Here Mr. Bailey Kettledrum hit himself hard on the bosom, and broke the glass of his watch.

"Mr. Kettledrum," said Rufus, rising, "your sentiments do you honour. Mine, however, is not an orchard, but an orchard-house."

"Ha, ha, good again! House in an orchard! yes, I see. Corklemore, hear that, my boy? Our admirable host—no, thank you, not a single drop more wine—I always know when I have had enough. Sir, it is the proud privi—prilivege of a man——Corklemore, get up, sir don't you see we are waiting for you?"

Mr. Corklemore stared heavily at him; his constitution was a sleepy one, and he thought he had eaten his dinner. His friend nodded gravely at Dr. Hutton; and the nod expressed compassion tempering condemnation.

"Ah, I see how it is. Ever since that fall from the hayrick, the leastest little drop of wine, prej— prej——"

"Prejudge the case, my lord," muttered Mr. Corklemore, who had been a barrister.

"Prejudicially affects our highly admired friend. But, sir, the fault is mine. I should have stretched forth long ago the restraining hand of friendship, sir, and dashed the si—si—silent bottle——"

"Chirping bottle, possibly you mean."

"No, sir, I do not, and I will thank you not to interrupt me. Who ever heard a bottle chirp? I ask you, sir, as a man of the world, and a man of common sense, who ever heard a bottle chirp?

What I mean, sir, is the siren—the siren bottle from his lips. What is it in the Latin grammar—or possibly in the Greek, for I have learned Greek, sir, in the faulchion days of youth ;—is it not, sir, this : *improba Siren desidia?* Perhaps, sir, it may have been in your grammar, if you ever had one, *improba chirping desidia.*" As he looked round, in the glow and sparkle of lagenic logic, Rufus caught him by the arm, and hurried him out at the garden door, where luckily no steps were. The pair went straight, or, in better truth, went first, to the kitchen garden ; Rufus did not care much for flowers ; all that he left to his Rosa.

"Now I will show you a thing, sir," cried Rufus in his glory, "a thing which has been admired by the leading men of the age. Nowhere else, in this part of the world, can you see a piece of ground, sir, cropped in the manner of that, sir."

And to tell the plain, unvinous truth, the square to which he pointed was a triumph of high art. The style of it was wholly different from that of Mr. Garnet's beds. Bull Garnet was fond of novelties, but he made them square with his system ; the result was more strictly practical, but less nobly theoretical. Dr. Hutton, on the other hand, travelled the entire porker ; obstacles of soil and season were as nothing to him, and when the shape of the ground was wrong, he called in the navvies and made it right.

A plot of land four-square, and measured to exactly half an acre, contained 2400 trees, cutting

either way as truly as the spindles of machinery;
there was no tree more than five feet high, the
average height was four feet six inches. They
were planted just four feet asunder, and two feet
back from the pathway. There was every kind of
fruit-tree there, which can be made by British
gardeners to ripen fruit in Britain, without artificial
heat. Pears especially, and plums, cherries, apples,
walnuts (juglans præparturiens), figs, and medlars,
quinces, filberts, even peaches, nectarines, and
apricots—though only one row, in all, of those
three; there was scarcely one of those miniature
trees which had not done its duty that year, or now
was bent upon doing it. Still the sight was beautiful; although far gone with autumn, still Cox's
orange-pippin lit the russet leaves with gold, or
Beurré Clairgeau and Capiaumont enriched the
air with scarlet.

Each little tree looked so bright and comely,
each plumed itself so naturally, proud to carry its
share of tribute to the beneficent Maker, that the
two men who had been abusing His choice gift,
the vine, felt a little ashamed of themselves, or
perhaps felt that they ought to be.

"Magnificent, magnificent!" cried Kettledrum,
theatrically; "I must tell the Dook of this. He
will have the same next year."

"Will he, though?" said Rufus, thinking of the
many hours he had spent among those trees, and
of his careful apprenticeship to the works of their
originator; "I can tell you one thing. He won't,

unless he has a better gardener than I ever saw
in these parts. Now let us go to the orchard-
house."

The orchard-house was a span-roofed building,
very light and airy; the roof and ends were made
of glass, the sides of deal with broad falling
shutters, for the sake of ventilation. It was about
fifty feet in length, twenty in width, and fifteen in
height. There was no ventilation at the ridge,
and all the lights were fixed. The free air of
heaven wandered through, among peaches, plums,
and apricots, some of which still retained their
fruit, crimson, purple, and golden. The little
trees were all in pots, and about a yard apart.
The pots were not even plunged in the ground,
but each stood, as a tub should, on its own inde-
pendent bottom. The air of the house was soft
and pleasant, with a peculiar fragrance, the smell
of ripening foliage. Bailey Kettledrum saw at once
—for he had plenty of observant power, and the
fumes of wine were dispersing—that this house
must have shown a magnificent sight, a month or
two ago. And having once more his own object
in view, he tripled his true approval.

" Dr. Hutton, this is fine. Fine is not the word
for it; this is grand and gorgeous. What a
triumph of mind! What a lot you must pay for
wages!"

"Thirteen shillings a week in summer, seven
shillings a week in the winter." This was one of
his pet astonishments.

"What! I'll never believe it. Sir, you must either be a conjuror, the devil, or—or——"

"Or a liar," said Rufus, placidly; "but I am none of the three. Jonah has twelve shillings a week, but half of that goes for housework. That leaves six shillings for gardening; but I never trust him inside this house, for he is only a clumsy dolt, who does the heavy digging. And besides him I have only a very sharp lad, at seven shillings a week, who works under my own eye. I have in some navvies, at times, it is true, when I make any alterations. But that is outlay, not working expense. Now come and see my young trees just arrived from Sawbridgeworth."

"Stop one moment. What is this stuff on the top of the pots here? What queer stuff! Why, it goes quite to pieces in my hands."

"Oh, only a little top-dressing, just to refresh the trees a bit. This way, Mr. Kettledrum."

"Pardon me, sir, if I appear impertinent or inquisitive. But I have learned so much this afternoon, that I am anxious to learn a little more. My friend, the Dook, will cross-examine me as to everything I have seen here. He knew our intention of coming over. I must introduce you to his Grace, before you are a week older, sir; he has specially requested it. In fact, it was only this morning he said to Nowell Corklemore—but Corklemore, though a noble fellow, a gem of truth and honour, sir, is not a man of *our* intelligence; in one word, he is an ass!"

"Haw! Nowell Corklemore, Nowell Corklemore is an ass, is he, in the wise opeenion of Mr. Bailey Kettledrum? Only let me get up, good Lord—and perhaps he told the Dook so. There, it's biting me again, oh Lord! Nowell Corklemore an ass!"

By the door of the orchard-house grew a fine deodara, and behind it lay Mr. Corklemore, beyond all hope entangled. His snores had been broken summarily by the maid coming for the glasses, and he set forth, after a dozen "haws," to look for his two comrades. With instinct ampeline he felt that his only chance of advancing in the manner of a biped lay or stood in his bamboo. So he went to the stick-stand by the back-door, where he muzzily thought it ought to be. Mrs. Hutton, in the drawing-room, was rattling on the piano, and that made his head ten times worse. His bamboo was not in the stick-stand; nevertheless he found there a gig-umbrella with a yellow handle, like the top of his fidus Achates. Relying upon this, he made his way out, crying "haw!" at every star in the oilcloth. He progged away all down the walk, with the big umbrella; but the button that held the cord was gone, and it flapped like a mutinous windmill. However, he carried on bravely, until he confronted a dark, weird tree, waving its shrouded arms at him. This was the deodara; so he made a tack to the left, and there was hulled between wind and water by an unsuspected enemy. This was Rufus Hutton's pet of all pet pear-trees, a perfect model of symmetry, scarce three feet six in height, sturdy, crisp, short-jointed, spurred from keel to truck, and carrying twenty great pears. It had been so stopped and snagged throughout, that it was stiffer than fifty hollies; and Rosa was dreadfully jealous of it, because Rufus spent so much time there. He used to go out in the summer forenoon, when-ever the sun was brilliant, and draw lines down the fruit with a wet camel's hairbrush, as the French gardeners do. He had photographed it once or twice, but the wind would move the leaves so.

Now he had the pleasure of seeing Nowell Cor-klemore flat on his back, with his pet Beurré Su-perfin (snapped at the stock), and the gig-umbrella between his legs, all a hideous ruin. The gig-umbrella flapped and flapped, and the agonised pear-tree scratched and scratched, till Nowell Corklemore felt quite sure that he was in the embrace of a dragon. The glorious pears were rolling about, some crushed under his frantic heels, the rest with wet bruises on them, appealing from human barbarism.

"Well!" said Rufus Hutton. He was in such a rage, it would have choked him to say another word.

"Haw! I don't call it well at all to be eaten up by a dragon. Pull him away for mercy's sake, pull him away! and I'll tell all about this busi-ness."

At last they got him out, for the matter was

really serious, and Rufus was forced to hide his
woe at the destruction of the pear-tree.   And after
all he had no one but himself to thank for it.   Why
did he almost force his guests to drink the third
bottle of sherry?

"Wonderful, perfectly wonderful!" exclaimed
Mr. Bailey Kettledrum, as Rufus was showing
them out at the gate, before having his own horse
saddled.   "The triumphs of horticulture in this
age are really past belief.   You beat all of us, Dr.
Hutton, you may depend upon it; you beat all of
us.   I never would have believed that trees ought
to be planted with their heads down, and their
roots up in the air.   Stupid of me, though, for I
have often heard of root-pruning, and of course
you could not prune the roots unless they grew in
that way."

Rufus thought he was joking, or suffering from
vinous inversion of vision.

"Remember, my good friend Hutton—excuse
my familiarity, I feel as if I had known you for
years—remember, my dear friend, you have
pledged your word for next Wednesday—and Mrs.
Hutton too, mind—Mrs. Hutton with you.   We
waive formality, you know, in these country
quarters.   Kettledrum Hall, next Wednesday—
honour bright, next Wednesday!   You see I know
the motto of your family."

"Thank you, all right," said Rufus Hutton;
"it's a deuced deal more than I know," he added,

going up the drive. "I didn't know we had a motto. Well, I'm done for at last!"

No wonder he was done for. He saw what Kettledrum had taken in the purest faith. All those lovely little trees, dwarf pyramids, &c., were standing on the apex. Jonah, after all the sherry given to and stolen by him, had laid them in by the heels with a vengeance. All the pretty heads were a foot under ground, and the roots, like the locks of a mermaid, wooing the buxom air.

CHAPTER XXV.

THAT evening Dr. Hutton started, on his long swift mare, for the Hall at Nowelhurst, where he had promised to be. He kissed his Rosa many times, and begged her pardon half as often, for all the crimes that day committed. Her brother Ralph, from Fordingbridge, who always slept there at short notice, because the house was lonely, would be sure to come (they knew) when the little boy Bob was sent for him. Ralph Mohorn—poor Rosa rejoiced in her rather uncommon patronymic, though perhaps it means Cow-horn—Ralph Mohorn was only too glad to come and sleep at Geopharmacy Lodge. He was a fine, fresh-hearted fellow, only about nineteen years old; his father held him hard at home, and of course he launched out all the more abroad. So he kicked up, as he expressed it, "the devil's own dust" when he got to the Lodge, ordered everything in the house for supper, with a bottle of whisky afterwards—which he never

touched, only he liked the name of the thing—and
then a cardinal, or the biggest meerschaum to be
found in any of the cupboards. His pipe, however, was not, like his grog, a phantom of the imagination ; for he really smoked it, and sat on three
chairs, while he " baited" Rosa, as he called it, with
all the bogeys in Christendom. It was so delicious
now to be able to throw her into a tremble, and
turn her cheeks every colour, and then recollect
that a few years since she had smacked his own
cheeks *ad libitum*. However, we have little to do
with him, and now he is a jolly farmer.

Rufus Hutton rode through Ringwood over the
low bridge where the rushes rustle everlastingly,
and the trout and dace for ever wag their pellucid
tails up stream. How all that water, spreading
loosely, wading over miles of meadows, growing
leagues of reed and rush, mistress of a world in
winter, how it all is content to creep through a
pair of little bridges—matter of such mystery, let
the Christchurch salmon solve it. Dr. Hutton went
gaily over—at least his mare went gaily—but he
was thinking (beyond his wont) of the business he
had in hand. He admired the pleasant old town
as he passed, and the still more pleasant waters ;
but his mare, the favourite Polly, went on at her
usual swing, until they came to the long steep hill
towards the Picked Post. As he walked her up
the sharp parts of the rise, he began to ponder the
mysterious visit of those convivial strangers. It
was very plain that neither of them knew or cared

the turn of a trowel about the frank art of gardening; that, of course, was only a sham; then what did they really come for? Rufus, although from childhood upwards he had been hospitable to his own soul, that is to say, regarded himself with genial approbation, was not by any means blindly conceited, and could not suppose that his fame, for anything except gardening, had spread through the regions round about. So he felt that his visitors had come, not for his sake, but their own. And it was not long before he suspected that they wished to obtain through him some insight, perhaps even some influence, into and in the course of events now toward at Nowelhurst Hall. They had altogether avoided the subject; which made him the more suspicious, for at present it was of course the leading topic of the county.

However, as they were related to the family, while he, Rufus Hutton, was not, it was not his place to speak of the matter, but to let his guests do as they liked about it. They had made him promise, moreover, to dine with the Kettledrums on the very earliest day he could fix—viz. the following Wednesday—and there he was to meet Mr. and Mrs. Corklemore. Was it possible that they intended, and perhaps had been instructed, to subject the guest on that occasion to more skilful manipulation than that of their rude male fingers?

"I'll take Rosa with me," said Rufus to himself; " a woman sees a woman's game best; though Rosa, thank Heaven, is not very Machiavellian. How very

odd, that neither of those men had the decency
to carry a bit of crape, out of respect for that
poor boy; and I, who am noway connected with
him, have been indued by my Roe with a hat-
band !"

Shrewd as our friend Rufus was, he could not
be charged with low cunning, and never guessed
that those two men had donned the show of
mourning, and made the most of it round their
neighbourhood to impress people with their kinship
to the great Nowells of Nowelhurst, but that their
guardian angels had disarrayed them ere they
started, having no desire to set Rufus thinking
about their chance of succession. As the sharp
little doctor began to revolve all he had heard
about Corklemore, his mare came to the Burley-
road where they must leave the turnpike. Good
Polly struck into it, best foot foremost, and, as she
never would bear the curb well, her rider had quite
enough to do, in the gathering darkness, and on
that cross-country track, to attend to their common
safety.

She broke from the long stride of her trot into
a reaching canter, as the moon grew bright between
the trees, and the lane was barred with shadow.
Pricking nervously her ears at every flaw or rustle,
bending her neck to show her beauty, where the
light fell clear on the moor-top, then with a snort
of challenge plunging into the black of the hollows,
yet ready to jump the road and away, if her challenge should be answered; bounding across the

water-gulley and looking askance at a fern-shadow ; then saying to herself, " It is only the moon, child," and up the ascent half ashamed of herself; then shaking her bridle with reassurance to think of that mile of great danger flown by, and the mash and the warm stable nearer, and the pleasure of telling that great roan horse how brave she had been in the moonlight——

" Goodness me! What's that ?"

She leaped over road and roadside bank, and into a heavy gorse-bush, and stood there quivering from muzzle to tail in the intensity of terror. If Rufus had not just foreseen her alarm, and gripped her with all his power, he must have lain senseless upon the road, spite of all his rough-riding in India.

" Who-hoa, who-hoa, then, Polly, you little fool, you are killing me! Can't you see it's only a lady ?"

Polly still backed into the bush, and her unlucky rider, with every prickle running into him, could see the whites of her eyes in the moonshine, as the great orbs stood out with horror. Opposite to them, and leaning against a stile which led to a footpath, there stood a maiden dressed in black, with the moonlight sheer upon her face. She took no notice of anything; she had heard no sort of footfall; she did not know of Polly's capers, or the danger she was causing. . Her face, with the hunter's moon upon it, would have been glorious beauty, but for the broad rims under the eyes, and

the spectral paleness.   One moment longer she
stared at the moon, as if questing for some one
gone thither, then turned away with a heavy sigh,
and went towards the Coffin Wood.

All this time Rufus Hutton was utterly blind to
romance, being scarified in the calf and thighs
beyond any human endurance.   Polly backed
further and further away from the awful vision
before her—the wife of the horse-fiend at least—
and every fresh swerve sent a new lot of furze-
pricks into the peppery legs of Rufus.

"Hang it!" he cried, "here goes; no man with
a ha'porth of flesh in him could stand it any longer.
Thorn for thorn, Miss Polly."   He dashed his spurs
deep into her flanks, the spurs he had only worn
for show, and never dared to touch her with.   For
a moment she trembled, and reared upright in
wrath worse than any horror; then away she went
like a storm of wind, headlong through trees and
bushes.   It was all pure luck or Providence that
Rufus was not killed.   He grasped her neck, and
lay flat upon it; he clung with his supple legs
around her; he called her his Polly, his darling
Polly, and begged her to consider herself.   She
considered neither herself nor him, but dashed
through the wild wood, wilder herself, not knowing
light from darkness.   Any low beech branch, any
scrag holly, even a trail of loose ivy, and man and
horse were done for. . The lights of more than a
million stars flashed before Rufus Hutton, and he
made up his mind to die, and wondered how Rosa

would take it.   Perhaps she would marry again,
and rear up another family who knew not the name
of Hutton; perhaps she would cry her eyes out.
Smack, a young branch took him in the face,
though he had one hand before it.   "Go it
again!" he cried, with the pluck of a man despair-
ing, and then he rolled over and over, and dug for
himself a rabbit-hole of sand, and dead leaves, and
moss.   There he lay on his back, and prayed, and
luckily let go the bridle.

The mare had fallen, and grovelled in the rotten
ground where the rabbits lived; then she got up
and shook herself, and the stirrups struck fire
beneath her, and she spread out all her legs, and
neighed for some horse to come and help her.   She
could not go any further; she had vented her soul,
and must come to herself, like a lady after hysterics.
Presently she sniffed round a bit, and the grass
smelled crisp and dewy, and, after the hot corn and
musty hay, it was fresher than ice upon brandy.
So she looked through the trees, and saw only a
squirrel, which did not frighten her at all, because
she was used to rats.   Then she brought her fore-
legs well under her stomach, and stretched her long
neck downwards, and skimmed the wet blades with
her upper lip, and found them perfectly wholesome.
Every horse knows what she did then and there, to
a great extent, till she had spoiled her relish for
supper.

After that, she felt grateful and good, and it
repented her of the evil, and she whinnied about

for the master who had outraged her feelings so
deeply.   She found him still insensible, on his back,
beneath a beech-tree, with six or seven rabbits, and
even a hare, come to see what the matter was.
Then Polly, who had got the bit out of her mouth,
gave him first a poke with it, and then nuzzled him
under the coat-collar, and blew into his whiskers as
she did at the chaff in her manger.   She was beginning to grieve and get very uneasy, taking care not
to step on him, and went round him ever so many
times, and whinnied into his ear, when either that,
or the dollop of grass half chewed which lay on his
countenance, revived the great spirit of Rufus
Hutton, and he opened his eyes and looked lan-
guidly.   He saw two immense black eyes full upon
him, tenderly touched by the moonlight, and he
felt a wet thing like a sponge poking away at his
nostrils.

"Polly," he said, "oh, Polly dear, how could you
serve me so ?   What will your poor mistress say ?"

Polly could neither recriminate nor defend herself ; so she only looked at him beseechingly, and
what she meant was, "Oh, do get up."

So Rufus arose, and dusted himself, and kissed
Polly for forgiveness, and she, if she had only learned
how, would have stooped like a camel before him.
He mounted, with two or three groans for his back,
and left the mare to her own devices to find the
road again.   It was very pretty to see in the moonlight how carefully she went with him, not even
leaping the small water-courses, but feeling her

footing through them. And so they got into the forest-track, some half mile from where they had left it; they saw the gleam of Bull Garnet's windows, and knew the straight road to the Hall.

Sir Cradock Nowell did not appear. Of course that was not expected; but kind John Rosedew came up from the parsonage to keep Rufus Hutton company. So the two had all the great dinner-table to themselves entirely; John, as the old friend, sat at the head, and the doctor sat by his right hand. Although there were few men in the world with the depth of mind, and variety, the dainty turns of thought, the lacework infinitely rich of original mind and old reading, which made John Rosedew's company a forest for to wander in and be amazed with pleasure; Rufus Hutton, sore and stiff, and aching in the back, thought he had rarely come across so very dry a parson.

John was not inclined to talk: he was thinking of his Cradock, and he had a care of still sharper tooth—what had happened to his Amy? He had come up much against his wishes, only as a duty, on that dreary Saturday night, just that Mr. Hutton, who had been so very kind, might not think himself neglected. John had dined four hours ago, but that made no difference to him, for he seldom knew when he *had* dined, and when he was expected to do it. Nevertheless he was human, for he loved his bit of supper.

Mr. Rosedew had laboured hard, but vainly, to persuade Sir Cradock Nowell to send some or any message to his luckless son. "No," he replied, "he did not wish to see him any more, or at any rate not at present; it would be too painful to him. Of course he was sorry for him, and only hoped he was half as sorry for himself." John Rosedew did not dream as yet of the black idea working even now in the lonely father's mind, gaining the more on his better heart because he kept it secret. The old man was impatient now even of the old friend's company; he wanted to sit alone all day weaving and unravelling some dark skein of evidence, and as yet he was not so possessed of the devil as to cease to feel ashamed of him. "Coarse language!" cries some votary of our self-conscious euphemism. But show me any plainer work of the father of unbelief than want of faith in our fellow-creatures, when we have proved and approved them; want of faith in our own flesh and blood, with no cause for it but the imputed temptation. It shall go hard with poor old Sir Cradock, and none shall gainsay his right to it.

Silence was a state of the air at once uncongenial to Dr. Hutton's system and repugnant to all his finest theories of digestion. For lo, how all nature around us protests against the Trappists, and the order of St. Benedict! See how the cattle get together when they have dined in the afternoon, and had their drink out of the river. Don't they flip their tails, and snuffle, and grunt at their own fine sentiments, and all the while they are chewing the cud take stock of one another?

Don't they discuss the asilus and œstrum, the last news of the rinderpest, and the fly called by some the cow-dab, and don't they abuse the festuca tribe, and the dyspepsia of the sorrel? Is the thrush mute when he has bolted his worm, or the robin over his spider's eggs?

So Rufus looked through his glass of port, which he took merely as a corrective to the sherry of the morning, cocked one eye first, and then the other, and loosed the golden bands of speech.

"Uncommonly pretty girls, Mr. Rosedew, all about this neighbourhood."

"Very likely, Dr. Hutton; I see many pleasant faces; but I am no judge of beauty." He leaned back with an absent air, just as if he knew nothing about it. And all the while he was saying to himself, "Pretty girls indeed! Is there one of them like my Amy?"

"A beautiful girl I saw to-night. But I don't wish to see much more beauty in that way. Nearly cost me my life, I know. You are up in the classics so: what is it we used to read at school?— Helene, Helenaus, Helip—something—teterrima belli causa fuit. Upon my word, I haven't talked so much Latin and Greek—have another glass of port, just for company; the dry vintage of '34 can't hurt anybody." John Rosedew took another glass, for his spirits were low, and the wine was good, and the parson felt then that he ought to have more confidence in God. Then he brought his mind to bear on the matter, and listened very attentively while the doctor described, with a rush of warm language and plenteous exaggeration, the fright of his mare at that mournful vision, the vision itself, and the consequences.

" Sir, you must have ridden like a Centaur, or like Alexander. What will Mrs. Hutton say? But are you sure that she leaped an oak-tree ? "

" Perfectly certain," said Rufus, gravely, " clean through the fork of the branches, and the acorns rattled upon my hat, like the hail of the Himalaya."

" Remarkable ! Most remarkable ! "

" But you have not told me yet," continued Dr. Hutton, " although I am sure that you know, who the beautiful young lady is."

" From your description, and the place, though I have not heard that they are in mourning, I think it must have been Miss Garnet."

" Miss Garnet ! What Miss Garnet ? Not Bull Garnet's daughter ? I never heard that he had one."

" Yes, he has, and a very nice girl. My Amy knows a little of her. But he does not allow her to visit much, and is most repressive to her. Unwise, in my opinion ; not the way to treat a daughter ; one should have confidence in her, as I have in my dear child."

" Oh, you have confidence in Miss Rosedew ; and she goes out whenever she likes, I suppose ? "

" Of course she does," said the simple John,

wondering at the question; "that is, of course, whenever it is right for her."

"Of which, I suppose, she herself is the judge."

"Why, no, not altogether. Her aunt has a voice in the matter always, and a very potent one."

"And, of course, Miss Rosedew, managed upon such enlightened principles, never attempts to deceive you?"

"Amy! my Amy deceive me!" The rector turned pale at the very idea. "But these questions are surely unusual from a gentleman whom I have known for so very short a time. I am entitled, in turn, to ask your reason for putting them." Mr. Rosedew, never suspecting indignities, could look very dignified.

"I'm in for it now," thought Rufus Hutton; "what a fool I am! I fancied the old fellow had no *nous*, except for Latin and Greek."

Strange to say, the old fellow had *nous* enough to notice his hesitation. John Rosedew got up from his chair, and stood looking at Rufus Hutton.

"Sir, I will thank you to tell me exactly what you mean about my daughter."

"Nothing at all, Mr. Rosedew. What do you suppose I *should* mean?"

"You *should* mean nothing at all, sir. But I believe that you *do* mean something. And, please God, I will have it out of you." Rufus Hutton said afterwards that he had two great frights that

evening, and he believed the last was the worst.
The parson never dreamed that any man could be
afraid of him, except it were a liar, and he looked
upon Rufus contemptuously. The man of the
world was nothing before the man of truth.

"Mr. Rosedew," said Rufus, recovering himself,
"your conduct is very extraordinary; and (you will
excuse my saying it) more violent than becomes
a man of your position and character."

"No violence becomes any man, whatever his
position. I am sorry if I have been violent."

"You have indeed," said Rufus, pushing his
advantage: a generous man would have said, "No,
you haven't," at seeing the parson's distress, and
so would Rufus have said, if he had happened to
be in the right; "so violent, Mr. Rosedew, that I
believe you almost frightened me."

"Dear me!" said John, reflecting, "and he has
just leaped an oak-tree! I must have been very
bad."

"Don't mention it, my dear sir, I entreat you
say no more about it. We all know what a father
is." And Rufus Hutton, who did not yet, but
expected to know in some three months, grew very
large, and felt himself able to patronise the rector.
"Mr. Rosedew, I as well am to blame. I am
thoughtless, sir, very thoughtless, or rather I should
say too thoughtful; I am too fond of seeing round
a corner, which I have always been famous for.
Sir, a man who possesses this power, this gift, this
—I don't know the word for it, but I have no

doubt you do — that man is apt to — I mean to——"

"Knock his head against a wall?" suggested the parson, in all good faith.

"No, you mistake me; I don't mean that at all; I mean that a man with this extraordinary foresight, which none can understand except those who are gifted with it, is liable sometimes, is amenable—I mean to—to——"

"See double. Ah, yes, I can quite understand it." John Rosedew shut his eyes, and felt up for a disquisition, yet wanted to hear of his daughter.

"No, my dear sir, no. It is something very far from anything so common-place as that. What I mean is—only I cannot express it, because you interrupt me so—that a man may have this faculty, this insight, this perception, which saves him from taking offence where none whatever is meant, and yet, as it were by some obliquity of the vision, may seem, in some measure, to see the wrong individual." Here Rufus felt like the dwarf Alypius, when he had stodged Iamblichus.

"That is an interesting question, and reminds me of the state of ἀρρεψία, as described in the life of Pyrrho by Diogenes Laertius; whose errors, if I may venture to say it, have been made too much of by the great Isaac Casaubon, then scarcely mature of judgment. It will give me the greatest pleasure to go into that question with you. But not just now. I am thrown out so sadly, and my memory fails me"—John Rosedew had fancied

this, by-the-by, ever since he was thirty years old—
"only tell me one thing, Dr. Hutton, and I am
very sorry for my violence; you meant no harm
about my daughter?"   Here the grey-haired man,
with the mighty forehead, opened his clear blue
eyes, and looked down upon Rufus beseechingly.

"Upon my honour as a gentleman, I mean no
harm whatever. I made the greatest mistake, and
I see the mistake I made."

"Will you tell me, sir, what it was? Just to
ease my mind. I am sure that you will."

"No, I must not tell you now, until I have
worked the matter out. You will thank me for
not doing so. But I apologise most heartily. I
feel extremely uncomfortable. No claret, sir, but
the port, if you please. I was famous, in India,
for my nerve; but now it seems to be failing me."

Rufus, as we now perceive, had fully discovered
his mistake, and was trying to trace the consequences. The beautiful girl whom he saw in the
wood, that evening, with Clayton Nowell, was not
our Amy at all at all, but Mr. Garnet's daughter.
He knew the face, though changed and white,
when it frightened his mare in the moonlight;
and, little time as he had to think, it struck him
then as very strange that Miss Rosedew should be
there. Bull Garnet's cottage, on the other hand,
was quite handy in the hollow.

CHAPTER XXVI.

At this melancholy time, John Rosedew had quite enough to do without any burden of fresh anxieties about his own pet Amy. Nevertheless, that burden was added; not by Dr. Hutton's vague questions, although they helped to impose it, but by the father's own observation of his darling's strange condition. "Can it be," he asked himself, and often longed to ask her, as he saw only lilies where roses had been, and little hands trembling at breakfast-time, "can it be that this child of mine loved the poor boy Clayton, and is wasting away in sorrow for him? Is that the reason why she will not meet Cradock, nor Cradock meet her, and she trembles at his name? And then that book which Aunt Doxy made her throw on the kitchen fire—very cruel I now see it was of my good sister Eudoxia, though at first I did not think so—that book I know was poor Clayton's, for I have seen it in his hand. Well, if it truly is so, there is nothing to be done, except to be unusually kind to her, and trust to time for the cure, and give her plenty of black-currant jam."

These ideas he imparted to the good Aunt Doxy, who delivered some apophthegms (which John did not want to listen to), but undertook, whatever should happen, to be down upon Amy sharply. She knew all about her tonsils and her uvula, and all that stuff, and she did not want John's advice, though she had never had a family; and thank God heartily for it!

On Monday, when the funeral came to Nowel-hurst churchyard, John Rosedew felt his heart give way, and could not undertake it. At the risk of deeply offending Sir Cradock, whose nerves that day were of iron, he passed the surplice to his curate, Mr. Pell, of Rushford; and begged him, with a sad slow smile, to do the duty for him. Sir Cradock Nowell frowned, and coloured, and then bowed low with an icy look, when he saw the change which had been made, and John Rosedew fall in as a mourner. People said that from that day the old friendship was dissevered.

John, for his part, could not keep his eyes from the nook of the churchyard, where among the yew-trees stood, in the bitterness of anguish, he who had not asked, nor been asked, to attend as mourner. Cradock bowed his head and wept, for now his tears came freely, and prayed the one Almighty Father, who alone has mercy, not to take his misery from him, but to take him from it.

When the mould was cast upon the coffin, black

Wena came between people's legs, gave a cry, and jumped in after it, thinking to retrieve her master, like a stick from the water. She made such a mournful noise in the grave, and whimpered, and put her head down, and wondered why no one said "Wena, dear," that all the school-girls burst out sobbing—having had apples from Clayton lately—and Octavius Pell, the great cricketer, wanted something soft for his throat.

That evening, when all was over, and the grave heaped snugly up, and it was time to think of other things and begin to wonder at sorrow, John Rosedew went to Sir Cradock Nowell, not only as a fellow-mourner and a friend of ancient days, but as a minister of Christ. It had cost John many struggles; and, what with his sense of worldly favours, schoolday-friendship, delicacy, he could scarce tell what to make of it, till he just went down on his knees and prayed; then the learned man learned his duty.

Sir Cradock turned his head away, as if he did not want him. John held out his hand, and said nothing.

"Mr. Rosedew, I am surprised to see you. And yet, John, this is kind of you."

John hoped that he only said "Mr. Rosedew," because the footman was lingering, and he tried not to feel the difference.

"Cradock, you know what I am, as well as I know what you are. Fifty years, my dear fellow, fifty years of friendship."

"Yes, John, I remember when I was twelve years old, and you fought Sam Cockings for me."

"And, Cradock, I thrashed him fairly; you know I thrashed him fairly. They said I got his head under the form; but you know it was all a lie. How I do hate lies! I believe it began that day. If so, the dislike is subjective. Perhaps I ought to reconsider it."

"John, I know nothing in your life which you ought to reconsider, except what you are doing now."

Sir Cradock Nowell began the combat, because he felt that it must be waged; and perhaps he knew in that beginning that he had the weaker cause.

"Cradock, I am doing nothing which is not my simple duty. When I see those I love in the deepest distress, can I help siding with them?"

"Upon that principle, or want of it, you might espouse, as a duty, the cause of any murderer."

The old man shuddered, and his voice shook, as he whispered that last word. As yet he had not worked himself up, nor been worked up by others, to the black belief which made the living lost beyond the dead.

"I am sure I don't know what I might do," said John Rosedew, simply, "but what I am doing now is right; and in your heart you know it. Come, Cradock, as an old man now, and one whom God has visited, forgive your poor, your noble son, who never will forgive himself."

But for one word in that speech, John Rosedew would perhaps have won his cause, and reconciled son and father.

"My *noble* son indeed, John! A very noble thing he has done. Shall I never hear the last of his nobility? And who ever called my Clayton noble? You have been unfair throughout, John Rosedew, most unfair and blind to the merits of my more loving, more simple-hearted, more truly noble boy, I tell you."

Mr. Rosedew, at such a time, could not of course contest the point, could not tell the bereaved old man that it was he himself who had been unfair.

"And when," asked Sir Cradock, getting warmer, " when did you know my poor boy Violet stick up for political opinions of his own at the age of twenty, want to drain tenants' cottages, and pretend to be better and wiser than his father?"

" And when have you known Cradock do, at any rate, the latter?"

" Ever since he got that scholarship, that Scotland thing at Oxford"—Sir Cradock knew the name well enough, as every Oxford man does— "he has been perfectly insufferable; such arrogance, such conceit, such airs! And he only got it by a trick. Poor Viley ought to have had it."

John Rosedew tried to control himself, but the gross untruth and injustice of that last accusation were a little too much for him.

" Perhaps, Sir Cradock Nowell, you will allow

that I am a competent judge of the relative powers
of the two boys, who knew all they did know from
me, and from no one else."

" Of course, I know you are a competent judge,
only blinded by partiality."

John allowed even that to go by.

" Without any question of preference, simply as
a lover of literature, I say that Clayton had no
chance with him in a Greek examination. In Latin
he would have run him close. You know I always
said so, even before they went to college. I was
surprised, at the time, that they mentioned Clayton
even as second to him."

" And grieved, I dare say, deeply grieved, if the
truth were told!"

" It is below me to repel mean little accusa-
tions."

" Come, John Rosedew," said Sir Cradock, magnanimously and liberally, " I can forgive you for
being quarrelsome, even at such a time as this. It
always was so, and I suppose it always will be. To-
day I am not fit for much, though perhaps you
do not know it. Thinking so little of my dead
boy, you are surprised that I should grieve for
him."

" I should be surprised indeed if you did not.
God knows even I have grieved deeply, as for a
son of my own."

" Shake hands, John; you are a good fellow—
the best fellow in the world. Forgive me for

being petulant.   You don't know how my heart aches."

After that it was impossible to return for the moment to Cradock Nowell.   But the next day John renewed the subject, and at length obtained a request from the father that his son should come to him.

By this time Cradock hardly knew when he was doing anything, and when he was doing nothing. He seemed to have no regard for any one, no concern about anything, least of all for himself. Even his love for Amy Rosedew had a pall thrown over it, and lay upon the trestles. The only thing he cared at all for was his father's forgiveness: let him get that, and then go away and be seen no more among them. He could not think, or feel surprise, or fear, or hope for anything; he could only tell himself all day long, that if God were kind He would kill him. A young life wrecked, so utterly wrecked, and through no fault of its own; unless (as some begin to dream) we may not slay for luxury; unless we have but a limited right to destroy our Father's property.

Sir Cradock, it has been stated, cared a great deal more for his children than he did for his ancestors. He had not been wondering, through his sorrow, what the world would say of him, what it would think of the Nowells; he had a little too much self-respect to care a fig for fool's-tongue. Now he sat in his carved oak-chair, expecting his

only son, and he tried to sit upright. But the flat-
ness of his back was gone, never to return; and the
shoulder-blades showed through his coat, like a
spoon left under the tablecloth. Still he appeared
a stately man, one not easily bowed by fortune, or
at least not apt to acknowledge it.

Young Cradock entered his father's study, with
a flush on his cheeks, which had been so pale, and
his mind made up for endurance, but his wits
going round like a swirl of leaves. He could not
tell what he might say or do. He began to believe
he had shot his father, and to wonder whether it
hurt him much. Trying in vain to master his
thoughts, he stood with his quivering hands clasped
hard, and his chin upon his breast.

So perhaps Adrastus stood, Adrastus son of
Gordias, before the childless Crœsus; and the
simple words are these.

"After this there came the Lydians carrying
the corpse. And behind it followed the slayer.
And standing there before the corpse, he gave
himself over to Crœsus, stretching forth his hands,
commanding to slay him upon the corpse, telling
both his own former stress, and how upon the top
of that he had destroyed his cleanser, nor was
his life now liveable. Crœsus, having heard these
things, though being in so great a trouble of the
hearth, has compassion on Adrastus, and says to
him——

"But Adrastus, son of Gordias, son of Midas,
this man, I say, who had been the slayer of his

womb-brother, and slayer of him that cleansed him, when there was around the grave a quietude from men, feeling that he was of all men whom he had ever seen the most weighed down with trouble, kills himself dead upon the tomb."

But the father now was not like Crœsus, the generous-hearted Lydian, although the man who stood before him was not a runagate from Phrygia, but the son of his own loins. The father did not look at him, but kept his eyes fixed on the window, as though he knew not any were near him. Then the son could wait no more, but spoke in a hollow, trembling voice:

" Father, I am come, as you ordered."

" Yes. I will not keep you long. Perhaps you want to go out" ("shooting" he was about to say, but could not be quite so cruel). "I only wish so to settle matters that we may meet no more." ·

" Oh, father—my own father!—for God's sake! —if there be a God—don't speak to me like that!"

" Sir, I shall take it as a proof that you are still a gentleman, which at least you used to be, if you will henceforth address me as ' Sir Cradock Nowell,' a title which soon will be your own."

" Father, look me in the face, and ask me ; then I will."

Sir Cradock Nowell still looked forth the heavily-tinted window. His son, his only, his grief-worn son, was kneeling at his side, unable to weep, too proud to sob, with the sense of deep wrong rising.

If the father once had looked at him, nature must have conquered.

" Mr. Nowell, I have only admitted you that we might treat of business. Allow me to forget the face of a fratricide, perhaps *murderer*."

Cradock Nowell fell back heavily, for he had risen from his knees. The crown of his head crashed the glass of a picture, and blood showered down his pale face. He never even put his hand up, to feel what was the matter. He said nothing, not a syllable; but stood there, and let the room go round. How his mother must have wept, if she was looking down from heaven !

The old man, having all the while a crude, dim sense of outrunning his heart, gave the youth time to recover himself, if it were a thing worth recovering.

" Now, as to our arrangements—the subject I wished to speak about. I only require your consent to the terms I propose, until, in the natural course of events, you succeed to the family property."

"What family property, sir?" Cradock's head was dizzy still, though the bleeding had done him good.

" Why, of course, the Nowelhurst property; all these entailed estates, to which you are now sole heir."

" I will never touch one shilling, nor step upon one acre of it."

"Under your mother's—that is to say, under my marriage-settlement," continued Sir Cradock, in the same tone, as if his son were only bantering, "you are at once entitled to the sum of 50,000*l*. invested in Three per Cent. Consols—which would have been—I mean, which was meant for younger children. This sum the trustees will be pre-pared——"

"Do you think I will touch it? Am I a thief as well as a murderer?"

"I shall also make arrangements for securing to you, until my death, an income of 5000*l*. per annum. This you can draw for quarterly, and the cheques will be countersigned by my steward, Mr. Garnet."

"Of course, lest I should forge. Once for all, hear me, Sir Cradock Nowell. So help me the God who has now forsaken me, who has turned my life to death, and made my own father curse me—every word of yours is a curse, I say—so help me that God (if there be one to help, as well as to smite a man), till you crave my pardon upon your knees, as I have craved yours this day, I will never take one yard of your land, I will never call myself 'Nowell,' or own you again as my father. God knows I am very unlucky and little, but you have shown yourself less. And some day you will know it."

In the full strength of his righteous pride, he walked for the first time like a man, since he leaped that deadly hedge. From that moment a change came over him. There was nothing to add to his happiness, but something to rouse his manhood. The sense of justice, the sense of honour—that flower and crown of justice—forbade him henceforth to sue, and be shy, and bemoan himself under hedges. From that day forth he was as a man visited of God, and humbled, but facing ever his fellow-men, and not ashamed of affliction.

CHAPTER XXVII.

WITH an even step, and no frown on his forehead, nor glimpse of a tear in his eyes, young Cradock walked to his own little room, his "nest," as he used to call it; where pipes, and books, and Oxford prints—no ballet-girls, however, and not so very many hunters—and whips, and foils, and boxing-gloves—*cum multis aliis quæ nunc describere longum est; et cui non dicta* long ago?—were handled more often than dusted. All these things, except one pet little pipe, which he was now come to look for, and which Viley had given him a year ago, when they swopped pipes on their birthday (like Diomed and the brave Lycian), all the rest were things of a bygone age, to be thought of no more for the present, but dreamed of, perhaps, on a Christmas-eve, when the air is full of luxury.

Caring but little for any of them, although he had loved them well until they seemed to injure him, Cradock proceeded with great equanimity to

do a very foolish thing, which augured badly for
the success of a young man just preparing to start
for himself in the world. He poured the entire
contents of his purse into a little cedar tray, then
packed all the money in paper rolls with a neatness
which rather astonished him, and sealed each roll
with his amethyst ring. Then he put them into a
little box of some rare and beautiful palm-wood,
which had been his mother's, laid his cheque-book
beside them (for he had been allowed a banking
account long before he was of age), and placed
upon that his gold watch and chain, and trinkets,
the amethyst ring itself, his diamond studs, and
other jewellery, even a locket which had contained
two little sheaves of hair, bound together with
golden thread, but from which he first removed,
and packed in silver paper, the fair hair of his
mother. This last, with the pipe which Clayton
had given him, and the empty purse made by
Amy's fingers, were all he meant to carry away,
besides the clothes he wore.

     After locking the box he rang the bell, and
begged the man who answered it to send old Hogstaff
to him. That faithful servant, from whom he had
learned so many lessons of infancy, came tottering
along the passage, with his old eyes dull and heavy.
For Job had gloried in those two brothers, and
loved them both as the children of his elder days.
And now one of them was gone for ever, in the
height of his youth and beauty, and a whisper was
in the household that the other would not stay.

Of him, whom Job had always looked upon as his future master (for he meant to outlive the present Sir Cradock, as he had done the one before him), he had just been scoring upon his fingers all the things he had taught him—to whistle "Spanka-dillo," while he drummed it with his knuckles; to come to the pantry-door, and respond to the "Who's there?"—"A grenadier!" shouldering a broomstick; to play on the Jew's-harp, with varia-tions, "An old friend, and a bottle to give him;" and then to uncork the fictitious bottle with the pop of his forefinger out of his mouth, and to decant it carefully with the pat of his gurgling cheeks! After all that, how could he believe Master Crad could ever forsake him?

Now Mr. Hogstaff's legs were getting like the ripe pods of a scarlet-runner (although he did not run much); here they stuck in, and there they stuck out, abnormally in either case; his body began to come forward as if warped at the small of the back; and his honest face (though he drank but his duty) was September'd with many a vintage. And yet, with the keenness of love and custom, he saw at once what the matter was, as he looked up at the young master.

"Oh, Master Crad, dear Master Crad, whatever are you going to do? Don't, for good now, don't, I beg on you. Hearken now; do'ee hearken to an old man for a minute." And he caught him by both arms to stop him, with his tremulous, wrinkled hands.

" O Hoggy, dear, kind Hoggy! you are about the only one left to care about me now."

" No, don't you say that, Master Crad; don't you say that, whatever you do. Whoever tell you that, tell a lie, sir. It was only last night Mrs. Toaster, and cook, and Mrs. O'Gaghan, the Irish-woman, was round the fire boiling, and they cried a deal more than they boiled, I do assure you they did, sir. And Mr. Stote, he come in with some rabbits, and he went on like mad. And the maids, so sorry every one of them, they can't be content with their mourning, sir; I do assure you they can't. Oh, don't 'ee do no harm to yourself, don't 'ee, Mr. Cradock, sir."

" No, Hoggy," said Cradock, taking his hands; " you need not fear that now of me. I have had very wicked thoughts, but God has helped me over them. Henceforth I am resolved to bear my trouble like a man. It is the part of a dog to run, when the hoot begins behind him. Now, take this little box, and this key, and give them yourself to Sir Cradock Nowell. It is the last favour I shall ask of you. I am going away, my dear old friend; don't keep me now, for I must go. Only give me your good wishes; and see that they mind poor Caldo: and, whatever they say of me behind my back, you won't believe it, Job Hogstaff, will you?"

Job Hogstaff had never been harder put to it in all his seventy years. Then, as he stood at the open door to see the last of his favourite, he thought of the tall, dark woman's words so many years ago. "A bonnie pair ye have gat; but ye'll ha' no luck o' them. Tak' the word of threescore year, ye'll never get no luck o' 'em."

Cradock turned aside from his path, to say good-bye to Caldo. It would only take just a minute, he thought, and of course he should never see him again. So he went to that snuggest and sweetest of kennels, and in front of it sat the king of dogs.

The varieties of canine are as manifold and distinct as those of human nature. But the dog, be he saturnine or facetious, sociable or contemplative, mercurial or melancholic, is quite sure to be one thing—true and loyal ever. Can we, who are less than the dogs of the Infinite, say as much of ourselves to Him? Now Caldo, as has been implied, if not expressed before, was a setter of large philosophy and rare reflective power. I mean, of course, theoretical more than practical philosophy; as any dog would soon have discovered who tried to snatch a bone from him. Moreover, he had some originality, and a turn for satire. He would sit sometimes by the hour, nodding his head impressively, and blinking first one eye and then the other, watching and considering the doings of his fellow-dogs. How fashionably they yawned and stretched, in a mode they had learned from a pointer, who was proud of his teeth and vertebræ; how they hooked up their tails for a couple of joints, and then let them fall at a right angle,

having noticed that fashion in ladies' bustles, when
they came on a Sunday to talk to them; how they
crawled on their stomachs to get a pat, as a pro-
vincial mayor does for knighthood; how they
sniffed at each other's door, with an eye to the
rotten bones under the straw, as we all smell
about for the wealthy; how their courtesy to one
another flowed from their own convenience—these,
and a thousand other dog-tricks, Caldo, dwelling
apart, observed, but did not condemn, for he felt
that they were his own. Now he hushed his bark
of joy, and looked up wistfully at his master, for
he knew by the expression of that face all things
were not as they ought to be. Why had Wena
snapped at him so, and avoided his society, though
he had always been so good to her, and even
thought of an alliance? Why did his master order
him home that dull night in the covert, when he
was sure he had done no harm? Above all, what
meant that moving blackness he had seen through
the trees only yesterday, when the other dogs
(muffs as they were) expected a regular battue,
and came out strong at their kennel doors, and
barked for young Clayton to fetch them?

So he looked up now in his master's face, and
guessed that it meant a long farewell, perhaps a
farewell for ever. He took a fond look into his
eyes, and his own pupils told great volumes. Then
he sat up, and begged for a minute or two, with a
most beseeching glance, to share his master's fortunes, though he might have to steal his livelihood,

and never get any shooting. Seeing that this could never be, he planted his fore-paws on Cradock's breast (though he felt that it was a liberty) and nestled his nose right under his cheek, and wanted to keep him ever so long. Then he howled with a low, enduring despair, as the foot-fall he loved grew fainter.

Looking back sadly, now and then, at the tranquil home of his childhood, whose wings, and gables, and depths of stone were grand in the autumn sunset, Cradock Nowell went his way toward the simple Rectory: he would say good-bye there to Uncle John and the kind Aunt Doxy; Miss Rosedew the younger, of course, would avoid him, as she had done ever since. But suddenly he could not resist the strange desire to see once more that fatal, miserable spot, the bidental of his destiny. So he struck into a side-path leading to the deep and bosky covert.

The long shadows fell from the pale birch stems, the hollies looked black in the sloping light, and the brown leaves fluttered down here and there as the cold wind set the trees shivering. Only six days ago, only half an hour further into the dusk, he had slain his own twin-brother. He crawled up the hedge through the very same gap, for he could not leap it now; his back ached with weakness, his heart with despair, as he stayed himself by the same hazel-branch which had struck his gun at the muzzle. Then he shivered, as the trees did, and his hair, like the brown leaves, rustled, as he knelt and prayed that his brother's spirit might appear there and forgive him. Hoping and fearing to find it there, he sidled down into the dark wood, and with his heart knocking hard against his ribs, forced himself to go forward.

All at once his heart stood still, and every nerve of his body went creeping—for he saw a tall, white figure kneeling where his brother's blood was— kneeling, never moving, the hands together as in prayer, the face as wan as immortality, the black hair—if it were hair—falling straight as a pall drawn back from an alabaster coffin-head. The power of the entire form was not of earth, nor heaven; but as of the intermediate state, when we know not we are dead yet.

Cradock could not think nor breathe. The whole of his existence was frozen up in awe. It showed him in the after time, when he could think about it, the ignorance, the insolence, of dreaming that any human state is quit of human fear. While he gazed, in dread to move (not knowing his limbs would refuse him), with his whole life swallowed up in gazing at the world beyond the grave, the tall, white figure threw its arms up to the darkening sky, rose, and vanished instantly.

. What do you think Cradock Nowell did? We all know what he ought to have done. He ought to have walked up calmly, with measured yet rapid footsteps, and his eyes and wits well about him, and investigated everything. Instead of that, he cut and ran as hard as he could go; and I know I should have done the same, and I believe more than half of you would, unless you were too much frightened. He would never turn back upon living man; but our knowledge of Hades is limited. We pray for angels around our bed; if they came, we should have nightmare.

Cradock, going at a desperate pace, with a handsome pair of legs, which had recovered their activity, kicked up something hard and bright from a little dollop of leaves, caught it in his hand like a tennis-ball, and leaped the hedge *uno impetu.* Away he went, without stopping to think, through the splashy sides of the spire-bed, almost as fast, and quite as much frightened, as Rufus Hutton's mare. When he got well out into the chase, he turned, and began to laugh at himself; but a great white owl flapped over a furze-bush, and away went Cradock again. The light had gone out very suddenly, as it often does in October, and Cradock (whose wind was uncommonly good) felt it his duty to keep good hours at the Rectory. So, with the bright thing, whatever it was, poked anywhere into his pocket, he came up the drive at early tea-time, and got a glimpse through the window of Amy.

"Couldn't have been Amy, at any rate," he said to himself, in extinction of some very vague ideas; "I defy her to come at the pace I have done. No, no; it must have been in answer to my desperate prayer."

Amy was gone, though her cup was there, when Cradock entered the drawing-room. "Well," he thought, "how hard-hearted she is! But it cannot matter now, much. Though I never believed she would be so."

Being allowed by his kind entertainers to do exactly as he pleased, poor Cradock had led the life of a hermit more than that of a guest among them. He had taken what little food he required in the garret he had begged for, or carried it with him into the woods, where most of his time was spent. Of course all this was very distressing to the hospitable heart of Miss Doxy; but her brother John would have it so, for so he had promised Cradock. He could understand the reluctance of one who feels himself under a ban to meet his fellow-creatures hourly, and know that they all are thinking of him. So it came to pass that Miss Eudoxia, who now sat alone in the drawing-room, was surprised as well as pleased at the entrance of their refugee. As he hesitated a moment, in doubt of his reception, she ran up at once, took both his hands, and kissed him on the forehead.

"Oh, Cradock, my dear boy, this is kind of you; most kind, indeed, to come and tell me at once of your success. I need not ask—I know by your face; the first bit of colour I have seen in your poor cheeks this many a day."

"That's because I have been running, Miss Rosedew."

"Miss Rosedew, indeed; and *now*, Cradock!

Aunt Eudoxia, if you please, or Aunt Doxy, with all my heart, now."

He used to call her so, to tease her, in the happy days gone by; and she loved to be teased by him, her pet and idol.

"Dear Aunt Eudoxia, tell me truly, do you think—I can hardly ask you."

"Think what, Cradock? My poor Cradock; oh, don't be like that!"

"Not that I did—I don't mean that—but that it was possible for me to have done it on purpose?"

"Done what on purpose, Cradock?"

"Why, of course, that horrible, horrible thing."

"*On purpose*, Cradock! My poor innocent! Only let me hear any one dream of it, and if I don't come down upon them."

An undignified sentence, that of Aunt Doxy's, as well as a most absurd one. How long has she been in the habit of hearing people dream?

"Some one not only dreams it, some one actually believes that I did it so."

"The low wretch—the despicable—who?"

"My own father."

I will not repeat what Miss Rosedew said, when she recovered from her gasp, because her language was stronger than becomes an elderly lady and the sister of a clergyman, not to mention the Countess of Driddledrum and Dromore, who must have been wholly forgotten.

"Then you don't think, dear Aunt Eudoxia, that—that Uncle John would believe it?"

"What, my brother John! Surely you know better than that, my dear."

"Nor—nor—perhaps not even cousin Amy?"

"Amy, indeed! I do believe that child is perfectly mad. I can't make her out at all, she is so contradictory. She cries half the night, I am sure of that; and she does not care for her school, though she goes there; and her flowers she won't look at."

Seeing that Cradock's countenance fell more and more at all this, Miss Rosedew, who had long suspected where his heart was dwelling, told him a thing to cheer him up, which she had declared she would never tell.

"Darling Amy is, you know, a very odd girl indeed. Sometimes, when something happens very puzzling and perplexing, some great visitation of Providence, Amy becomes so dreadfully obstinate, I mean she has such delightful faith, that we are obliged to listen to her. And she is quite sure to be right in the end, though at the moment, perhaps, we laugh at her. And yet she is so shy, you can never get at her heart, except by forgetting what you are about. Well, we got at it somehow this afternoon; and you should have heard what she said. Her beautiful great eyes flashed upon us, like the rock that was struck, and gushed like it, before she ended. 'Can we dare to think,' she cried, 'that our God is asleep like Baal—that He knows not when He has chastened His children beyond what they can bear? I know that he, who is now so trampled and crushed of Heaven, is not tried thus for nothing. He shall rise again more pure and large, and fresh from the hand of God, and do what lucky men rarely think of—the will of his Creator.' And, when John and I looked at her, she fell away and cried terribly."

Cradock was greatly astonished: it seemed so unlike young Amy to be carried away in that style. But her comfort and courage struck root in his heart, and her warm faith thawed his despair. Still he saw very little chance, at present, of doing anything but starving.

"How wonderfully good you all are to me! But I can't talk about it, though I shall think of it as long as I live. I am going away to-night, Aunt Doxy, but I must first see Uncle John."

Of course Miss Rosedew was very angry, and proved it to. be quite impossible that Cradock should leave them so; but, before very long, her good sense prevailed, and she saw that it was for the best. While he stayed there, he must either persist to shut himself up in solitude, or wander about in desert places, and never look with any comfort on the face of man. So she went with him to the door of the book-room, and left him with none but her brother.

John Rosedew sat in his little room, with only one candle to light him, and the fire gone out as usual: his books lay all around him, even his best-loved treasures, but his heart was not among them. The grief of the old, though not wild and passionate

as a young man's anguish, is perhaps more pitiable,
because more slow and hopeless. The young tree
rings to the keen pruning-hook, the old tree groans
to the grating saw; but one will blossom and bear
again, while the other gapes with canker. None of
his people had heard the rector quote any Greek or
Latin for a length of time unprecedented. When
a sweet and playful mind, like his, has taken to
mope and be earnest, the effect is far more sad
and touching than a stern man's melancholy. Iron-
works out of blast are dreary, but the family
hearth moss-grown is woeful.

Uncle John leaped up very lightly from his
brooding (rather than reading), and shook Cradock
Nowell by the hand, as if he never would let him
go, all the time looking into his face by the light of
a composite candle. It was only to know how he
had fared, and John read his face too truly.
Then, as Cradock turned away, not wanting to
make much of it, John came before him with
sadness and love, and his blue eyes glistened
softly.

"My boy, my boy!" was all he could say, or
think, for a very long time. Then Cradock told
him, without a tear, a sigh, or even a comment,
but with his face as pale as could be, and his
breath coming heavily, all that his father had said
to him, and all that he meant to do through it.

"And so, Uncle John," he concluded, rising to
start immediately, "here I go to seek my fortune,
such as it will and must be. Good-bye, my best
and only friend. I am ten times the man I was

yesterday, and shall be grander still to-morrow." He tried to pop off like a lively cork, but John Rosedew would not have it.

"Young man, don't be in a hurry. It strikes me that I want a pipe; and it also strikes me that you will smoke one with me."

Cradock was taken aback by the novelty of the situation. He had never dreamed that Uncle John could, under any possible circumstances, ask him to smoke a pipe. He knew well enough that the rector smoked a sacrificial pipe to Morpheus, in a room of his own up-stairs; only one, while chewing the cud of all he had read that day. But Mr. Rosedew had always discouraged, as elderly smokers do, any young aspirants to the mystic hierophancy. It is not a vow to be taken rashly, for the vow is irrevocable; except with men of no principle.

And now he was to smoke there—he, a mere bubble-blowing boy, to smoke in the middle of deepest books, to fumigate a manuscript containing a lifeful of learning, which John could no more get on with; and—oh Miss Eudoxia!—to make the hall smell and the drawing-room! The oxymoron overcame him, and he took his pipe: John Rosedew had filled it judiciously, and quite as a matter of course; he filled his own in the self-same manner, with a digital skill worthy of an ancient fox trying on a foxglove. All the time, John was shyly wondering at his own great force of character.

"Now," said John Rosedew, still keeping it up, "I have a drop of very old Schiedam—Schnapps I think, or something—of which I want your opinion; Crad, my boy, I want your opinion, before we import any more. I am no judge of that sort of thing; it is so long since I was at Oxford."

Without more ado, he went somewhither, after lighting Cradock's yard of clay—which the young man burnt his fingers about, for he wouldn't let the old man do it—and came back like a Bacchanal, with a square black-jack beneath his arm, and Jenny after him, wondering whether they had not prayed that morning enough against the devil. It was a good job Miss Amy was out of the way; the old cat was bewitched, that was certain, as well as her dear good master. Miss Doxy was happy in knowing not that she was called " the old cat" in the kitchen.

CHAPTER XXVIII.

"Now, Craddy, my dear, dear boy," said Uncle John, when things had been done with lemon and cold water, and all that wherein discussion so utterly beats description, "you know me too well to suppose that I wish to pass things lightly. I know well enough that you will look the hard world full in the face. And so should I do, in your case. All I wish is that you should do it, not with spite, or bile, or narrowness, but broadly as a Christian."

"It is hard to talk about that now," said Cradock, inhaling charity, and puffing away all acrimony; "Uncle John, I hope I may come to it as my better spirit returns to me."

"I hope it indeed, and believe it, Crad; I don't see how it can be otherwise, with a young man of your breadth of mind, and solid faith to help you. An empty lad, who snaps up stuff because he thinks it fine, and garbles it into garbage, would become an utter infidel, under what you have suffered. With you, I believe, it will be otherwise; I believe you will be enlarged and purified by sorrow—the night which makes the guiding-star so much the clearer to us." John Rosedew was drinking no Schiedam—allow me to explain— though pretending rare enjoyment of it, and making Cradock drink a little, because his heart was down so.

After they had talked a pipeful longer, not great weighty sentiments, but a deal of kindly stuff, the young fellow got up quietly, and said, " Now, Uncle John, I must go."

" My boy, I can trust you anywhere, after what you have been telling me. Of human nature I know nothing, except"—for John thought he did know something—" from my own little experience. I find great thoughts in the Greek philosophers; but somehow they are too general, and too little genial. One thing I know, we far more often mistrust than trust unwisely. And now I can trust, you, Cradock; in the main, you will stand upright. Stop, my boy; you must have a scrip; I was saving it for your birthday."

" You don't despise me, I hope ?" said Cradock; "you don't think me a coward for running away so? After what has happened to-day, I should go mad, if I stopped here. Not that that would matter much; only that, if it were so, I should be sure to do it."

John Rosedew had no need to ask what he

meant by the last two words, for the hollow voice told him plainly. But for him, it is likely enough that it would have been done ere this; at any rate, in the first horror, his hand alone had prevented it. The parson trembled at the idea, but thought best not to dwell upon it.

" ' Reformidare mortem est animi pusillanimi,' but ' reformidare vitam' is ten times worse, because impious. Therefore in your case, my boy, it is utterly impossible, as well as ignoble towards us who love you so. Remember that you will break at least two old hearts you owe some duty to, if you allow your own to be broken. And now for your viaticum; see how you have relieved me. While you lived beneath Hymettian beams in the goods of Tyre and Cyprus, I, even I your god-father, knew not what to give you. The thought has been vexing me for months, and now what a simple solution! You shall have it in the original dross, to pay the toll on the Appian road, at least. the South-Western Railway. Figs to Athens, I thought it would be, or even as eels to Copaïs; and now ' serves iturum Cæsarem.' I believe it is at the twenty-first page of my manuscript, such as it is, upon the Sabellian elements."

After searching in three or four drawers—for he was rather astray at the moment, though gene-rally he could put his hand, even in the dark, upon any particular one of his ten thousand books—he came upon the Sabellian treatise, written on backs of letters, on posters, on puffing circulars, even on

visiting-cards, and cast-away tradesmen's tickets;
and there, at the twenty-first page or deltis, lay a
50*l*. Bank of England note, with some very tough
roots arranged diamond-wise on the back, and
arrows, and hyphens, and asterisks, flying about
thickly between them. These he copied off, in a
moment, on a piece of old hat-lining, and then
triumphantly waved the bank-note in the air.
It was not often poor Uncle John got hold of so
much money; too bitterly knew Aunt Doxy how
large was the mesh of his purse.

While Cradock gazed with great admiration,
John Rosedew, with his fingers upon his lips, and
looking half ashamed of himself, went to a cupboard, whose doors, half open, gave a glimpse of
countless sermons. From among them he drew a
wide-mouthed bottle of leeches, and set it upon the
table. Then he pulled out the stopper, unplugged
it, and lo! from a hole in the cork fell out two
sovereigns and a half one. As this money rolled
on the table, John could not help chuckling a
little.

" Ha, good sister Eudoxia, have I overreached
thee again? Double precaution there, you see,
Crad. She has a just horror of my sermons, and
she runs at the sight of a leech. ' Non missura
cutem'—be sure, not a word about it, Crad. That
asylum is inviolable, and sempitern, I hope. I shall
put more there next week."

Cradock took the money at once, with the deepest
gratitude, but no great fuss about it; for he saw

how bitterly that good man would feel it, if he were small enough to refuse.

I shall not dwell upon their good-bye, as we have had enough valediction; only Cradock promised to write from London, so soon as he could give an address there; then leaving sadness behind him, carried a deal of it with him. Only something must yet be recounted, which befell him in Nowel-hurst. And this is the first act of it.

While he was in his garret packing a little bag of necessaries, forced upon him by Miss Doxy from John's wardrobe and her own almost indiscriminately, and while she was pulling and struggling up-stairs with John, and Jemima, and Jenny—for she would have made Cradock, if she could, carry the entire house with him—he, stowing some things in his pocket, felt what he had caught up so hastily, while flying out of the wood. He examined it by the candlelight, and became at once intent upon it. It had lain beneath a drift of dead leaves backed by a scraggy branch, whence anything short of a grand "skedaddle" would never have dislodged it.

And yet it was a great deal too pretty to be treated in that way. Cradock could not help admiring it, though he shuddered and felt some wild hopes vanish as he made out the meaning. It was a beautiful gold bracelet, light, and of first-rate workmanship, harmonious too with its purpose, and of elegant design. The lower half was a strong soft chain of the fabric of Trichinopoli, which bends like the skin of a snake; the front and face showed a strong right arm, gauntleted, yet entirely dependent upon the hand of a lady. No bezilling, no jewel whatever, except that a glorious rose-shaped pearl hung, as in contest, between them.

Cradock wondered for some little time what could be the meaning of it. Then he knew that it was Clayton's offering to the beloved Amy. No doubt could remain any longer, when he saw in the hollow of the back the proposed inscription pencilled, " Rosa debita," for the dead gold of the lady's palm, " Rosa dedita" for the burnished gold of the cavalier's high pressure. With ingenious love to help him, he made it out in a moment. " A rose due, now a rose true." That was what it came to, if you took it in punster fashion. Just one of poor Viley's conceits.

Cradock had no time to follow it out, for Miss Eudoxia then came in with a parcel as big as a feather-bed, of comforters, wrappers, and eatables. But, after he had left the house, he began to think about it, in the little path across the green to the village churchyard. He concluded that Amy must have been in the wood that fatal evening. She must have come to meet Clayton there; and yet it was not like her. Facts, however, are facts, as sure as eggs are eggs; though our knowledge makes no great advance through either of those aphorisms. But a growing sense of injury—though he had no right to feel injured, however it might be—this sense had kept him from asking for Amy, or leaving the flirt a good-bye.

He entered the quiet churchyard, with the moon rising over the tombstones, a mass of shadow cast by the great tower, and some epitaphs pushing well into the light, like the names which get poked into history. The wavering glance of the diffident moon, uncertain yet what the clouds meant, slipped along the buttressed walls, and tried to hold on at the angles. The damp corner, where the tower stood forth, and the south porch ran out to look at it, drew back like a ghost who was curtseying, and declining all further inquiry. Green slime was about, like the sludge of a river; and a hundred sacred memories, growing weary and rheumatic, had stopped their ears with lichen.

Cradock came in at the rickety swing-stile, and, caring no shadow for ghost or ghostess, although he had run away so, took the straight course to the old black doorway, and on to the heart of the churchyard; for he must say good-bye to Clayton. All Nowelhurst still admired that path; but those who had paved and admired it first were sleeping on either side of it. The pavement now was overlapped, undertucked, and crannied, full of holes where lobworms lived and came out after a thunderstorm, and three-cornered dips that looked glazed in wet weather, but scurfy and clammy in drought. And some of the flags stole away and gave under, as if they too wanted burial, while others jerked up, and asserted themselves as

superior to some of the tombstones. There in the
dark, no mortal with any respect for his grandfather, nor even a ghost with unbevilled soles, could
go many steps without tripping.

Who will be astonished, then, when I say that the
lightest and loveliest foot that ever tripped in the
New Forest not only tripped but stumbled there ?
At the very corner where the side walk comes in,
and the shade of the tower was deepest, smack
from behind a hideous sarcophagus fell into Cradock's arms the most beautiful thing ever seen.
If he had not caught her, she must have cut the
very sweetest face in the world into great holes
like the pavement. Stunned for a moment, and
then so abroad, that she could not think, nor even
speak—"speak nor think" I would have said, if
Amy had been masculine—she lay in Cradock's
trembling arms, and never wondered where she
was. Cradock forgot all despair for the moment,
and felt uncommonly lively. It was the sweetest
piece of comfort sent to him yet from heaven.
Afterwards he always thought that his luck turned
from that moment. Perhaps it did ; although
most people would laugh who knew him afterwards.

Presently Amy recovered, and was wroth with
herself and everybody. Ruddier than a Boursalt
rose, she fell back against the tombstone.

"Oh, Amy," said Cradock, retiring; "I have
known it long. Even you are turned against
me."

"I turned against you, Mr. Nowell! What right have you to say that of me?"

"No right to say anything, Amy; and scarcely a right to think anything. Only I have felt it."

"Then I wouldn't give much for your feelings. I mean—I beg your pardon—you know I can never express myself."

"Of course, I know that," said Cradock.

"Oh, can't I, indeed?" said Amy; "I dare say you think so, Mr. Nowell. You have always thought so meanly of me. But, if I can't express my meaning, I am sure my father can. Perhaps you think you know more than he does."

"Amy," said Cradock, for all this was so unlike herself, that, loving that self more than his own, he scarce knew what to do with it; "Amy, dear, I see what it is. I suspected it all along."

"What, if you please, Mr. Nowell? I am not accustomed to be suspected. Suspected, indeed!"

"Miss Rosedew, don't be angry with me. I know very well how good you are. It is the last time I shall ever see you, or I would not restore you this."

The moon, being on her way towards the south-east, looked over the counter-like gravestone, and Cradock placed on the level surface the bracelet found in the wood. Amy knew it in a moment; and she burst out crying—

"Oh, poor Clayton! How proud he was of it! Mr. Nowell, I never could have thought this of you; never, never, never!"

"Thought what of me, Amy? Darling Amy, what on earth have I done to offend you?"

"Oh, nothing. I suppose it is nothing to remind me how cruel I have been to him. Oh no, nothing at all. And all this *from you*."

In a storm of sobs she fell upon Jeremy Wattle's tombstone, and Cradock put one arm around her, to prevent her being hurt.

"Amy, you drive me wild. I have brought it to you only because it is yours, and because I am going away."

"Cradock, it never was mine. I refused it months ago; and I believe he gave it—you know what he was, poor dear—I believe he transferred it, and something else—oh no, I can't express myself—to—just to somebody else."

"Oh, you darling! and who was that other? What a fool he must have been! Confound it, I never meant that."

"I don't know, Cradock. Oh, please keep away. But I think it was Pearl Garnet. Oh, Cradock, dear Cradock, how dare you? No, I won't. Yes, I will, Crad; considering all your misery."

She put up her pure lips in the moonlight—for Cradock had got her in both arms by this time, and was listening to no reason—her sweet lips, pledged once pledged for ever, she put them up in her love and pity, and let him do what he liked with them. And the moon, attesting a thousand seals hourly, never witnessed one more binding.

After all, Cradock Nowell, so tried of Heaven, so scourged with the bitterest rods of despair, your black web of life is inwoven now with one bright thread of gold. The purest, the sweetest, the loveliest girl that ever spun happiness out of sorrow, or smiled through the veil of affliction, the truest and dearest of all God's children, loving all things, hating none, pours into your heart for ever all that fount of love. Freed henceforth from doubt and wonder (except at her own happiness), enfranchised of another world, enriched beyond commercial thoughts, ennobled beyond self, she blushed as she spoke, and grew pale as she thought, and who shall say which was more beautiful? Cradock could tell, perhaps, if any one can; but he only knew that he worshipped her. And to see the way she cried with joy, and how her young bosom panted; it was enough to warm old Jeremy Wattle, dead and buried nigh fourscore years.

Cradock, all abroad himself, full of her existence, tasting, feeling, thinking nothing, except of her deliciousness, drew his own love round to the light to photograph her for ever. Poor Clayton was dead; else Crad would have thought that he deserved to be so, for going away to Pearl Garnet: but then the grapes were sour. How he revelled in that reflection! And yet it was very wrong of him.

Amy stood up in the moonlight, not ashamed to show herself. She felt that Cradock was poring upon her, to stereotype every inch of her; and yet she was not one atom afraid. She knew that no man ever depreciates his own property, except in the joke which is brag. It is a most wonderful thing, what girls know and what they *won't* know. But who cares now for reflections?

Her thick hair had all fallen out of her hat, because she had been crying so; her delicate form, still so light and girlish, leaned forward in trust of the future, and the long dark lashes she raised for her lover glistened with the deep light under them. Shame was nestling in her cheeks, the shame of growing womanhood, the down on the yet ungathered fruit of love. Then she crept in closer to him, to stop him from looking so much at her.

"Darling Cradock, my own dear Cradock, don't you know me now? You see, I only love you so because you are so unlucky, and I am so dreadfully obstinate."

"Of course, I know all that, my pet; my beauty inexpressible. And, remember that I only love you so because you are such a darling."

Then Amy told him how sorry she was for having been so fractious lately; and that she would never be so again, only it was all his fault, because she wanted to comfort him, and he would not come and let her — here the softest gleam fluttered through her tears, like the Mazarine Blue among dewdrops — and that only for the veriest chance, and the saucer she had broken — but what of that, she would like to know; it was the surest sign of good luck to them, although it was the best service—only for that, her Crad would have gone—gone away for ever, and never known how she loved him; yes, with all her heart, every single atom of it, every delicious one, if he *must* know. And she would keep it for him for ever, for ever; and be thinking of him always. Let him recollect that, poor darling, and think of his troubles no more.

Then he told her how Uncle John had behaved —how nobly, how magnanimously; and had given every bit of money he possessed in the world for Cradock to start in life with. John Rosedew's only child began to cry again at hearing it, and put her little hand into her pocket in the simplest way imaginable. "Yes, you will, dear;" "No, I won't;" went on for several minutes, till Amy nestled quite into his bosom, and put her sweet lips to his ear.

"If you don't, I will never believe that you love me truly. I am your little wife, you know; and all that I have is yours."

The marriage-portion in debate was no more than five and sixpence, for Amy could never keep money long; so Cradock accepted the sweet little purse, only he must have a bit of her hair in it. She pulled out her little sewing-case, which she always took to the day-school, and the small bright scissors flashed in the moonlight, and they made a great

fuss over them. Two great snips were heard, I
know; for exchange, after all, is no robbery.

Then hand in hand they went together to see
poor Clayton's grave, and Cradock started as they
approached, for something black was moving there.

"Little dear," said Amy, as the doggie looked
mournfully up at them, "she would starve if it
were not for me. And I could not coax her to eat
a morsel until I said, 'Clayton, poor Clayton!'
And then she licked my hand and whined, and
took a bit to please me. She has had a very nice
tea to-night; I told you I broke the saucer, but
that was all my own clumsiness."

"And what has she got there? Oh God! I
can't stand it; it is too melancholy."

Black Wena, when it was dark that evening, and
Clayton must have done dinner, had stolen away
to his dressing-room, and fetched, as she had been
taught to do, his smoking-jacket and slippers. It
took her a long time to carry the jacket, for fear it
should be wet for him. Then she came with a
very important air, and put them down upon his
grave, and wagged her tail for approval. She was
lying there now, and wondering how much longer
till he would be ready.

Cradock sobbed hysterically, and Amy led him
softly away to the place where his travelling-bag
was.

"Now, wait here one moment, my poor dear,
and I will bring you your future companion."

Presently Amy came back, with Wena following

the coat and the slippers. "Darling Cradock, take her with you. She is so true and faithful. She will die if she is left here. And she will be such a comfort to you. Take her, Cradock, *for my sake.*"

The last entreaty settled it. Cradock took the coat and slippers, and carried Wena a little way, while she looked back wistfully at the churchyard, and Amy coaxed and patted her. They agreed on the road that Amy Rosedew should call upon Miss Garnet to restore the bracelet, and should mark how she received it; for Amy had now a strong suspicion (especially after what Cradock had seen, which now became intelligible) that Pearl knew more of poor Clayton's death than had been confessed to any one.

"My own Cradock, only think," said Amy; "I have felt the strongest conviction, throughout, that you had nothing to do with it."

"Sweetest one," he replied, with a desperate longing to clasp her, but for Wena and the carpet-bag, "that is only because you love me. Never say it again, dear; suspense, or even doubt about it, would kill me like slow poison."

Amy shuddered at his tone, and thought how different men were: for a woman would live on the hope of it. But she remembered those words when the question arose, and rejoiced that he knew not the whole of it.

And now with the great drops in her eyes, she stood at her father's gate, to say good-bye to her love. She would not let him know that she cried;

but Wena was welcome to know it, and Wena licked some tears off, and then quite felt for Amy.

"Good-bye, my own, my only," said Cradock, for the twentieth time; even the latch of the gate was trembling; "God loves us, after all, Amy. Or, at any rate, He loves you."

"And you, and you. Oh, Cradock! if He loves one, He must love both of us."

"I believe He does," said Cradock; "since I have seen you, I am sure of it. Now I care not for the world, except my world in you."

"Dearest darling, life of my life, promise me not to fret again."

"Fret, indeed, with you to love me! Give me just one more."

Cradock, with a braver heart than he ever thought to own again (and yet with a hole and a string in it, for, after all, he did not own it), being begged away at last by the one who then went down on her knees, only to beg him back again,—that hapless yet most blessed fellow strode away as hard as he could, for fear of running back again; and the dusky trees closed round him, and he knew and loved every one of them. Then the latch of the gate for the last time clicked, when he was out of sight, and the laurustinus by the pier, beginning to bud for the winter, glistened in the moonlight with a silent storm of tears.

END OF VOL. I.

LONDON:
PRINTED BY C. WHITING, BEAUFORT HOUSE, STRAND.

www.ingramcontent.com/pod-product-compliance
Lightning Source LLC
Chambersburg PA
CBHW021258050726
47498CB00003BB/896